D1055192

Try to Remember

Try to Remember

A NOVEL

Zane Kotker

Random House New York

This is a work of fiction. Names, characters, places, and incidents are the product of the author's imagination or are used fictitiously. Any resemblance to actual events, locales, or persons, living or dead, is entirely coincidental.

 Published in the United States by Random House, Inc., New York, and simultaneously in Canada by Random House of Canada Limited, Toronto.

ISBN: 0-679-44042-9

Random House website address: http://www.randomhouse.com/

Printed in the United States of America on acid-free paper
24689753
First Edition

For Molly Friedrich,
high-wire artist

Acknowledgments

Thanks to my writing students at Smith College (1990 and 1991), who first taught me the difference between our generations, and to the powers that be at the MacDowell Colony, Yaddo, and the National Endowment for the Arts for past pleasures and sustenance. To my husband, Norman Kotker, for the reading of several books now, and to writers Shirley Abbott and Lyman Gilmore for the same; to writers Mel Gussow, Joann Kobin, Kitty Hickcox, and Sheri Holman for their first time as readers, and to my daughter, Ariel Kotker, for the same. And to Sally Arteseros, Frances Jalet-Miller, Olga Seham, Page Dickinson, Margaret Wimberger, Beth Pearson, and, most critically, my editor, the ever resourceful Kate Medina.

Try to Remember

1990

There was no inkling of anything but the ordinary as Claire made a last survey of the narrow townhouse, searching for things that might belong to either daughter. On the top story of the house, she crossed old floorboards and appeared briefly in an oak-framed mirror, middle-aged but in the professional manner, short hair made blond again, brown eyes with the faintest liner. There was still a waistline and she moved with the expectation that something remained of her sexual life; here was a woman pleased with what lay around her. Reaching the hallway, she took the steep stairs with experienced thighs and ignored the third floor, where the girls would check their own rooms, one exquisitely cluttered and the other a spartan barrack. On the second floor she glanced toward the front room where light from the big windows lay comfortably on the pale patterns of a Chinese rug: Was there a misplaced book, some tapes, perhaps a scarf? Nothing, nor in the dim family room behind it, a sweet room over the garden with worn peach-colored carpet that maybe after they'd repaid the college loans they could replace. Family room, it was called, yet they'd spent most of their time on the first floor. The stairs leveled out beside a formal dining room with its chandelier missing a bulb—mine is a used more than an empty nest, Claire assured herself. The real family room was back here in the kitchen. Everything had happened in this large honey-colored room. Beside the fireplace, in front of the modern galley, among the four high stools, the sagging couch, and the two old bentwood rockers, this is where they'd raised the girls. What a lovely room, too, strewn with magazines and flowerpots—and there she was, the secondborn, their June graduate who was leaving today, Bess.

She wore her hair, or part of it, in a ponytail, which she was busy detaching from a buckle of her utilitarian backpack, and then she was walking slowly across the floor to the fireplace. She was saying good-bye, Claire realized, to all her familiars—the old iron fireplace tools, the hanging baskets of Star of Bethlehem, the photograph on the mantel where the four of them sat permanently intertwined, the girls still small. In the picture time stops and every family member touches another, some two: an arm around a shoulder, a hand upon a knee, linked elbows, one animal in four parts, that's a family, or temporarily. Bess turned to Claire and said, "Guess I've got it all." This was not the daughter Claire had worried much about.

They headed out of the kitchen together, though Claire stopped and went back to return the butter to the refrigerator. *It's going to be hot today.* Later on, it would be that pause she'd remember, banal and ordinary, as if in turning back she'd somehow veered off course into the wrong future. Because that's where she was when Phoebe came running in to pour a last cup of tea into a travel mug. The firstborn had her father's red hair and an energy that made the kitchen hum. Claire had had that energy once, still did, inside, somewhere. She'd learned to push it down and quell it because a mother must move forward effectively, quietly pacifying whatever jumps and jerks or threatens to fall apart. Phoebe doesn't know that yet, Claire told herself, adding with a touch of rue: She'll find out. The firstborn and her father had long ago been so close that Claire had found it necessary to teach herself not to mind. She'll find out that a mother must think without alarm of yet another leaking thermos or a teacher's report that reads, "immature for five." Claire smiled at that. She herself was definitely immature for fifty, far too young for any years called Golden.

"Phoebe!" she called after the light-footed girl and gathered up a paperback of Herman Hesse's *Magister Ludi* from the top of the refrigerator with

"Phoebe Fairchild" written dashingly across the title page. She felt the years roll off her: There's nothing to worry about. They're fine, the girls, off to New York together, fine. Even though Phoebe doesn't seem too thrilled at carting Bess into her life and even though Bess has always followed after that red-haired firecracker who seldom looked her way. They're grown up now. Stay calm a couple minutes more and the number of items animate and inanimate for which you've been responsible for a quarter of a century will reduce. Your old self will bubble up. Call it the Yellow Years, shine on.

Outside, a wiry man with surprisingly white hair waited by a car. Harvey had already loaded Bess's enormous carpetbag into the trunk, as well as her stereo and tapes, which were packed in a very heavy box with recently devised—he'd made them himself—rope handles and wheels. He liked to take care of his daughters. This was not the way he'd left home for Korea, except for maybe the sharpness of the morning light. He'd carried a fifty-pound duffel bag to the bus station because his father had taken the car to get to his job on the late shift. Only his mother had stood by the door to wave and he'd had to lug the duffel manfully without limping or leaning until he got around the first corner and out of her sight where life could begin. Now it was his turn to be left behind.

Bess came out of the house and stood unmoving, looking up and down the cobbled sidewalk. What was she doing? He watched her take a step, her movements considered, unerringly right, like her mother's. His own were quick, sometimes too fast, sometimes a beat behind.

"Lots of room!" he called out to Bess and indicated the open trunk. She shrugged as she stepped into the street. Maybe a little scared, he told himself. She was the kind that hung back at first, played guard instead of forward, looked things over. The firstborn was more like himself, center forward or wing, plunge in and see.

Phoebe ran out of the house toward the car, her carroty hair crinkled by one of those processes known to women that gave it a rippling effect like something out of Botticelli, if he had the painter right. He'd had that color hair once, too, boy's version. And Phoebe had the same blue eyes he saw in the mirror every morning and once or twice a year in the face of his aging mother, where they no longer conferred the light of understanding. Phoebe handed him a shabby fringed shoulder bag for the trunk and he felt that great mystery, that biological pull toward what's genetically familiar—his girl.

Claire came out of the house last, turned, and stood back to the car as she locked up the house. He admired her serenity—his wife did not fluster. He looked at his watch. They were on time. He shut the trunk, walked around to the driver's door, and lowered himself into the seat.

"We're hitting bottom, Dad," Bess said in her full, satisfying voice behind him. It was an old family joke from their days at the lake when, in the boat, he'd mistaken the branches of a moldering tree beneath them for the shoreline.

"Next stop, life," he replied, easing off the cobblestones and heading toward Rittenhouse Square.

"God, Daddy, relax!" Phoebe said in her breathier, anxious voice.

Did he appear tense?

Claire, moving in to handle the moment, said, "Okay, your new housemates are two guys from Yale . . ."

"Daryl and Ibrahim," Phoebe replied with a hairline mix of politeness and impatience. "Plus Nora, who's brilliant. She graduated fourth in her college."

At Yale '88, not bad.

"You watch out for those two guys, Bess," Harvey said, hearing too late the 1950s leer in his voice. Silly, outdated. And it wasn't simply the sexual difference between his and his children's generation to watch out for; there was also the sister stuff. Boys had been falling over Bess since she reached eighth grade. Not Phoebe, who could be testy and selfish, who stood for her own rights before anybody else's. He'd taught her that. If she'd been a boy, it would have worked out fine.

Bess was going on correctively about today's men and women in her droll, throaty hum: "Now, what was it you guys called it, Dad? 'Dating'? No dating with housemates nowadays, remember?"

Harvey crossed Market to JFK and onto the elevated boulevard that spanned the Schuylkill to the white-columned railroad station on Thirtieth Street, where he pulled into a parking space. Inside the great marble expanse, they walked side by side, the parents in the middle with Harvey pushing the stereo and balancing the carpetbag. Beside him, Phoebe twisted an ankle above her fairly gala shoes and flung out a hand toward her father's arm, balanced herself, continued on. Claire adapted her pace to Bess's so that halfway across the station those two were walking just a bit behind the other two. Strangers might have noticed in the striated light of the cathedral space how alike Claire and Bess were in movement, how alike Harvey and Phoebe. There are variations of these alignments in all families, even, sometimes, when children are adopted; but such simplifications can be misleading. A happy family, one might judge; why isn't mine like that? Another would hazard only that this was a family that had not known tragedy.

Downstairs by the tracks, steam whooshed from under the cars' couplings and conductors called out, *Smoking! No Smoking!* "Good-bye, honey," Harvey said, giving Phoebe a quick embrace. "Keep on showing 'em your stuff in the Big Apple." Claire thought she saw Phoebe stiffen at this cliché, then she was embracing her daughters and Phoebe was raising her shoulderbag with a little salute before starting up the metal steps. Harvey hugged Bess and began to lift her box for her, wheels and all, up the steps until she pulled on his sleeve to stop him. "Thanks, Dad. I'll do it."

He smiled and let go and then Bess was climbing up and out of sight, too, lugging the stereo after her. They were gone and there was no way to peer inside the car. Harvey stood on the platform, unable to help his children further. Claire put her arm through his, knowing that it would hit him now; he'd been glum for weeks when Phoebe first left home for New York. She did her griefs beforehand and so felt lighter now. Parenting was over, the little faces gone: Oh, brave new world, step carefully.

2

In the taxi Phoebe felt relief to get back to her own city and away from the pull of home and its beckoning comforts. To Bess she pointed out the Empire State Building, Washington Square Park, and the Lower East Side, realizing too late that she was sounding ever so much like Dad. It wasn't as if Bess had never been in the city before. They'd come with their parents to see the Christmas lights and the United Nations and all that. And once they'd stood in front of a building in Greenwich Village where Dad and Mom had met, each renting an apartment so small they'd never unpacked their books. Her parents knew nothing from tiny!

She stopped the driver in front of a four-story brownstone not unlike the one they'd left, except that this was dirty and run-down. Never mind, in Manhattan you could call it a find, though Bess wouldn't realize that yet. Bess would be expecting so much more of her—a bigger place, a decent job, maybe even a guy. And Peter, if he showed up, wouldn't be the right guy.

"My place in Rockaway was nicer," Phoebe found herself suddenly explaining. "But the subway ride was impossibly long." Actually it'd been Andrew and Sophie making love behind the wall of her room that had caused her to flee. Study others, her acting coach had insisted, but Andrew and Sophie? Please, no!

They trundled the stereo up over the curb and outside the barred windows, where Phoebe produced her keys. "The silver goes into the gate. The gold here in the door." Bess nodded, the little sister, obedient, and Phoebe was suddenly glad to have her, glad to welcome her to New York. After all, she wouldn't be a secretary forever and maybe there'd be a message from the tryouts at NYU. Not that she wanted to act anymore, but you don't exactly start out directing from scratch. She led the way into a broken-tiled foyer and then into an inner hallway where she noticed the damp, moldy smell that usually escaped her.

She was steering past the stairway when Bess called out, "I thought you said upstairs."

"Did I say that?"

"Mom asked you what floor—she said, 'Not the first floor, I hope'—and you said, 'Oh, no, Mom, not a chance.' "

Phoebe laughed. "I didn't want her on my case, I guess. She calls me up every time some big fire makes the New York news. It's here, in back." She turned two more locks and opened the door of her apartment onto a blank wall so close they had to tilt the wheeled carton to get into the hallway. "That's the guys' room," she said of the first door they passed. She hadn't told her parents that the guys were gay—that sort of thing turned them into such right-wingers—but had she mentioned it to Bess?

"That's Nora's," she said of the second door, also closed. "And here's mine." She liked her room a lot and opened the door with confidence onto a space whose every bit of wall was covered with jewelry or hats or graphics hanging from thumbtacks, nails, racks: "Voilà."

"Hey, nice!"

She needn't apologize for this part of her life. One entire wall was hung with a huge blowup of the poster from the production of *Macbeth* she'd directed senior year with sardonic, wiry Andrew, front and center. You'd think a woman could find herself an intelligent man at Yale, only most of the guys in theater arts had been gay, except for Andrew, who was accommodating enough to be bisexual. Your work is too personal, her coach told her; go out and live.

"Isn't that your old roommate?"

"Lady Macbeth? The very one."

"What's she doing now?"

"Yale Drama." Practically the hardest grad school to get into—while she was hanging by the thumbs about a two-line part in a student film Peter had found posted at NYU! Oh, what was the matter with her? She used to be the one to win the prizes.

At least she had a window. A window in Manhattan! It was narrow but it looked out on a courtyard covered with ivy.

"Hey, great," Bess said. "Ivy."

"There's rats under the ivy." It wasn't an apology, being a simple urbanity.

Bess turned from the window. "Nice room, but I see what you mean, it's kind of small for two, isn't it?"

"This is big for New York!" Phoebe threw her shoulder bag onto the narrow futon. "We can both fit on here okay."

"I see. This is big, then. Nice."

"I know a guy who's sleeping in a closet for four-fifty a month. This humble abode costs me six hundred a month, half what I earn at Miss Hinckley's."

"It's fine."

"Put your bag on top of the laundry basket. You can use it for a bureau."

"It's great."

With a chill, Phoebe realized that Bess was forcing it, the way Mom would do. She took a fresh look at her haven in Manhattan. Actually, it was kind of as if Mom and Dad had come to visit. She loved them but could she never escape them?

Bess restated her plans. "I'm not staying very long, you know, only a couple of weeks."

"No problem." Except it was. She'd sworn up and down to Nora that Bess's visit would last one week at the very most.

Bess stood studying the antique brass clothes rack until Phoebe realized too late that it was filled to overflowing with her own clothes. "I'll clear that off. Come on, you can unpack later."

The kitchen was really amazingly decent and Phoebe felt better, even though the message machine's red light wasn't blinking. No callback. Maybe tomorrow. The walls were hung with pegboards and pans, the counters fairly clean. She set out chips and salsa, hummus and pita. She filled the teakettle and placed it on the stove's one working burner. "Tonight we'll go out and get a *Times* and a *Voice.* I got my first job out of the *Times.* Nora got me Miss Hinckley's, though. You gotta make yourself a network."

Bess sat at the small green table, feeling like her old self, Little Bess—the sometimes guest on Phoebe's imaginary TV show, "Phoebe the Magnificent." She'd forgotten how to watch her step.

When the kettle whistled, Phoebe poured the water into a nice little pot she'd bought at the Vietnamese store. She handed a mug to Bess, who was actually okay for a Puritan. Studying others, she bent herself to the observation of her sister, who was sitting across the table carefully ignoring the littered ashtray, the slew of tapes piled on the table, topped by a newspaper clipping from an Arabic paper and a photograph of Nora as a three-year-old in a bathing suit, the very summer that Nora's trouble began. Such an innocent, Bess, but solid and appealing, and she ate daintily, her thick blond hair, her perfect olivey skin, none of the white freckled stuff a redhead has to deal with. Now even the kitchen was beginning to take on a lesser look, with Bess sitting in it.

It was almost one o'clock when a door in the hallway opened and Nora moved noisily toward the bathroom. Phoebe was relieved to have something so dramatic as Nora to present to her sister.

"Nora's on antidepressants, that's why she shuffles like that."

"What's the matter with her?"

"I don't know if she wants to talk about it."

Bess sat up straighter. "Come on, that's mean!" Then she made herself settle back. She'd learned long ago not to bite at Phoebe's bait, not to win at Monopoly, not to want to win.

A short big-breasted person with curly black hair appeared at the threshold and gave them a quizzical look. Bess wondered if Nora had even been told of her arrival.

"This is Bess, remember? My sister."

"Oh, yeah. Hi."

"She's staying a couple of weeks. Like Jeff." That last just popped into Phoebe's head, but it was perfect. Nora's friend Jeff had spent two weeks on Nora's floor so he wouldn't have to go home and come out to his parents.

"So." Nora shrugged, looking at neither of them. "It's morning again."

"Morning it is," Bess replied cheerfully.

Phoebe could tell that Bess was listening her hardest, which was, as usual, a little too hard. That is, Bess was modifying herself toward Nora's stronger personality, and you can't do that. Being yourself is warfare. You've got to project what you are, if you want to stay alive. It was taking her a while to learn that, what with Mom never having an opinion unless Dad had it first. Good news: Since living with Nora, she was learning to hold her own. Except with Peter.

Nora moved immediately to The Topic. "Donna's got me so doped up I walk funny when I first get up. But God bless Donna. Without her, I'd still be wandering in the dark. Hey, without her, I wouldn't even know what's hung me up."

"Donna is her therapist," Phoebe explained, pleased with the thought that Nora would probably tell all to Bess now and that it would take a couple of hours at least. Nora's tale was compelling enough to wipe out the damp smell of poverty and the fact that you're a secretary in a comptroller's office. You have to work at it, to rise above your surroundings. Art is what we do with carroty hair or white, freckled skin or pale blue eyes that water so fast in the light.

3

Bess woke cramped against a wall. A shower was running and she could hear traffic loud nearby. Where? New York!

She turned away from the wall toward a room where in one spot green beads hung next to purple feathers stuck in a peach-colored hat. James would take one look and sink into a fit about abundance. Wherever her sister lived things seemed to rise up and proliferate, while she herself preferred the kind of space you find in a museum, with things coming to rest, balanced and still. If there were less stuff in this apartment, maybe Nora wouldn't mind that she . . .

Nora. A sense of something foul came over her. Last night Nora told them that her mother had tied her to a table when she was small, with her legs fixed onto some funny kind of wooden bar. Nora said her mother had snapped on the big lamp over the table . . .

Phoebe came through the doorway wrapped in a towel and, dressing hurriedly, shot sentences down toward the futon. "I'm late. The guys have gone and Nora's out by midafternoon. Bagels in the freezer. So long! Good luck!"

Standing, Bess found the floor gritty under her feet. Phoebe was flying;

what was the matter? She seemed unreachable, glassed over. The guys were okay. Big, hairy Daryl worked over in New Jersey in his parents' chain of retail stores, while the smaller, sleeker Ibrahim manned a camera at a TV studio out in Queens. But Nora! Nora had left law school and was tending bar at a place called the Open Eye.

"Do you believe it?" she'd asked Phoebe last night after Nora had gone off to work.

Phoebe's face had taken on an older-sister look. "Wake up, this stuff has been kept under wraps for centuries. Did you know that one out of four girls is sexually abused by the time she's fourteen?"

"No kidding. I only know one, from last summer. So how did we and all our friends escape?"

Phoebe made the old joke, "We lived in Philadelphia." They'd laughed and for a minute Bess had been able to shed a growing wariness.

Dressing quickly now, she gathered up her new keys and her backpack and her subway map and left for the Time Life building in midtown, where she had her first job interview and where Mom had landed a job two weeks after she graduated from Smith. A corporation? James would be shocked. Adrianna, too. She looked up at the lofty building before pushing through the door: New York was just an experiment, a get-started year. In the elevator a black guy with a single earring stood holding a picture spread of the city under the words THE ROTTING OF THE BIG APPLE. He gave her an appreciative look and she returned it.

In a small office a woman wearing half glasses explained that *Time* had just let go a lot of staffers. If they hired anyone now, it would be those same trained staffers coming back, only part-time, without health insurance. The woman gave a little smile.

An hour and a half later Bess emerged from a similar small office at Reader's Digest General Books, having talked with a similar woman in similar half glasses who'd spent the whole time inquiring about Bess's experiences at Wesleyan because her son was debating whether to apply there or to Harvard. "My friend James tried both and he didn't like Harvard *or* Wesleyan," Bess obliged her. "He says they're both filled with middle-class kids pretending they want to help the poor." That woman, too, gave Bess a funny little smile.

It was a discouraging morning but Bess tucked into a stationery store to buy a little flowered book of blank pages and then into a coffee shop, where she wrote into it the names of everyone she knew in New York. There were eighteen in all, her network. Who was Phoebe to think she didn't know about networks? A maid at the first phone number said Cara was in Jamaica for two weeks. Phil's mother at the second said he'd flown to British Columbia to fight forest fires for big pay. Sasha was up in Vermont for the summer and Toma in Nigeria indefinitely. Okay, not to worry. She sat back down and ordered a grilled cheese.

Her friends were responding to the worst job market in history the same way she was, by treating themselves to a final adventure before life took hold. If there weren't any jobs in New York, she'd head west. That's where her friend Adrianna wanted to go as soon as she got back from Scotland, where her family was spending the semester. Jobs were better out there. James's travels were another matter. Bess drank a lot of coffee.

On the next page of the flowered book she inscribed the motto of her biology class, THINK SMALL BUT CAREFULLY. That was hard to apply to the job market. Technology had changed everybody's jobs. Production had gone over to service. With statistics, you could measure the effects. You could get at what she loved most, the invisible truth under things. Except she didn't have the patience for real science.

When she'd killed enough time to allow for Nora's absence from the apartment, she went back underground. In the hard-walled tunnel, the cars came rattling and she was all alone in the crowd and suddenly missed the presence of familiar faces. She'd call the rest of her list tonight. Half the placards were in Spanish and she tried to decipher them.

Aboveground she stopped at a fairly inviting-looking flower shop. There was a small dark-skinned woman behind the counter with a ring in her nose. Her mother would die if she pierced her nose. She bought a huge bunch of dahlias—rosy-orange, van Gogh yellow, and musky pink, the kind her mother liked to fill the house with every fall. Too expensive, but they'd called out to her—Buy me, Bess! That's the Economic Imperative for you—Dad's favorite phrase.

Then back to the streets, the strangers and the traffic impinging. Why did Phoebe like New York so much? Didn't she ever get lonely? It seemed so vast and poor. Of course there was North Philadelphia, too, and the whole long ruin of Ridge Avenue where she'd driven abreast of James as he'd walked the blocks slowly, practicing to be poor. He had courage. She did not. Home seemed miles and years away and only cowards could return.

In the kitchen she found Phoebe sitting in front of the phone—her pale skin blotchy, as if she'd been crying.

"What's the matter?"

"The matter? Nothing's the matter. Great flowers! Any luck?"

4

Harvey suffered less over Bess's departure than he had over Phoebe's—both girls were educated now and that ended a major financial responsibility. They were on their own. No grad school, he'd done $150,000 on their colleges and it would take him five years to pay off the $67,000 loan before he could start saving for retirement. In his office, he gazed out over his desk toward a framed photograph of Phoebe and Bess so young that when he'd tripped the shutter he'd had no idea how they'd look grown. They were fishing off the dock at the lake out in Jersey and the sunlight made a triangle on Bess's small bent head as she labored with bait; it glistened off Phoebe's wet bathing suit as she cast out past the edge of the snapshot. A companion photograph of Claire showed her as young as his girls were now, wearing a straw hat and leaning over a railing with the Statue of Liberty behind her. He'd hardly thought of Claire as some man's child when he'd noticed that round face, those brown eyes, and that pleasing body in the elevator of his apartment building on Cornelia Street. He'd spoken to her first beside the mailboxes. "No checks, no love letters," he'd opened urbanely, riffling through his envelopes. "Bills," she'd replied, holding up two letters. "That time of the month," he'd answered without thinking of the phrase's other connotation, and she'd actually blushed. It was 1961, after all. "I'm sorry," he rushed in. "I mean . . . I'm Harvey, 3F." She was Claire, 2F. Days later, focusing through the shutter on that round face in the ferry spray, he'd felt all the other girls drop away and there she was, standing at the center of his life.

He turned on his computer. Like himself, the whole East Coast was in hock. He no longer searched for real estate to sop up with the annual profits of Sommers & Neugeboren, Life Insurance. Money had stopped flowing; the Japanese and Arabs had quit developing and weren't even buying trophy buildings. Everyone was running in place, managing and renovating. He must now get the maximum performance out of existing properties and dump the losers. Yesterday he'd called at a shopping center in Germantown where two young black men had leased adjoining storefronts for a literacy center that they'd flanked and supported with a beauty parlor and a dry cleaning shop. Graffiti covered the verticals, broken glass glittered in the parking lot. They were paying their bills on the thirtieth instead of the first, a bad sign. He ought to drop them. But he couldn't. Once he'd dreamed of working for racial equality. Raising kids, you don't get much chance. Now that the girls were grown, maybe he could try again.

Claire vowed to wait for an invitation before visiting the girls. She wouldn't hover, she reminded herself as she threaded through the back corridors of the museum and zigzagged among storage stacks to a stringent scattering of desks along the back wall. Research curator—not something to brag about at the Smith College reunion but after all she'd taken ten years out at home to raise her kids. They weren't so polite as kids raised by a nanny but they were curious and passionate and she didn't regret the long afternoons of snagged mitten clips, though she'd like to branch out now, try something new.

"How're the girls?" asked her neighbor, Winnie, a photographer hired two years before in the push for diversity.

"Bess has a job in a flower shop and says her hands are always freezing from the water. How's Cathy?"

Winnie's seventeen-year-old daughter had installed her boyfriend in her bedroom and Winnie said, "They've put their teddy bears together on the pillow."

They laughed, the white woman and the black woman, both trying to appear more relaxed than either felt in the daily acting out of the equality both had longed for as girls.

"At least she's protected," Winnie went on, looking down at her light box. "We got that part right in the seventies."

"We got work right, too," Claire responded. "At my age my mother was taking long naps and getting depressed about her empty nest."

"Well, mine was teaching fourth grade," Winnie replied with an edge that suddenly divided them.

Claire changed the subject. "Who are you up to?"

"Adriaen Van Ostade."

About work there was no undercurrent. "Oh, one of my favorites. I love that interior painting of the family by the hearth, the mother sitting in the basket to nurse the child."

"The shadowings on this one are unbelievably delicate," Winnie responded with enthusiasm. "But it's a wash and I'm having trouble keeping the contrasts up high enough. I hate to admit it but the camera doesn't do quite so delicate a job as the human hand."

Claire, too, admired the realistic renderings of the Dutch painters, their landscapes so mysterious, their skies rounded with so much god-filled space—indeed those skies had been the subject of her master's thesis. How she'd love to travel to the low countries—maybe when the debts were paid. Maybe alone? Throw herself into it, unprotected, uninfluenced by Harvey's constant presence.

Midafternoon she got a call from a collector in Baltimore. He'd heard about her from a friend on the museum board who'd actually sent him the Xerox of an old journal article of hers on the particularities of Jan Van Goyen's skies. Did she know of someone who'd make a good director of his holdings? She recommended Amy Broderick.

"She's down there in Baltimore."

"I was hoping, maybe yourself."

"She's down there. I'm up here."

"Ah yes, Philadelphia," he said, with the barely spoken irony she enjoyed.

Walking the two miles home in October's shine, she wondered if maybe she could handle a job or a commute like that. She bought sesame noodles and salad and stuffed them into her string bag. At home Harvey was in a good mood and family life engulfed her as he talked.

"I had to kill a loan in Willow Grove. But it wasn't so bad, the guy was actually sort of relieved."

"What was the problem?"

"Same old stuff, the recession."

They'd eaten so many meals here with the girls tiny, tired after instructive jaunts to mountains and sandy beaches, or home with relief from the orthodontist. They'd laughed at beginner jokes that weren't so funny and stood in their slippers to cast a cold eye on young men with artificial dreadlocks and real bulges in their jeans. At this very table they'd searched the entire English language for the right words to provoke thought and quell temper, to develop exactly the right amount of conscience, that is, not enough as that which sent Andrew Goodman to his death in a swamp in Mississippi.

". . . and Wilson Goode, he's really putting Philadelphia on the dead list."

"Winnie's son works for him."

"Why don't our daughters get jobs at the mayor's office?"

"We could call them and ask."

He laughed at that. But it was more than a week since they'd heard from the girls, so after supper when Harvey was crinkling the *Inquirer*, Claire stood at the wall phone by the counter and dialed Phoebe, who sounded strange. Then her voice became the old challenging, energetic song that Claire knew so well. Yes, it was great having her own room back now that Bess was gone. That voice? Oh, that was Peter. Oh, just someone who'd stopped by with a bag of steamed clams. There was laughter in the background, a cackle of sorts. Oh, that was just the guys, and Nora. Nora was having one of her little parties. At a nod from Claire, Harvey, across the room, picked up the long-corded mantel phone bought long ago so they could all talk to the grandparents together.

"Yo, Freebie," he said. Putting down the paper, he settled with pleasure into the sense of purpose her voice restored to him. They'd always been close. "Couldn't be better. I've saved a literacy storefront. How about you?"

"Same old job."

"Did you ask for that performance review?"

She gave a funny little laugh. "That's not exactly appropriate for Miss Hinckley's, Dad. Besides, I don't intend to stay on in this dump."

"What do you intend to do?"

"I don't know. Maybe I'll go into literacy storefronts. Maybe I'll win the lottery and go to film school. Maybe I'll hang up now."

He took a breath. "Don't hang up, honey. What's wrong?"

"Nothing, this is just a bad time to talk."

"Okay. Call us in a few days."

"What do you think?" Claire said when he'd hung up. "Didn't she sound a little depressed?"

"Maybe a little. Sounded like a party. That could be it."

"You don't think she was drunk, do you?"

"Drunk, why would you say that?"

"The forced hilarity in the background. Drugs?"

"I don't know." He searched his wife's face, its high rounded brow, the dark eyes. It wasn't like Claire to worry inappropriately, though there'd been times when the houseful of women had seemed to him awash in hysteria. Phoebe had sounded rude to him, more than anything else.

"You dial," Claire said, and recited Bess's new number at the northern edge of Manhattan. Phoebe was okay, the twenties had their ups and downs. That's all.

Bess wanted money.

"I know it's hard, honey," Harvey said. "But that's not what we agreed."

Claire readied herself, knowing he'd be turning the phone over to her soon.

"But that's what it's about, honey," he went on, with growing tightness in his voice. "That's why you have to get a job! Any job, it doesn't have to be the perfect job. You don't just borrow in life, Bess. In life you have to learn to pay your own way. Here, talk to your mother."

Claire picked up and the voice she heard sounded peeved: "God, Mom, he doesn't get it. Things are *expensive* here. I know you have to have a job, for Pete's sake! You have to have a place to live first! This room is five-fifty a month, plus a month's rent in advance, which I've got. But now they're telling me I'm supposed to come up with a month's security, too. That's sixteen-fifty, Mom! I only have eleven-fifty left from the job this summer. Does he want me to sleep on the street?"

Claire asked about the apartment, the roommates, and said, "We'll send you a thousand dollars, honey." She hung up and faced an annoyed Harvey.

"Why'd you do that?"

"That's what parents are for."

"I thought they're to teach kids about the real world."

"What's unreal about this? The place has entry fees."

"She should have planned better."

"She must be planning pretty well if she still has eleven-fifty from her summer job."

"Phoebe doesn't ask for money."

"She ought to now and then. She's too proud."

"How will Bess learn if we keep giving her everything?"

"How did the Rockefeller kids learn?"

Whoops, Claire hadn't meant to compare Harvey to the Rockefellers. But she *had* been wondering how the rich managed to teach their kids about money. She'd watched Bess's wealthy friend James Buttenwieser rinse his own dishes and put them in the washer.

Harvey didn't answer. He'd crinkled his way back into his newspaper, worrying about whether he'd dropped $150,000 on educations that had rendered his children spoiled as well as dreamless. Phoebe no longer spoke of working in the theater and Bess appeared content to wander the world with her knapsack. He wished his girls had dreams, big ones, the bigger the better. You start with a dream and work down. His girls didn't seem to be starting at all.

Claire could tell he was hurt and she knew him to be a man who required small but immediate attentions.

"You're looking very Robert Redford," she said. The offer of a job and a little irony to boot had put her in the mood.

"Ah, Simone," he replied, glancing up over the paper. "The young Simone," he added quickly.

She laughed. "Simone Signoret was never young."

Later they climbed up to the fourth floor and took showers, each looking up through the five-hundred-dollar skylight at the distant darkness and the present stars. Life is short. They made love in their new, slower way, and did not notice the luster of the white sheets in the old glass of the mirror, which would have reflected them in their calmed pleasures to anyone crossing the room. No one else was in the room though. They were alone till the holidays.

In a cubbyhole for secretaries, Phoebe pulled the edges off the new brand of tractor-feed paper. It was satisfying, much easier and neater than the last brand. She said that again to herself and then smiled to the TV audience and mouthed, *Buy this brand.* She smiled again, made eyes at the imaginary camera. Oh, this was such a fun, wonderful, creative, important, worthwhile, inspiring, life-saving job at the Hinckley School!

Maybe Dad was right, try Teach America, try film school, try law school. Except after a few years as a lawyer, she'd be just like Dad, sold out, dead—his John Lennon haircut shorn off for his first really decent job interview in, what could it have been, 1964? Besides, he wasn't paying for grad school. She'd have to borrow. It was life she needed anyway, not school. Your work is too personal, live.

She could quit and tend bar. Nora said the only problem was the older guys who stared down your cleavage. They never touched you but they talked on and on twenty minutes past closing time every night staring at your breasts. Her own cleavage was nothing to get excited about, though Andrew had said—the one night they'd had together—that her breasts were perfect, perfection. Too bad she'd heard him saying the same thing to Sophie right through her wall.

Ibrahim had the best job she knew of. He'd been hired on what he liked to call Quota Day. He could do Lebanese, Egyptian, Gay, and Other. Try Native American, he'd told her, but her father's stories of early intermarriage with the tribes on the Chesapeake would never cut it.

Here she was, a daddy's girl, and everybody in women's studies said daddy's girls do so well. Not one kind word from NYU, a standard reject. Something was holding her back. Maybe she had a fatal flaw. Hamlet's? Agamemnon's? Orestes'? They were all men, of course, the West incarnate. Maybe her fatal flaw was . . . Phoebe, come to attention! The boss passeth through!

Mr. Reed opened the glass door on which was painted in peeling black letters, BUSINESS OFFICE, COMPTROLLER. Mr. Reed extended a foot and then another foot into the airless, windowless cubicle. She looked up dutifully. Mr. Reed spoke. "Hi, Felina." It was his little joke.

You gotta hold your own. She replied with her little joke. "Mr. Reed, I presume?" Oh, God, the working world. Then he was off in a cloud of dandruff and she put the letters she'd processed into a stack and headed out. The good thing about this job was leaving at four o'clock. The kids were already gone to their nannies by then, nannies who'd stood so long in creased white uniforms outside the door, waiting to teach the little ones the class system.

Down in the subway Phoebe Fairchild: Most Likely to Succeed pressed her token into the slot, moved against the turnstile, her red hair going a sickening lavender under the fluorescents. PREGNANT? a sign in the advertising slots asked. God, I hope not. Asians, Africans, Hispanics filled the seats. Really, it was so boring being white. Maybe that was her flaw. She'd never known what to do in grade school at the yam festival. And at Yale, well, she'd had to take constant heat for the sins of the West. Worse, men thought WASPs were made of ice.

She was not. She could still remember the thrill that went through her in high school the first time Vince Lamberra kissed her—as an experiment—in front of the Vibration Transference exhibit at the Franklin. And Pop Termolian, God, why had she done that? A hippie cook twice her age? Because he knew everything, that's why, and because he adored her.

Phoebe, Phoebe, he'd whisper, out on the beach by the breakers at night, my phoenix. She'd been surprised he knew a word like that.

Changing trains at Grand Central, she walked through an underground tunnel past an incredibly handsome black man in tatters playing a saxophone under a huge ad that showed white people who had curled their hair and acquired thousands of dollars' worth of tennis equipment drinking and otherwise living a darling life. That's not me! Not me! she tried to project to her fellow travelers.

At her own apartment, and what's this? No resistance met her turning key—the door was opening! It was the guys, coming out.

"See you Monday, princess," announced Daryl, in his New Jersey jeans with the deliberate hole at the knee.

"Tonight's the night for ABC," advised Ibrahim in biking shorts, raising his fingers. "Bogart at ten."

She gave them high fives and went in. They were off for the weekend and she'd be alone for three whole nights. The place smelled of dead smoke and beer, meaning Nora. The red light on the answering machine was blinking. Peter had called! She put down her pocketbook, draped herself over the chair, shook her hair out behind her, adopted the air of Katharine Hepburn in an oldie, pressed the button and heard Nora's mother pleading, *Please dear, call us, Our letter came back Return to Sender. Please, please.*

The next message was for Nora, too. *Dr. Donna Phillips here. I cannot meet with Nora Mercer on Tuesday. Call for rescheduling.* And then the beeps and buzzes and no more messages.

Peter had said he might come by. He seldom called till around ten, which meant you had to stay in the whole evening. *His* life mattered, he was always onstage. Maybe that's what appealed to her about him. Was that her flaw? To be always a watcher? That's not a flaw. It's a talent. After all, actors must know the self, directors others. The drugs, though, they scared her. But his body, hers with it, and the way he held her . . . Friday evenings were so hard.

She made scrambled eggs and ate them at the table, where she discovered that Arabic letters upside down looked Japanese. There was a yellowing newsprint picture of Tiananmen Square. Jamaican music came from the pipe that ran vertically through the kitchen. Welcome to worldwide competition. Welcome to real life. Cleaning up at the sink, she felt uncomfortable with her back exposed in the empty kitchen.

It was not yet half past six. Would he call? You could not predict Peter. Once in the subway he'd leaned over her and kissed her on the top of the forehead and said, "Because you have the heart of a Girl Scout, and not because of your beautiful sexy hair."

She leaned back and shook her hair out. Peter definitely wasn't the kind of guy you could count on. That kind tended to resemble Roger Blaustein, who taught fourth grade at the school. Her parents would like Roger. Maybe she'd call them tonight. No, not until she had some news, good news.

It was less lonely in the bathroom, redoing her eyeliner. Peter had said next time he'd bring some downers, just a little bit of something. She'd like it, he'd promised.

I don't want anything. I'm fine.

I know, you're fine. You're very fine, Phoebeebeebee, the finest. But this'll slow us down. You'll like it. It'll keep you from thinking. You think too much.

Everybody tries everything once. You have to. Otherwise, how do you know? You have to study all of human emotion. Coke she'd tried and ended up putting in the same category as champagne and caviar, expensive and bubbly, sort of out of sight. But she could accept a downer, one, to try it. Hey, what's that?

The doorbell. No kidding.

Then he was there on the other side of the glass bubble, distorted, and then he was pressing his tongue against the bubble. She opened the door and there he was, tall, bright, radiating self-love.

"Ho, Beebee."

He touched her right away, already on something. No need to talk when you're on something. From his mouth to hers, he slipped her a small hard pellet, the downer. She let it glide down her throat, her hips moved toward his. It wasn't something serious out of John Sayles with Peter, it was always something very Philip Kaufman, something very Henry and June against the wall. But this time, slow.

On the futon they lay together in an altered state that was hardly love.

They touched gently, so very very gently, and everything came peacefully. There was no hurry, no rhythm, or rather the rhythm was to such a cadence that the space between the beats seemed timeless, perfect, forever. His long fingers caressed her, his Scandinavian coloring pleased her, but where was she? Not here, not as herself, only watching.

"I need a place to stay, babe," he said afterward. "Can I hang out here with you?"

Weeks later he was still there, occupying far more space than Bess had, never washing the sheets, showering exactly when Nora claimed the bathroom. East Germans were flooding into West Germany and westerners were evacuating Kuwait but Peter stayed on. It got to be late October and there she was, totally naked, in the shower, with Nora all puffed up and pulling back the curtain with a flourish, shouting.

"No, no, no, not another day!" It was like a scene out of *Psycho*. "Not another day! He goes or you go. Daryl agrees with me!"

Phoebe grabbed a towel. "I pay my rent!"

"And his, it appears. You're an idiot! Take a look at yourself! There's gotta be a reason for what you're doing."

Here was a test of projection, of personality. She was Nora's equal. She would outshout her: "I want some privacy!"

"So do I! He goes. Today!"

"He's my lover! Why shouldn't I have him? Ibrahim and Daryl have each other!"

"They both pay. Listen, he's out by tonight or you're out! Call the locksmith. Or I will. Your stuff will go on the stoop along with his."

Was this little Nora, the whiz of her Foucault class? "Nora, what's with you?"

"You're the one with the blanket over your face. Wake up. The man is using you."

She could see herself in a blanket, lying on the prairie like someone out of *Dances With Wolves*. It was funny, sort of. But she didn't laugh. What she wanted was to cry. "Nora, I'm scared of him."

"I'll help you. Come on, I'll look up the locksmith in the Yellow Pages."

Phoebe saw that Nora's dark eyes did not waver, that Nora's small body stood upright, that she herself had lost the contest. Nora knew how to get what she wanted. She didn't. She was a loser. Nora, a winner. Nora would help her. She needed help. Resolve left her. She went limp. Tears gathered in her eyes.

"Buck up, woman."

"I don't know what's wrong," Phoebe managed to choke out. She sat down on the closed toilet. "I think I'm just getting the tiniest bit depressed."

"The whole fucking world is what's wrong," Nora said. "You have to fight back. These bastards will take every inch they can get. Florence Rush did not lie: Men screw us to teach us our place in society. Now, get the phone book. I've already arranged with the guys to take Peter out tonight. I've convinced him he wants to experience life in a gay bar. They're leaving about ten and will stay with him a couple of hours, then they'll proceed off to one of their little forays without him and he'll come home alone. Tell the locksmith ten-thirty. It'll be overtime, but that's the best way. We don't want fisticuffs."

Phoebe nodded her head.

"You need help," Nora said. "Not to worry. I know where you can find it."

Therapy. Phoebe'd often imagined herself in therapy, especially after Liz Tsui had gone to Dr. Lucy in junior high and begun to get the good parts in the plays. She stood in an apartment building near St. Marks Place looking at a shiny plaque that said SAHRA MEEHAN, M.S.W. Sahra, that sounded, maybe, Bengali? Exciting. Well, no matter what, the woman had a master's degree, and a master knows what to do.

Opening the door, she stepped into a narrow waiting room in which a humidifier hummed and spit. God, this place was damp. She wondered if the pale spot on her chair could be mildew. A framed diploma informed her that Sahra Meehan had received her MSW this very year from the Warburg School of Social Work. She'd heard of the Warburg. When a door opened, a disappointingly ordinary-looking woman who was at least ten years her senior invited her in.

"Phoebe Fairchild? This way, please."

The voice was good, strong and assured; the woman wore black balloon pants and a brown shirt, maybe silk, very New York—Mariel Hemingway, without the eyebrows.

Two wicker chairs faced each other in front of a wall on which hung a pair of masks, tragedy and comedy as carved by Native Americans. If only she could have had Nora's doctor, Dr. Donna Phillips. Dr. Phillips was famous. She'd been on *Good Morning America.* The good doctor wouldn't, however, treat the roommate of a client.

Phoebe took a seat next to a tiny table bearing a box of tissues in a metal container. Give us a break. Maybe she shouldn't have come. She hated decorative tissue boxes. She rested her eyes on the one beautiful thing: a light green Chinese vase containing those tall grasses that grow beside highways. Oh, what are they called? What? What? Fragmites? Fragmatites? My life has fallen into fragmatites. She allowed her crinkly hair to drift comfortingly over the edge of her face and she waited.

Sahra Meehan wanted to like this client referred to her by the Warburg Clinic but on first sight, no. That great mane of red hair had been permanented on number twos, the smallest rods, the ones her mother dreaded having to roll. The eyes were downcast and somehow the client stirred up anxiety in her own gut. Rapport is essential. If you don't have it, you're not supposed to take the client. This summer she'd turned down a referral and the young man had eventually been diagnosed as schizophrenic. What a relief. You don't want schizophrenics. But this was her first referral from the clinic where she dreamed of making staff. Try and try again.

"Something brings you in for help?"

"It's men, I guess," the client said, looking into her lap, mumbling her words. "I've been . . . having a relationship with this guy named Peter. He's . . . very creative, but trouble, in a way. . . . Anyhow, I let him stay with me. But my roommates . . . I guess you don't know Nora?"

"No." Sahra shook her head.

It was hard to talk to someone with decorator tissues. "They said he had to leave. And I guess . . . although I'm attracted to him, I don't really *like* him. I mean, you can't trust Peter. He . . . he does a little drugs." She looked at her hands. Really, she had to do better than this. "Nothing much, but . . . you know, it's not always clear if he's going to show up. And he says he hasn't slept around much, not enough to be dangerous, but somehow . . ." She raised her eyes to Sahra Meehan's, which were a remarkable light green. "Somehow you know he's the type that might not even tell you if he were positive. I mean HIV positive?"

Sahra nodded. A good thing to worry about; you can't trust anyone. Now, who did this person remind her of? Someone back home in upstate New York.

Phoebe felt estranged from those green eyes. This whole thing was starting to feel sort of ridiculous, unreal. "I called the locksmith . . . even though it seemed so cruel, so final, not to mention expensive. When Peter came back and pounded on the door, I watched through the peephole. The look on his face . . . like out of the Irish Republican Army, I mean, ready to kill? Then he stopped pounding and just stood there, looking so alone, so abandoned, and that was worse, much worse."

Loss—Sahra Meehan felt her first connection to Phoebe Fairchild. The winter her father walked out on them in Watertown, New York, in all that snow, she'd stood night after night in the living room by the window calling out, Here he comes now! This car now!

Phoebe suddenly felt welcome and she tucked some hair behind an ear and let more of her face into the open. "He can be a sweet guy, really. But then he started in again, you know, kicking the door? That scared me. I'm just no judge of men at all! So that's why I'm here, I guess. I always choose the wrong guy."

Sahra had chosen the wrong guy, too. Quite a few things rated higher on her happy list than Brian Untermeyer: endive with French dressing for one. She smiled and said, "You were right to come, Phoebe. This can be a confusing time of life, the twenties. But it's a great time to organize, take charge of ourselves, find our true identities. Go on. You're doing fine. What else?"

Phoebe smiled back, then her forehead wrinkled. "I'm, like, tired all the time? And I hate my job. It's menial of the brain. And I don't have any money. I can't imagine how I'll pay you."

"Let's don't worry about payment right now," Sahra said, and a look she couldn't decipher crossed Phoebe's face. "Tell me a bit about your family."

Phoebe moved on, though she could see her mother wincing at that "let's don't." Really, grammar is such a pointless distinction, such an old-fashioned nicety! "Oh, they're okay, really. Very privileged, you know, very establishment. Half my friends at school were on scholarship. They were the poor boys and I was the rich girl, except my parents aren't really rich, just comfortable."

Sahra was thinking of that awful wallpaper with pictures of camels walking over every inch and of hanging around with Maria Demas and talking about the smartest, best-dressed girls from Watertown High. . . . Sherry Knight, that's it! This is Sherry Knight. That's what her gut had been trying to tell her. Okay, she got it. Countertransference examined, she could get past herself. She could keep this client! First, to concentrate on Phoebe and take a shot at diagnosis. The new rules demanded one almost immediately.

Phoebe's sentences were coming more easily. "They're very straight people, you know. My father's a good guy, I guess you could say. I'm sort of a daddy's girl." She gave a laugh, apologetic. "I mean he always let me know that he admires me. He came to all the plays I ever acted in and he always brought flowers."

Sahra's father had never reappeared but so what. She'd had her mother, good old Agnes. Where was Phoebe's mother?

Phoebe felt funny talking about her parents. They were okay, pretty nice, actually. But therapy is about parents, isn't it? So she did what she could. "My mother makes herself so subservient to my father. I hate that. It's always Yes, honey, yes, honey. But he is sort of terrific, in his clumsy way." She felt the therapist was really listening now and she tossed back her hair and began to hit a stride. "Of course, they know nothing of the real world. My mother never in her life had to rip tractor-feed paper to support herself. They do try, though. In fact, they try a little too hard. They're always so understanding. Sometimes I've wondered if they'd even forgive me for serial murder. They're always *there.*"

Failure to separate?

"They expect a lot of me. And I'm not doing so well. Bess made me feel so . . . She's my sister. She's beautiful. She's just come to New York. I put her up for a little while but Nora went apeshit and I was glad, sort of, when Bessie left. She and Mom were always, like, a pair?"

Dysfunctional family alignment?

"It got so hard to keep up a front with Bess. I don't know why, I've been crying a lot since she came and I never used to do that. It's just so lonely in

New York sometimes. It's so big. And I hate my job. Did I say that, Sarah? Dr. Meehan? What do I call you, anyway?"

"Sah-ra," she said, deepening the first syllable the way her yoga instructor had done—mispronouncing her given name and simultaneously letting her know that we can be what we want in life, if we'll just take charge of ourselves.

"Sah-ra," Phoebe repeated. "Nice. Okay. I guess the most important thing is that I want to be a film director, but how do you get there? I'm a paltry little secretary. So all in all, I'm here to figure out what I'm doing wrong. Nora said it would help."

Sahra's eyes moved toward the clock: 4:39. "That's an excellent beginning, Phoebe. We should be able to work together. One last question. Is there anything you're not telling me?"

"Sure, lots!"

"Some big, dark secret?" This was the generalized intake question on sexual abuse and she'd almost forgotten to ask it.

Phoebe thought of all the times she'd hated Bess and envied Liz Tsui. "No."

"Okay. Now, my sessions run at sixty dollars an hour. Have you got insurance?"

"I think so. Maybe. At work?"

"Check it out. It's probably five hundred dollars a year and that's plenty right now, since it's already November. Next week, then, at this same time?"

Sahra walked her client to the exit door, automatically imagining a more grown-up hairstyle for her—gathered low at the nape, a few tendrils to soften the face. Her mother had always said, *You want to help them, dearie? You give them a haircut that will stop their friends dead in the street.*

Back in her office, Sahra clasped her hands behind her back and began her stretches, warned by Dr. Mundiger of what could happen to a therapist's body after years in The Chair. Your work does affect your body—Agnes Meehan had come home every night with shoulders aching and ankles swollen. She'd stick a meatloaf in the oven and put her legs up on a chair. She'd open a beer and ask Sara, as she was called then, to massage her shoulders. Please, dearie—her mother's nightly stories of tumors and infidelities began—find something that pays better than this, although it's great work, hairdressing, great work, we're the priests of the brush and comb. And she had found her work. Approaching forty, she'd probably never bear children but never mind, a good therapist brings young adults into the world a second time. She'd be the Good Mother to other people's children. She'd fix heads instead of hair, her mother's old joke that had annoyed her for years. You need eighteen clients to survive and now she had six. If she did well with Phoebe, there'd be others from the clinic.

Phoebe had so much going for her. What had put her off track? Making notes on a possible analysis, Sahra looked up several categories in the manual to check their numbers: *Depressive Disorder (311). Generalized Anxiety Disorder (300.02).* Or was it *Adjustment Reaction with Anxious Mood (309.24)*? Or maybe *Adjustment Disorder with Mixed Anxiety and Depressed Mood (309.28)*? She jotted down key words: *Hates job, chooses losers. Needs to separate. Jealousy? Loss?* She'd build Phoebe up, give her some confidences. First, a more realistic goal—she'd wanted to be a talk-show host herself. Get real, Phoebe. Take a step at a time. Sometimes all these young women needed was a little meatloaf and a cheering squad, but of course their mothers were always flying back and forth to the Cayman Islands. Okay, she'd do her best. Here she was helping Sherry Knight. That was a laugh. If she knew where her old friend Maria Demas was, she'd call her up and tell her!

7

Thanksgiving, and the girls weren't coming home. They were going to dinner at some friend of Phoebe's in New York. Claire and Harvey cut back the darkened stalks of lilies and long-fragrant phlox behind the house. They recalled to each other their last visit to Phoebe's place in Rockaway, when, driving home, they'd laughed at how painfully clear it was that their daughter couldn't wait for them to leave—exactly as they'd once felt about their own parents' visits.

"At least she invited Bess," Claire said. "They must be getting on."

"Must be."

"Maybe Phoebe's in love. That's why she sounds funny on the phone."

"Hope so."

They'd promised each other not to dwell on the girls today. After the cutting came the bulbs and they'd waited too late this fall. It wasn't easy for Harvey to tease the spade into the hardened if still-unfrosted earth. From a paper bag Claire took one narcissus bulb and stuck it into the hole he dug, then another. They worked well together. Now and then the wind played against a string of brass bells Bess had hung outdoors.

Beyond the withered perennials stood a cherry tree, some lilac bushes, and farthest off a collection of tired rosebushes hanging on to a trellis against the back wall of the lot. Above these dry remnants they could see their neighbors in the kitchen of the abutting house stuffing a turkey. It pleased both of them that they were not doing a turkey. It reminded them of the time before the children when not doing holiday things had made them feel rebellious and powerfully grown-up.

Last, they mulched the garden, the damp air reddening their cheeks. Their bare dirt-caked hands stiffened in the chill and they named the warm places they would visit five years from now when the college debt was paid—Crete, Sicily, maybe Arizona, not Florida.

"Definitely not Florida!"

"It's wall-to-wall shuffleboard."

It was a happy morning, with the usual reservations. When Harvey looked at Claire, he saw home and home is not the only thing he'd dreamed of as a boy. When Claire looked at Harvey, she felt a slight sense that she must perform for him, block out part of herself, pretend, exaggerate. Still, she smiled when she put her blackened hand into his and pulled herself to her feet. There was the old thrill of standing beside a tall, well-made man.

Inside they showered, dressed, and, because it was Thanksgiving, telephoned what was left of their parents. Upstairs in the bedroom where the comforter was rumpled and clothes were strewn about, Claire dialed her father in Florida. He lived beside a golf course with his second wife, the jovial New Age Linda.

"Hi, Dad. How are you? . . . Good. Good. Linda? . . . Good. . . . Oh, fine. We've just mulched the garden. . . . They're spending Thanksgiving in New York. Some friend of Phoebe's. . . . Yes, Bess went along with her. . . . Yes, nice they can be together. . . . Oh, Bess is working in a flower shop. . . . Yes, I know she was an honors student but . . . yes. I'll tell her. . . . Yes, Phoebe's still at the school. . . . Well, she isn't planning to stay there forever. You can't just walk into film directing, you know. It's the same old story—no license without experience, no experience without a license. . . . No, we're going out to dinner. . . . That's nice. . . . Yes, to you, too, and to Linda."

She hung up. Somehow there was simply nothing to say to Dad anymore. His life had grown impersonal. All history of home had faded. If only her mother were alive. She'd never been that close to Edie Walsh Monroe but lately she suspected her mother would have understood the vague melancholy of ceremonial days, even if she'd never known why a girl would want to pierce her ears. Or perhaps she had known, perhaps that's why she'd forbidden it.

When Harvey finished shaving and took his turn at the bedside phone, Claire was leaning over brushing her expertly cut hair downward to give it bounce. He reached a tape at his sister's house in Minneapolis. Phyllis and Ben must be with one of their daughters, both of whom were married now. His sister and he—not a son between them! He left his message and then punched in his mother's numbers and gave her name to the receptionist at Lakeside Rest. Breathing he heard, tight breathing, and then the old, familiar voice.

"Hello?"

"Hi, Mother. It's me, Harvey."

"Hello there?"

"Hi, Mother. It's me, Harvey, your son."

"Hello, son."

"How's everything there, Mother?"

"We're having mashed potatoes with gravy."

"No turkey?"

"Turkey?"

"We're not having turkey here, either, Mother. How are you?"

"I am fine. Who is paying the bills here?"

"The bills, Mother?" He couldn't say the state. That would break her heart after how hard she'd worked to keep her nest egg intact. Nine months at Lakeside and *pffft*. "I am." It was true enough; he bought the extras.

"And who, may I ask, is I?"

"Your son, Harvey."

"Harvey is paying the bills? Good Lord, I hope he's doing a good job!" She hung up.

Harvey put the receiver quietly into its cradle. Claire swung the hair back to look at him. He sat on the bed like a small boy whose house has been swept away. It wasn't his mother's lack of confidence in him—he'd grown used to that. It was that other, the basic absence that collects around you when there is no mother to keep you entire and together in her mind.

Claire stopped brushing. It was just like last time.

"Didn't she know you?"

"No."

"I'm sorry," she said, then added with a laugh, "Who could ever figure you out anyway? My mystery man!"

He stood up, resumed something of the world. "Come on, kid. Let's go."

They seated themselves in the dining room of the small inn in Amish country where they'd once signed in as man and wife before the fact. That was in the heady days of the early 1960s when nice girls were still deciding whether to buy themselves diaphragms and join the revolution. Yes, I said, I said yes, yes, I will buy a diaphragm, Claire repeated to herself with an inner laugh. For Harvey, yes. For Jerry before him, no, no diaphragm. Only romance, only swept away. The smile left her face. At least she'd done that much for her girls, informed them, prepared them. Maybe they'd never have to go through an abortion the way she had. But if she hadn't done it, her two girls would never have been born. Why hadn't Phoebe returned their call this week? Something was wrong with Phoebe. Something was veiled, off, not working. She remembered the last time she'd seen her alone, in the kitchen before they'd driven off to the train, turned, seen her; she'd been fine, hadn't she? Claire had meant not to, but she spoke of the girls again across the table.

"Do you think they're okay?"

"Hey, we're not calling them, remember? We're waiting to see if they call us."

"How can they? We're not there."

"They'll talk to our machine. We called our parents, didn't we?"

Harvey looked across at Claire, whose dark eyes received him. This was home. And how lucky he was. He'd watched marriages over the years. Most people stopped talking to each other, but Claire had remained his friend. She was the one person in the world to whom he truly spoke, with whom he risked all—well, almost all. He examined the menu. "We won't be eating all this German stuff in Crete."

"We'll be eating on a balcony," she joined in. The image of the northern lowlands where she might wander alone had faded weeks ago. "There'll be sunshine all over the balcony. It will be eighty-four degrees." Maybe Phoebe's ancient need to make conflict or—to put it in a better light, to stand up for herself no matter what—would wither away. Maybe Bess would stop relying so much on her friends with their self-denying and alternatingly self-indulgent ideas. She took in the room, the candlelight, the Olde Inne and its accoutrements. They'd been in love when they'd first come here: Harvey's hair red then and worn like John Lennon's. Hers had been darkening but cut à la Sassoon. How malleable we all are in the culture of our time, thinking ourselves to be individuals, when really, we're every one of us peas in the soup du jour.

The man across the table was full of energy. He was talking to her, and she nodded as he spoke, but somehow she was thinking of her mother, who'd lived in a kind of silence like this, smiling, nodding, encouraging. Where had Edith Walsh's keen, unused mind wandered as she listened to Lester Monroe—out to her garden of Protestant peas? To her yellow cat asleep in the hammock? To her daughter, Claire, on an abortionist's table next to a sinkful of blood? No, she'd never told her mother about that. You can't grow up until you stop telling it all to your mother.

"So if I keep on floating these two guys and don't dump them," the energetic, white-haired man was saying, "we could maybe work together at the mall in something like the community-development centers Bobby Kennedy started up."

Oh, ask not what you can do for the country, ask how to put the heart to rest when you want someone, anyone, to ask you how you're really doing in these strange years when it seems your life is over and all the time it hasn't, somehow, begun.

Phoebe stood on a faded Persian rug in front of an elevator in a huge lobby, glad that Sahra had urged her to stay in the city for Thanksgiving. The Blausteins, 11J. This could be fun. Maybe they'd be exotic like Daryl's parents, with fringes and candles—a sort of Hebrew Thanksgiving. "Is there anything you're not telling me?" Sahra had asked again last time, as if expecting her to come up with something they both knew was there, something dark and exciting. Yes, there is. I pray to be Ibo.

Roger opened the door. She took in his brown hair, his tiny old-fashioned Ben Franklin eyeglasses. Beyond him she glimpsed an expanse of not-so-faded Persian rugs and a view of the reservoir in Central Park and light, glorious light, on the fragile reddened tips of the bare tree branches out beyond the glass. And Roger had told her he was a socialist.

"Yo, Roger. Nice to view you in your natural habitat."

"Thank God you're here." He was an only child, responsible to his parents on every holiday, Jewish, Christian, and state. "Even before the appetizers, we've run out of subject matter."

"It's not exactly socialist Sweden, your place."

He indicated the surround. "Sometimes I wish I could get a short, life-threatening disease. Nothing mutilating. I'd recover. And then I'd never have to apologize for all this."

She laughed a little, suggesting that she knew the feeling.

He led her into a small kitchen to introduce her to his mother, who had two wings of gray in her short straight hair and a kindly manner. Phoebe surveyed the stack of dinner plates warming on top of the stove, the array of pots. It looked a lot like home.

"Can I help?"

"Not yet, dear, maybe later." Mrs. Blaustein picked up pot holders and headed toward the stove. Roger led her into the dining room to introduce her to his father, who was opening two bottles of zinfandel.

"So you're Phoebe from Yale," he said, wiping his hands on a linen napkin before shaking hers. She could see the hope on his face: Maybe Roger has a Girl. It was an exact match for her father's expression: Maybe Phoebe has a Guy.

"And you're Mr. Blaustein from the courts of law?"

He laughed, and she felt okay. She shouldn't feel this nervous. After all, she was hardly interested in Roger, nor he in her. He was merely seeking surcease of pain and she was merely trying to establish her own identity, as Sahra put it. Never mind the occasional clichés, Sahra got the main point: We're here to win. Trust Sahra not to self-destruct among the nuances.

"You can help out by eating the appetizers," Roger suggested, putting his hand on her shoulder to lead her into the living room with its many books. She might as well have gone straight to Philadelphia. Roger sat on the couch in front of a tray of marinated mushrooms. "Have ten or twenty."

On the wall behind them hung one of those blowups of a *New Yorker* cover that shows nothing between the Palisades and the Golden Gate Bridge. Okay, her parents would not have framed that.

She took a mushroom. "Bess should be here in a few minutes. They're closing the shop at one."

Roger took a mushroom. "Wow, kid, I'm so relieved you're here."

Maybe he was okay. Phoebe resettled the Renaissance hair that had fallen over her shoulder. She thought of a couple of things to put on the conversational table but they seemed ever so slightly like her mother placating her father and Sahra had told her to watch herself carefully on that score. You're done with them, Phoebe. Let's get to you. Who is Phoebe? Listen to yourself, your true self. God, it made conversation impossible. Roger was leaning forward now, close.

"I can tell Dad liked you. He doesn't usually laugh like that."

"Oh. Well."

The bell rang and Roger went off to the door. Thank God, a moment to get a grip. All this self-examination can rob you of spontaneity. But you gotta learn. A director must know everything an actor knows. In one of her weirder moments Sahra had suggested she think about aiming at something easier than directing, like maybe advertising or camera work.

She heard voices—his, Bess's—from the foyer. Then from the kitchen with Mrs. Blaustein's voice added, then from the dining room with Mr. Blaustein's. Then back into the living room but something had altered in Roger. A kind of valence was almost visible between him and Bess. Oh God, the old story, just like high school with Vince Lamberra! Never mind, you don't want Roger.

Everything grew jollier. Maybe it was the drinks. Mr. Blaustein sure looked contented pouring it out. And Mrs. Blaustein dug right into her crystal glass. They sat at the table with Roger across from her and Mr. Blaustein at the end, carving. Over them hung a too vast chandelier that didn't have a single missing bulb. She thought of her own parents, alone in front of a turkey, abandoned.

Turkey skin! Her mother would never allow that. Her mother's cranberry sauce would have nice little gobs of real cranberries in it. Oh, what was the matter? Her throat was filling up with tears. "Relax and go with the tears," Sahra had said. "It isn't good to keep them inside of you. They're chemically poisonous."

"We used to go up to Connecticut to my grandparents'," Roger was explaining as his gaze moved at a slant past her to Bess. "Over the bridge and through the New Haven tunnel to grandmother's house we go."

"That's Christmas." Phoebe heard herself correcting but Roger paid no mind. Actors learn to tell the exact point at which they've lost the audience. She tried eating. Maybe it was Thanksgiving, anyway? She was losing her grip.

"More turkey, Phoebe?" Mr. Blaustein was looking happy, very happy.

"Tell us about your family, girls," Mrs. Blaustein put in, just as their mother would have. "I mean women, young women." She laughed at herself then, with her hand to her breast. "I mean Bess and Phoebe. Tell us about your parents."

Phoebe let Bess answer, as she tried to shake off the sense of her own dining room at home. Mom smoothing things down, Dad blustering. It wasn't Dad she missed. She'd finished Dad, Sahra was right about Dad. It was Mom.

"They must miss you today," Mrs. Blaustein said, smiling at both of them but mostly Bess.

"Tell you what, I'll treat you to a phone call," Mr. Blaustein added. "I always let visiting young people call home."

"You do? So does my Dad!" These were the first words that came out of Phoebe's mouth without forethought. But she didn't want to call her parents from here. She was afraid she might cry. She turned toward Bess. "They were going out to Bala-Cynwyd for dinner, remember?"

"Oh, yeah," Bess replied obediently. "They were going out to dinner. We'll call them later. Thanks, anyway."

Phoebe held up her glass and Mr. Blaustein poured more of that rather stunning zinfandel all around. "To our parents!" Phoebe toasted, touching her glass with Bess's and then Mr. Blaustein's and then Mrs. Blaustein's and then Roger's. She looked right straight at him through those tiny silly little eyeglasses of his and—tightening her solar plexus to put a compelling energy into her voice—delivered the best line she could think of: "May they get a life in the global economy!" To which Mr. Blaustein replied, "Hear! Hear!"

When the pumpkin pie was being cut, Phoebe glanced at her watch and said, "Oh my God, but I've got to leave, I promised my housemates I'd be there for a little champagne this evening. Not to worry, Bess. You stay as long as you want. . . . Yes, yes, I will have a little pie and some coffee for the road. It's been lovely, really lovely."

On the first subway, she sat across from a man who was reading a newspaper folded in front of his face so that a picture of George Bush appeared just where the man's face should be. She had the creepiest feeling that if he lowered the paper, it would be Dad sitting there. On the second subway, one of those crazy guys who hadn't shaved in years sat across from her munching on his own gums. When the third subway pulled in to her station, Phoebe stood, adjusted her shoulder bag, pulled up the collar of her coat, and assumed her city posture: Here we go, into real life. The wild crinkly hair spilled out over the collar but the look on her face said, *Don't touch me, I'm carrying mace.*

Thank God, the guys were at home and Nora wasn't—she was tired of Nora and not just because she talked about Dr. Phillips as if she were so much better than Sahra. In the hallway Phoebe called out a greeting and the guys came into the kitchen, which was a chaos of dishes and pans. They started warming up leftovers and doing Gene Kelly imitations. She shook off her coat, pushed back her flyaway hair, and sat at the table with a cup of tea. At last a sense of warmth began to creep up from her feet. The guys started in on the Yellow Brick Road, turning into tin men before her eyes, creaking and halting. She could just see Vince Lamberra doing his Mister Rogers imitation, hanging his arms funny from his shoulders and putting one hand into the sleeve of an imaginary button-down sweater. She laughed until the tears ran out of her eyes, warm and oddly comforting.

9

Waiting for Phoebe Fairchild to arrive for her fourth session, Sahra Meehan reviewed the instructions of her supervisor, Dr. Carl Mundiger, in their weekly consult at the Warburg School. He'd raised the possibility of childhood sexual abuse in her new case. Phoebe? Why? she'd asked him, surprised, and he'd pointed to the classic signs. You've got a little drug use, a little promiscuity, lots of depression, and failure to make a lasting relationship; you may have trouble at work. Had Sahra asked Phoebe about insomnia or eating disorders? I'll ask again about sleeplessness, but I've asked her twice if there's something she hasn't told me and she says no. Don't ask her generally, ask directly. Remember your seminar work last year: Survivors need permission, repeated permission to remember abuse. After all, they've worked so hard to repress it. And do it this week—we can't wallow around like tired old analysts on Park Avenue. Dr. Phillips does it in the first session.

Dr. Phillips, always Dr. Phillips!

And give her the book, he'd called out when she was halfway to the door. It helps. She thought she should wait and build Phoebe up first, teach her some comfort measures. Survivors can grow distraught, she knew from her course with Dr. Phillips. Especially when the memories start coming. Phoebe, in her opinion, was simply stuck in an identity crisis. But that's what she loved about the Warburg—its therapists would have believed Maria Demas about what her father had done to her in the shed behind the house when nobody else in the world believed her, not even Agnes Meehan. So when she heard the outside door of her office open, Sahra placed a copy of *The Courage to Heal* under her chair.

In the client chair by the decorator tissues, Phoebe had a treat for Sahra. "Peter called me. Yes, Peter. I knew you'd love that!" When the expected concern appeared on Sahra's face, Phoebe couldn't help but drag it out and tease her therapist a little. "He begged to see me and I felt so terrible. He's human, isn't he? Creative people like that deserve a little extra consideration. I mean, look at Hart Crane. Look at Janis Joplin. So I met him in Carl Schurz Park, in the freezing cold, and we sat on those benches by the river? He told me the saddest story, that his father had been shot and paralyzed years ago in one of those drive-by things." Disbelief appeared on Sahra's face, as Phoebe had known it would. "So I said to myself, 'Sahra would tell me that the man is bullshitting me.' And he was. Because then I remembered that Peter had also said he'd hiked up Mount Rainier with his dad this last summer. So, hey! I'm doing okay, *n'est-ce pas?*"

"You're doing great." Sahra gave a rare and satisfying laugh.

"Thanks." Phoebe shrugged. "Couldn't have done it without you!" That was the treat, her thanks to Sahra, for teaching her to listen to herself instead of others.

"You did that work, not me," Sahra replied generously. "You really can work when you put your mind to it. And now I'm giving you a real assignment. First, a couple of questions. How're you sleeping?"

Phoebe felt herself sag a bit in the chair because the fact was, she wasn't sleeping very well. "I fall asleep and then I wake up about two o'clock. I lie there till, maybe, five? Some nights I can hear the guys making it down the hall. I go over and over in my head how to get from where I am in life to where I want to be. Even if I'm never the world's best director, I'd like to work in drama somehow. What if I never can? What if this is it? A secretary, a subsection of Mr. Reed's brain. I lie there until the light comes and then I fall back to sleep for an hour or so. At work I'm falling asleep over WordPerfect. I lost an entire file pressing *N* instead of *Y*. Mr. Reed was not a happy man."

Sahra didn't smile this time; in fact, she appeared strained. "How about eating? Are you eating regular meals?"

Phoebe decided to keep it short. "You sound like my mom!" And when she said that, a look of pleasure appeared in Sahra's light eyes.

"What are you eating, then?"

"Mostly grilled cheese, like Dr. Kevorkian." Phoebe laughed but Sahra looked worried. Oh, God, Sahra was going to think she was suicidal or something!

"And your mood?"

"Don't worry. It's a joke. But oh . . ." Here she let the crimped hair cascade over one side of her face for the comfort of it. She was disappointed, she'd wanted points for her clear-sightedness in Carl Schurz Park, not the third degree. "I reached a sort of crying peak on Thanksgiving and now I'm just feeling kind of, oh, I guess, numb. Bess is seeing Roger but like I said last week, I don't care."

Sahra's straight brown hair fell over her shoulders as she leaned forward. "Phoebe, there's a question I want to raise. It's just a question. Something to consider, to explore."

Phoebe felt alarm. She was mentally ill? Incurable?

"You know, Phoebe, a lot of the trouble you're having is common to a certain syndrome. You've been describing the symptoms of this syndrome for a month now. Depression, fatigue, the inability to form a lasting relationship, lack of success at work, trouble realizing goals—sound familiar? Now, add insomnia and a certain lack of confidence and also that you're easily intimidated by authority figures. The only trouble you don't have from the list is an eating disorder. A lot of cheese sandwiches isn't quite the same as bulimia."

Phoebe straightened her neck. She certainly was not intimidated by authority figures.

Sahra kept on. "I'm wondering if you might have this syndrome in your history."

"What syndrome is that?"

"Phoebe, did anyone in your childhood ever approach you sexually?"

"What?"

"Take it easy." Sahra leaned farther. "When this happens, it's common not to remember. In fact, most people don't, at first."

Phoebe took in her breath. This couldn't be happening!

"Now, I'm sure a Yale graduate would understand how the horrible things we don't want to remember can be kept way down deep below memory—it's called repression. Our body remembers for us—a pain, some discomfort in the thighs, or a sense that you're gagging, the feeling of something unwanted in your mouth, your throat. . . ."

Sahra could not mean this!

"These reminders can appear in dreams, in doodlings, or simply as a deep confusion, or as fear, even a vague rage. I wouldn't expect you to draw up any scenes from childhood right off. It can take years—"

"Sahra! What's the matter with you?"

"Men have been doing this to their daughters for ages. You don't have to be afraid to tell."

God, that *is* what she meant! "You mean like Nora's mother?"

"I really don't know Nora."

"My father wasn't like that!"

"I'm only suggesting that you ask yourself the question. This really is upsetting you, isn't it?" Sahra sat back and considered Phoebe's response. Upset itself could be another sign. Could it be true, then? Dr. Mundiger's hunch? This wasn't turning out the way she'd thought. Incest would help explain her client's masochistic relationship with Peter and even that odd lover of Phoebe's, Pop Termolian, forty years that summer to her twenty. If this were true—oh, it was sad, so sad. What man would do that? It made her so mad! Phoebe was staring at her.

Sahra had reread her course notes and sections of various texts the night before and spoke with them in mind. "You don't remember now, Phoebe, but are you remembering everything you've got inside that impressive head of yours? Kids cope by forgetting. Later, they get these little hints of memory. It's okay to look at it. Do you have any blank spots in your memories? Any memories that seem to have an aura of mystery around them? Start there. So often those spots are where we hide things too painful to face. Try to focus on those spots and bring them closer. Are you outside playing dolls? Climbing a jungle gym? Digging in a garden?

Running by the ocean? Remembering can start with the smallest thing, a glimpse, a whisper. Trust whatever you can get hold of. Work from there. Okay, I'll stop." She reached to the floor and picked up the book. "Take this home with you. Read a few pages."

Phoebe put her hand out. Here was Sahra, her rock, the center of her week, the only person in New York who gave a flea what happened to her, gone all weird like that doctor in that film oh what was it—he's the doctor and he's good until the girl is lying on the table for the surgery and he picks up the scalpel and pushes up—no, he takes it off—his white mask and there's the face of the enemy there, the one who has been pursuing her—a face with a leer and a laugh, a crazy maniacal laugh—and she's already drugged and can't move, can't scream. Why was she so upset? She wasn't upset. She was calm, very calm. Her parents were from Philadelphia—total and complete squares who didn't even know they were over the hill, that's all. That's all that was wrong with them.

10

Phoebe waited till Friday and then, cross-legged on her futon, opened the book to a chart entitled "How Can I Know If I Was a Victim of Child Sexual Abuse?" The authors, two women, named Ellen and Laura, said you could ask yourself if, as a child or teenager, you'd been "Touched in sexual areas?" No. Absolutely not. Don't be crazy. Well, do you count seventeen, with Vince, a teenager? Oh, that was sex, not sexual abuse. "Shown sexual movies" . . . Only last week she'd nearly had an orgasm when Richard Gere picked up Debra Winger as if she were a child during a rerun of *An Officer and a Gentleman.* That's strange. Isn't it strange? A man picking up a child turned her on? . . . "forced to listen to sexual talk?" There were only her mother's long technical descriptions of how you get your period. "Made to pose for seductive or sexual photographs?" Nope, Ellen, no, Laura, that was my sister whom the man in Rittenhouse Square wanted to photograph. "Subjected to unnecessary medical treatments?" Mom sometimes suggested Kaopectate, but it's sort of necessary, sometimes, before you go onstage. "Forced to perform oral sex?" Did Peter count? He hadn't forced her. It was just that she didn't know how and she'd asked him to show her. "Raped or otherwise penetrated?" No, I mean, Vince really had to work at it; I was a virgin. "Sexually tortured?" Oh, stop! "Made to watch sexual acts or look at sexual parts?" Mom told me to get a mirror and look at myself the summer before eighth grade and it was not a glorious sight. "Bathed in a way that felt intrusive to you?" When Pop Termolian stood me in the shower and sprayed me all over with the hand-held shower it felt, well, wonderful. That man knew everything, including how to bludgeon chicken into Chicken Kiev and how to do something blissfully intrusive—another man with a teenager. Did you notice that? "Objectified and ridiculed about your body?" Oh. Suddenly she felt hot all over. She stretched her legs out on the comforter. Bowlegged, flat-chested, red-haired, and freckly. Yes, she'd always felt ridiculed about her body. That's what she loved about acting, partly. You could be anyone you wanted, you could transform yourself into someone beautiful. She was starting to feel a little nauseous, actually. It was late. Maybe she should eat supper. She stood up, carrying the book, and kept reading. "Goaded into sex you didn't really want?" Those last nights with Peter she hadn't really wanted to. "Come on, baby, you frigid or something?" He'd forced her, maybe you could say. She walked into the kitchen and saw the note she'd written herself: *Call Bess.* "Told all you were good for was sex?" Never. If only.

Holding the fragrant freesia from the damage pile at the flower shop, Bess let herself into her ugly but safe apartment up near the Cloisters. Things were even more strained with Phoebe now, because of Roger. He was hardly worth it, a much too home-centered man. He'd even described the kids he wanted and they already had names! Jeremiah. Tess. He reminded her of Dad. A man's passion should not be for his own family but for the truth, like James's. She pushed aside the madras spread and entered the former living room, now her bedroom. In damp stocking feet, she padded across the straw mat and laid the freesia on the mantelpiece next to James's latest postcard:

The round globe
empty of people
you and me.
Warm, somewhere.

They meant nothing, these cards—she had a three-year collection of them.

Turning her FM on, she padded toward the kitchen past the bedroom where Brooke, the vegan, labored over her lesson plans for Teach America to the sound of Dinosaur Jr. In the kitchen Cara was eating salsa and chips and listening to Peter Tosh.

"Eh, Bess, that's you, now?" she called out in imitation Jamaican.

"Guess again."

Cara smiled and went on. "Hey, your sister called. She sounded excited. She wants to get together Sunday."

She'd wait till tomorrow to return the call. Roger was coming over and she didn't want to have to go into that with her sister.

Phoebe stirred the black beans on the burner. "Your father may have stood in the bathroom doorway, making suggestive remarks. . . . You had the feeling your stepfather was aware of your physical presence every minute." Not a chance. Dad was a prude. I don't have a stepfather.

She moved the beans off the burner and lay a tortilla on it. "If you are unable to remember any specific instances like the ones mentioned above but still have a feeling that something abusive happened to you, it probably did. (see page 81.)"

She spread the beans on the tortilla and skipped to page 81 because who could help it? "If you don't remember your abuse, you are not alone. Many women don't have memories, and some never get memories. This doesn't mean they weren't abused."

Someone was opening the front door. Daryl! She hurried to finish the section: "If you have unfamiliar or uncomfortable feelings as you read this book, don't be alarmed. . . . On the other hand, if you breeze through you probably aren't feeling safe enough to confront these issues."

Not safe enough? Tucking the book under her arm to hide the title, she carried the plate to her room, stuck some Enya in the CD player, slid the book under her futon, and sat down, the princess on the pea. I feel safe enough, she told herself. She remembered lots about her childhood: the kitchen with hot chocolate on the stove, the garden with its rosebushes in back, the zoo with the white lions, the lake in New Jersey and another lake somewhere. Near mountains? Where was that? In New England? It was hilly. When it rained you could see rainbows in the drizzle, as if God were making each one for you personally. The whole place shimmered. Everything there possessed an aura of mystery. An aura is what Sahra had said to look for. Where was that lake? She'd ask Bess on Sunday. When we are young the world has many different ways of seeming—who'd said that to her? When? It was a man's voice with the sound of water nearby. She wasn't afraid. She felt safe, very safe. Daryl was in the apartment. It wasn't as if she were here alone.

11

On Saturday Bess and Roger moved around the city pretending they were tourists, speaking fake German on the top of the Empire State Building and fake Italian at the South Street Seaport. It reminded her of how Dad used to take her to his office and they'd pretend she was a secretary. On Sunday Bess neatened up her few possessions for Phoebe, but when her sister arrived she hardly looked at the flower and the postcard on the mantel or at the page of perfectly rendered Latin capitals she'd found in a secondhand bookstore. There were dark circles under Phoebe's eyes as if she'd been awake for a week. Nor did Phoebe want to chat for long with Cara or Brooke. They walked over to the Cloisters.

"Are you okay?" Bess asked on the street. "You've seemed kind of weird since Thanksgiving." Well, that was stupid. She hadn't meant to rub it in about Roger.

"Weird?" Phoebe sounded detached. "Yeah, weird is sort of exactly it. I've been doing some weird thinking. I'll tell you about it later. Let's just walk."

They reached the Cloisters and entered into one of its high-ceilinged rooms containing tapestries. They walked behind a father whose little boy was trailing his hand along the medieval fringe that hung from a fabric. Some of the fringe fell off in his hand and he held it up to show his father. The father grabbed the fringe, stuck it in his pocket, picked up the boy, and walked speedily off.

"He's outta here!" Phoebe whispered. "And somehow I don't think he's on his way to Security."

Bess laughed. Her real sister was coming back. She quickened her pace to match Phoebe's and repeated, "But are you okay?"

Phoebe stared straight ahead as they walked through the stone interiors, past the dark hangings on the walls. "I've got a question for you. It's just a question."

"Shoot." Turning, Bess studied the profile, which was all of her sister's face being allowed her. Phoebe needed a new permanent or something; her hair was flattening out.

"You know this Sahra I'm seeing?"

"The therapist? The one that isn't Nora's?"

"Well, I guess you could put it that way. She's just as good as Nora's. Well, Sahra has been . . . she's been asking me to think back about Dad. She wonders if. . . . You see, the symptoms I have fit into a package. . . ."

Bess got the funniest feeling in the pit of her stomach. Phoebe never stumbled around like this. Phoebe always gave her opinions vivid expression whether she had the facts or not. Now her whole speech had gone fumbly.

"What are you talking about?"

When they passed from inside the dark halls to the cloistered walk around the open courtyard, Phoebe finally turned to face Bess. Her forehead was wrinkled and her fair skin raw in the cold. "You know, Bess. You know what I mean. She wants to know if Dad, you know, did things to me."

Bess stopped walking. All the air in the world seemed to swirl about in her head. She had seldom contradicted her older sister—there were always such violent consequences. Now she didn't hesitate. "You're out of your mind."

Phoebe came to an echoing halt. They stood together on the four-sided walk that bordered the courtyard. "Oh, Bess, that was my first response, too! But I've been reading this book and I've decided to at least investigate. You know, I've got some of the signs—all the stuff about not being able to get my life off the ground? This could be what's holding me back. Sort of like a fatal flaw. And lately I'm losing weight."

"What are you living on? Coffee?" Bess waited for the retaliatory blow.

"I eat fine!" The old fire came into Phoebe's eyes, then died, kaput. "Listen, Bess, listen to me. I know it's unlikely but these things happen in the best of families. And we . . . we press them under in our memories so it won't hurt so much. Remember that summer when we were in Minneapolis and Abby got scratched by the cat and Aunt Phyllis and Uncle Ben took us all to the emergency room?

"Sort of."

"Abby kept telling us the cat had scratched her, but when she got to the doctor and showed him her wrist there were these two little holes punched in her skin. And it was only then that Abby remembered that the cat had actually sunk its fangs right into her wrist."

"I don't get it."

"That's what they mean by repression. It was so awful—her own cat's fangs sinking into her wrist like a snake's—that she forgot it, pushed it under, repressed it."

"She remembered at the hospital."

"That's not the point! The point is, she'd forgotten it. Now think back to that hiking trip we took up in the mountains. That was New Hampshire, wasn't it? It was beautiful there, remember? The mountains closing in around you, the silence of the lake. The whole place had a sort of aura about it? Remember the tents, how they were set way out away from the bathrooms?"

"What trip?"

"When we were little. I think I was in third grade or something. You must have been in first. They took us up there in the car to the cog railway—"

"Oh, yeah, I remember."

"Well, then we slept out for a whole week, in the tent. It had little windows, remember, with flaps that pinned up?"

"Ummhmm."

"Well, one night Dad got up to pee, only he didn't go to the bathrooms. He stood right out there. And he . . . he took it out, and peed right there by the window and I could see everything."

"Took what out?" Bess knew, of course, but she was so annoyed at this—the pussyfooting, the whole thing. It made her reckless.

"His penis." Phoebe reddened at this pronunciation and Bess recalled how determined her older sister and her mother had always been to use the correct terms for the genitals.

"You mean he took his prick out to pee?" Bess wanted to laugh, except it was so terrible. She wasn't at all used to correcting her sister, not to mention speaking of her father in such terms.

"If you don't want to listen . . ." Phoebe looked down and scuffed at something with her boot. This wasn't like Phoebe; Phoebe attacked head-on.

"I'm listening, Feeb. But this is crazy. Dad's problem is he's such a straight shooter. Whoops, under the circumstances, that might not be the right way to put it. But you know as well as I do that Dad is practically a Sunday-school teacher about sex. Dad having sex with a kid? I'd sooner believe he'd had a sex-change operation." Bess found herself laughing—really, this was all so crazy.

"You're not listening. You don't have to have been penetrated or anything like that! It doesn't even have to be physical. It's enough if your father stood in the bathroom doorway and looked at you funny, or if he was always, you know, especially aware of you when you were in the room."

Bess stopped laughing. There was such sorrow and at the same time such agitation in her sister that Bess grew serious. "I'm listening."

"Well, you remember how he looks at you? His eyes go all lightened up and something just floods over his face."

"That's the way he looks at you, kid, the blessed firstborn. He looks at me as if I were an afterthought."

"You're first with Mom!" Phoebe replied, sticking her hands in her pockets.

"Mom loves you just as much, Phoebe. It's only that Mom and I are a lot alike and you and Dad are a lot alike."

"We are not!" Phoebe said in a choked voice. "I'm really a lot like Mom. Mom and I both like Chagall and we both like Mel Gibson and we . . ."

Bess stood there unable to believe they were back to their kid fights. She let Phoebe run down. It was the safest way. The next thing she knew, Phoebe was asking a new question.

"Did he ever touch you, you know, in an intimate manner?"

"Intimate! He's my father. He held me on his knee, he picked me up off the swings, he put me to bed. Did he ever put a hand or—as you put it—a penis on me in a sexual manner? No, absolutely no. You know Dad."

But Phoebe didn't stop. She pulled a book out of her pocket and handed it to Bess. "If he did, Bess, you can count on me. I'm here for you."

Then she went on about how this therapist of hers had told her how to put a little furniture into the blank rooms of her memory. Bess began to feel tired. This was indeed like old times. You never could get Phoebe to listen to your side of the argument. Or how you felt about something. It was only how Phoebe felt that mattered. Phoebe the Magnificent had to keep telling you how she felt over and over, so that in the end Little Bess turned into something inarticulate and stupid. In fact Little Bess standing at the Cloisters felt all of her body seep downward, felt the corners of her mouth, the corners of her eyes, her breasts, the arches of her feet somehow lowering. She could melt into the ground and Phoebe would go on talking and talking, so eternally caught up in herself. Only now she was pressing some book into Bess's hands.

"Just read it and tell me what you think," Phoebe concluded. "I need you, Bess. You've got a level head." Then abruptly she stopped talking and started walking and they made it side by side all the way to the subway stop without saying another word.

At home Daryl and Ibrahim were in the kitchen eating ice cream from matching Ben & Jerry cartons. Here were her friends, the last two of them now that Bess hadn't taken her seriously.

"Ah," Ibrahim said, "the English girl. She walks in beauty like the night."

"Ask him his good news," Daryl directed, his hairy legs bare under the cutoffs.

"What is it?" Phoebe replied as she put water on for tea and popped bread into the toaster.

"Our studio won a little prize. And that puts us in the running for some decent grants."

"Good news!" She sat down and pulled her hair behind her neck. If only she had the money for a new permanent. "So you're celebrating?"

"That we are," Daryl acknowledged. "First the ice cream, then a few adventures out and about in the cool of the evening. Nora's been gone all day to some wild het event."

"Good."

"Feebala, dear, we've got a question."

"Shoot."

"Do you believe her?"

It was Ibrahim who asked, the one she liked. In fact, if the truth be told, she found this small gay man rather attractive—the dark skin, the white teeth, the nice turn of phrase, the energy. Was that weird of her? Everything had grown so weird. She worked at her hair before she replied, her fingertips worrying its lack of kinkiness.

"I didn't. Then I did. Such strange things happen. Did you know that one out of four girls is abused by age fourteen?"

"Sounds about right. Men are such beasts!" Ibrahim spoke tongue in cheek and she liked that about him, too. "So glad I have you." He blew a smile at Daryl, who grimaced on receipt. "Now, angel," Ibrahim went on, to her. "Whether it's true or not, we're kind of tired of Nora. It's awful to have to be so quiet when she's sleeping. And she's forever in the bathroom. We're thinking of changing the arrangements down here."

She stopped fiddling with her hair. "How?"

"How about we leave and you two take over the lease or you two leave and we take over the lease?"

"Huh? What have you guys got against me?"

"Your sexual persuasion," Daryl said, popping the empty ice cream carton into the wastebasket.

"I'm neat, I'm clean, I don't stay up late."

"You brought that handsome Viking here and we had to change the locks."

"He's gone. Verboten. Out. He's history. And I paid for the lock and the keys, all four sets. It about broke me."

Ibrahim simply continued. "We like you, angel. It's Nora who's so tiring. Really tiring. She just wears a man out."

She'd never known Ibrahim could be like this, so calculating, so cold.

Then Daryl made it all the clearer: "The thing is, we've met these guys who are looking for a place."

"I see," she said. "I get it."

"You won't feel bad, angel?"

"I'll need time."

"You got it," Daryl said.

"And you know," Ibrahim added, "Now that the grant's a possibility, I can ask around at the studio, the way you wanted, for a nice little job.

Ready to hire a props researcher? I'll bruit it about. I know this fabulous redhead. And the boss'll ask me how she'd be on the Colonial period. Great, I'll tell him. Her very ancestors were here stealing it from the natives and all that."

"Now, that's good news." Phoebe buttered her toast. Two could play at calculation. "Tell them I'm fabulous. Tell them I'm perfect and I'll forgive you for the eviction notice."

"It's a deal."

The guys moved out for the evening, leaving the apartment empty of anything breathing except herself and maybe the radiator.

They made her so furious! Did Nora know about this? Nora made her furious! She didn't want to be stuck here or anywhere else with Nora. And Bess! Well, if it were true about Dad, she'd have to protect Bess from him whether Bess believed it or not. She'd stand by her sister even if her sister didn't stand by her. Hang on, hang on. She was sounding as if she thought it was true, and she didn't. It was only that when she struggled to remember, she couldn't. And that was a sign. That meant you had to look harder.

Dad would not have touched her. He'd been a hero to her. He'd taught her to walk on the railroad tracks. "Keep your head in the bottom of your feet," he'd said, to make her laugh. He'd taught her to swim. "The worst thing you're ever going to find in this water is a lot of kid pee." Before supper he would put his hand under her chin and tilt her head up and say, "I'll have a dish of those baby blues." But what else had he taught her? Something she'd pushed under in her mind?

She turned on the big paper globe of a lamp and sat down on her futon. There *was* a mystery about the past, the whole of it. A hovering, a blankness. There seemed to be a humming to it, like the humming of bees around roses. Could she actually be hiding something about Dad in her memory? Her mind kept returning to the night in the campsite. Why? What was she trying to tell herself? She pulled off her boots and got into the sweats she liked to sleep in. He'd stood there and taken out his penis and peed in the dark—only it was moonlight and she could see everything, the dark hair, the dark penis, his hand upon it, and her father's eyes gazing right into the tent through the window, right into her face. He should not have looked into the tent like that, into the corner where her mattress was, into her very eyes. Really, that was wrong for a father.

You'd think Bess would have listened to her a little bit. Yet what exactly had Dad done? Nothing, really. That was the blank spot.

You have to break through the blocks that keep the memory hidden away. You have to be brave. That's how you heal.

Cross-legged, she switched the lamp off. The lights of the city made a gray-orange glow in the courtyard, which was nothing but a dark spot with rats in it. Okay, she'd sit here and try to enlarge one of the blank spots in her memory. New Hampshire, that seemed the likeliest place to begin. If nothing happened, she'd know once and for all that it wasn't true and she'd make Sahra stop bugging her. She held out her hands, palms down, and looked at them, the way Pop Termolian had taught her. Stare at the back of your hands and ask Coyote to let you become alert inside your dreams. She stared at what she could make out of the tendons of her fingers. When she looked up and into the space right in the middle of her vision, she saw her father standing out there, beyond the tent. At the edge of her vision she could still see her futon and the walls of her room but in the center of her vision she could look out through the tent flap and there he was looking in at her. Then he moved. He moved. Oh holy Christ, he was moving! He stood at the door of the tent. She could hardly breathe. He opened the flap of the tent and motioned her out. She stood in her pajamas and walked out where it was cold, the sand under her feet. They walked side by side and she put her hand into his and he walked her down to the edge of the sand and then very slowly, he took off her pajamas. No! No! Her whole body filled with something black and the pulse of her life beat in her throat. She snapped on the light and for a minute, the scene by the lake was still there, in the middle of her room, and then it was gone. She was back on her futon but crouched in the corner at the bottom, breathing high and shallowly. No! No! He couldn't have! He wouldn't have! She'd seen it, though. She'd actually felt the sand beneath the back of her knees. No! No! She screamed aloud this time into the empty, echoing apartment.

13

"What's happened, Phoebe?" Sahra was surprised at the pale skin, the lips red in the paleness.

"I don't . . ."

The city's sounds were more muted than usual by the first falling of snow on the streets and window ledges and Sahra waited with a sense of apprehension.

"I can't . . ."

Incredible! Sahra understood what was coming. Dr. Mundiger had called it. This poor child! But it was too fast. It was supposed to take months, years. The safety measures, they weren't in place! Stay calm, Sahra told herself. She knew from past experience with Phoebe that she mustn't let her own anxiety show or Phoebe would pick up on it. She picked up so easily on the slightest clue. If it was true, the appropriate emotion to model would be not fear but anger. "Take your time, slowly now. We have time."

"You won't believe this," Phoebe finally began, tears gathering at her lower eyelids. "I was in my apartment but somehow this . . . this memory was there, too, and I saw it, the whole scene, like a film. It was along the lines of what you were saying, the book, too. I mean, well, I saw it twice, once before I went to bed and once when I woke up in the dark." She uncrossed her legs, recrossed them, looked over at Sahra.

Sahra's face gave Phoebe a still place in the whirl of the unfamiliar. Last week, things had been simple: Here is Canada, here is Chile. This week, everything had shifted. She must tell it to Sahra. "My father led me to the side of the lake onto this soft sand? He settled me on the sand and parted my legs. I could feel the sand underneath the backs of my knees. He said, 'Honey, this will hurt just a little bit but I want you to learn how to do this because it'll make you be a wonderful wife someday.' I saw his penis erect and dark by the moonlight. It looked so big to me! Because I was so little. He took my hand and put it around his penis and said with a kind of a moan, 'Oh, honey, that feels so good, so good.' He held the penis to the place between my legs—that's all I knew about it, a place—and then he pushed gently in and then not gently at all. Fiercely, it hurt! Oh, how could he? My father! A man who pretends to be ordinary and upright!"

"He calls himself a father. What a thing to do, that bastard!"

A darkness rose inside Phoebe. "It really happened, then?"

"It happened."

Phoebe felt limp, empty. "You sure?"

Sahra no longer needed Dr. Mundiger to tell her that total and frequent validation is essential. She'd been doing her homework. "Absolutely. We don't make up memories like that."

Tears filled Phoebe's throat. "It wasn't a dream or something?"

"Believe me, it's true."

"I don't see how I could have forgotten that."

"That's the repression we talked about. You were so clever, Phoebe, even when you were a little kid. That's how you protected yourself from knowing."

The tears came over Phoebe's eyelids, down her cheeks. "But he was good, my father. I mean, really, he was."

"One side of him perhaps. Not the other. It's like flipping a nickel, they say. One side of him gave what it ought to, the other side took what it shouldn't."

Phoebe dropped her face into her hands.

"You can heal, Phoebe."

"It's . . . so . . . hard."

"You can make it."

"It's so horrible. It's just horrible!"

"Hey, look up a minute."

In the air Sahra made an enclosing sphere with her hands. "See this space? We're here in this bubble. We're safe. You made it here."

Phoebe swallowed tears. This wasn't what she wanted. She wanted Sahra to say, no, you're fooling yourself. Now there was no way back to the known world.

"But my dad? I mean, he was a great dad."

"You deserved a great dad. Sad to say, you didn't get one."

"If it's true . . . everything has changed."

Sahra nodded yes. "Your healing is beginning now. It begins the instant you accept this as true."

"What if . . . it was only once?"

"Once is enough." Oh, the experts were so right, these survivors need endless confirmation! "Even if there was no penetration."

"There was . . . penetration."

"You see? Your body knows."

Phoebe sobbed now, unable to calm herself, hands over her face.

Sahra gave her time, lots of time. This was a natural grief. It had to be felt. She'd feel it with her client, as good therapists do. Validation, that's what survivors need. Her voice took on a crooning. "Oh, Phoebe, you won't have to hide part of yourself anymore. That's what you lost, you lost the little girl who underwent that betrayal. And today you're starting to reclaim her. Today you can start to be whole. You're strong. You can take charge of your life. Look at you! Look what you've done!"

"What I've . . . done?"

Sahra leaned forward to give what comfort she could without touching her client. She'd have to find out everything there was to know about survivors. She loved this poor girl and was afraid for her. "Now, Phoebe, we have to talk about safety. When you unbury a memory, you move into an emergency stage."

Phoebe sat with her hands over her face.

"This is hard work. Very hard. You must be good to yourself." That Dr. Mundiger! He must be some kind of genius. "Don't expect too much of yourself right now. Give yourself all the comfort you can. Here's a workbook. It will tell you how to soothe yourself. Call me if you need to. Call me anytime, Phoebe, day or night. You can make it, Phoebe. You can make it."

And then it was time for Phoebe to go out into a new world, where she put her right foot onto the pavement and then her left. The normal, comforting snow had stopped. Remnants of it glittered under the streetlights. How can you tell the real world from the not? She walked a few blocks. She started running. She ran from Third to Second with people looking at her. No wonder she had nothing! This is what had held her back! This terrible greed of her father's! She ran a few more blocks, breathless, slowed down. Once upon a time there was a little girl whose father was a fine, successful man but he had used her for his own needs and nobody knew a thing about it. They walked on the railroad tracks and went canoeing, he even tried to teach her hoop shots through the basket in the garden. You would think that this garden was paradise. But it was not. Because even though she doesn't remember everything yet, he was waiting for it to grow dark in the garden. He was waiting by the rosebushes. Phoebe, Phoebe, Phoebe, your name is the song of a bird.

14

Nutmeg with its fine haziness and clove with its dark pungency filled Claire's kitchen as she sifted flour and hummed along with Joan Baez on an old vinyl. She was sorting out the oldies because fifty is the age to strip down, distill, and move on. The collector from Baltimore had come back to her about a job. He hadn't liked the woman she'd recommended, or her approach. Amy Broderick lacked a sense of history, he'd complained. Would Claire consider coming down to talk to him? His collection was mostly drawings and prints, never so alive to her as paintings. She added cinnamon, more nutmeg. After Christmas she'd broach the idea to Harvey. They'd talk it over. Not now. Christmas would be a reprieve from any complicated decisions about herself. With the girls home, she could be a mom again. You don't have to focus on yourself when you're a mom. You can get by on empathy and doing for others.

She eased the cake onto the middle shelf of the oven, happy to remember how when she was first baking for Harvey she collected those little guidelines: bake a cake on the middle shelf, don't salt the meat. Why don't you salt the meat? her mother would inquire those few times she could afford to come east to visit. Women of her mother's generation always salted meat. Women of her daughters' generation wouldn't even touch meat with a fork. She belonged to the generation in between: We are the women who still eat meat but don't salt it. I know history. She closed the oven door gently: no harsh actions around a baking cake.

She gathered up the baking utensils, rinsed them under the satisfying spray. A pleasing light passed through the glass bottles Phoebe had once arranged in the window. The girls were finally coming home and, really, she must watch out. It was too late to mother anymore. She'd never managed to soften Phoebe's outer shell nor to give strength to her inner jelly. She'd never managed to shake Bess into being her own person instead of following after her endless string of friends. Okay, forget it. It was too late. Her job was over. I hereby let go of that job. They'll have to manage further improvements by themselves.

You can't evolve while your mother is watching. To look up from this—at that time—*new* kitchen counter and see Harvey escorting Edie Walsh Monroe through the doorway with that suitcase, oh! To look up and find that so-early graying mother surveying her and judging her—as caught forever in the coils of key lime pie—too much! The Great Claire who left us all behind in Cedar Rapids? You've come to this? Cooking soufflés and folding laundry? Even the good things could be tainted by her mother's unspoken judgment: The very babies gurgling beside the fireplace underwent a sea change. She'd wanted to scream out, "Don't touch my life! Don't see me! Don't know me!" That's because she hadn't been safe yet, in her own self. Marriage at twenty-three—it's too young.

You're only free to be yourself when you can step outside your mother's ken or stop responding to it and she hadn't managed that while her mother was alive. Only later, when her mother was dead. Now here she was, at those same separation years from the other side. It was hard to imagine that her daughters could possibly feel her to be the danger she'd felt her mother to be, but of course they must. It was natural. That's the last requirement of the mother job: to sustain being dumped. She must remember not to look too carefully at them. Not to let her eyes cross, glaze over, penetrate. She must give them distance, space. After they left, she'd decide about Baltimore. Take a pied-à-terre down there, commute twice a week. Go to the movies alone. Expensive. Expansive?

Phoebe summoned Bess to a bar on lower Broadway and Bess arrived first, entering a dim room where a couple her age were drinking beer with their knees touching and everybody else was potbellied. She sat in a booth equipped with a chrome-ridged record selector from the fifties. She hadn't spoken to Phoebe for a week or so and hoped she wouldn't be too annoyed that she hadn't read past page one in that book. Who had time—what with working late to prepare for the holidays, and Roger around? Anyway, maybe Phoebe'd forgotten all that craziness by now. Her ear was drawn to the voices on the flickering screen above the bar where a woman was telling Sally Jessy Raphael how her father had bound her wrists as a child and hung her on a spike in the basement. Another woman said her father had chained her to the base of a radiator. Show me the spike, Professor Zolbrod would have said in biology. Show me the mark on the radiator.

Phoebe arrived, still bearing that pale, tight look, and sat down across the booth. She started talking immediately, too fast, all out of joint. When Bess made out that Phoebe was actually saying Dad had raped her that night on the camping trip, she flung out her hand.

"Stop! I don't want to hear it."

"I'm not supposed to stop! The more you talk about it, the greater distance it puts between you and the pain."

"You sound like somebody on Sally Jessy! How could you say that? How could you think that of Dad?"

"Look what he did to me!"

"Not a thing, I bet."

"He did! I saw it before my eyes!"

"I'm not going along with this, Phoebe! I may be your little sister but I don't believe everything you dig up! This is another one of your games—showtime, remember? I'm not playing this one. Forget it. Which train are you taking?"

"Home? I can't go home!"

"Why not? We always go home for Christmas."

"How can I? I'd see Dad."

"How can you? You know Dad wouldn't touch you!"

Phoebe blinked. "He might give me some kind of look, you know, meaning he remembers what I remember. Then what would I do?"

It hit Bess that this was going to be larger than she'd thought. Phoebe was scared. Something was going on. This wasn't big sister. This wasn't Phoebe the Magnificent. This was someone entirely strange and new. She tried to find a comfort for her sister. "I'll be there, Feeb. You can sleep in my room with me."

"I could?"

"Sure. Remember how you used to let me sleep in your room?"

"With your blanket? When you had the bad dreams."

"And we can go home on the train together, too. Maybe you just need a break from New York. Maybe things will look different at home."

Phoebe's face was breaking into a grimace that made Bess get up and shove in next to her and put her arm around her. She wanted to wrap her sister in a blanket the way Phoebe had done for her when she was small and scared and had pulled her blanket across the third-floor hallway into her big sister's bed. Bessie? Phoebe would say on those nights. It's okay, Bessie, I'll take care of you. It's just a dream, a dream. This is just a dream, too. Isn't it, Feeb? Isn't it? Oh, Christ! It had better be!

If Phoebe didn't go home, Bess reasoned in the morning, maybe she'd stay in the city with her, make sure her sister had somewhere to go for Christmas. Not out to Montauk with Roger, though. She dialed home to test the waters.

"Bessie, my love," her father said. "What's up?"

My love? Was that a normal thing to say?

"Just thought I'd better warn you. Mr. Kaplan wants me working Christmas Eve, though he's trying to get his nephew in instead. If he can't, it'll be, you know, something like one-thirty in the morning before the train gets in."

"Not a problem. We'll be at Thirtieth Street."

"Maybe I could come . . . Christmas morning, instead?"

"Now, Bess, a girl has to sleep at home Christmas Eve or how else can her parents slip down in their pajamas to fill her stocking?"

Their pajamas? Oh, Dad, she wanted to say, grow up. Watch out. The craziest thing is happening. But she couldn't.

Her mother came on, "Have you seen much of Phoebe?"

"No." Bess turned from the madras curtain toward the snow-covered windowsill and opted for sins of omission. "Her school doesn't go on vacation till Friday. And she's being squeezed out of that apartment, so she's busy looking for another."

"Tell her to call us anyway, we're way too far out of touch."

"Okay." When Bess hung up she knew she had to go home. Someone had to show up. Someone had to protect them.

15

Dr. Mundiger had assured Sahra that terror is normal in survivors.

—They're all terrified, wouldn't you be?

—She was so shaken when she called.

—You've broken the abscess, Sahra. It needs to drain.

—You know, I've been reading but I still don't feel prepared.

—You're really doing quite well. There's a survivor workshop this weekend. Take it. Sit in on a survivor support group.

—One more question. Her sister wants her to go home for Christmas.

—Not yet! Not until she can confront them.

—But she seems really stalled, Dr. Mundiger.

—Carl. If she sinks into inertia, it's best to get her to confront.

—Okay, Carl. Thanks.

When Sahra opened the door, Phoebe stood bedraggled in a skimpy coat that symbolized the Fairchilds to Sahra. Couldn't they afford more than that for their daughter?

"I'm sorry I had to call you in the middle of the night," Phoebe began with something close to tremor, "but it was so awful, the pictures. I can hardly stay in my room. I've got this window that looks out on a garden but I told you that on the phone, didn't I?"

"You sure did."

"God, I can't lie in that room another minute! It's a damn good thing I'm leaving that apartment."

"How did it go with your sister?"

"She looks at me like 'there goes Phoebe again.' "

To join an accuser in her doubt, the experts all agreed, is like encouraging a suicide in her plans: "Your father abused you, Phoebe."

"How do you know? Maybe these pictures are dreams or visions or something."

"I know by your symptoms. And by the memories that you're finally strong enough to endure."

Hope faded as Phoebe searched in the chaos, more and more uncertain of what was steady ground and what illusion. "My mother always said I had this great imagination."

"There you go!"

"What do you mean?"

"That repression engine of yours. It sure wants to take over, doesn't it? Believe me, there is no shield from this, Phoebe. Without reliving the pain, you can't get well. You've broken the abscess." She cleared her throat. "It needs to drain."

Phoebe couldn't meet Sahra's eyes. "How about this? There isn't any sequence to the . . . memories. I don't even know if the lake in the mountains came first. It might have been the garden."

"That's very normal. These memories come in fragments. You sort it out later. I'll help you. Together we'll come to know exactly what happened in your childhood."

"But it's so awful!"

"Your own revulsion testifies to its truth."

Fatigue rolled over Phoebe; she'd hardly slept these last two weeks. "Will I ever be entirely sure?"

"One day."

"How do I get there?"

"By telling people. And there is increasing evidence that acting as if it happened will help, too, even if you're not one hundred percent sure."

Acting, the real world. Phoebe remembered high school with sweet comfort. "We used to have these debates. Do you act from the inside out, or from the outside in? Liz Tsui did a terrific job with the outside-in approach, but I did best with inside-out."

Sahra didn't respond.

"There's one last thing that doesn't make sense—why did my childhood always seem so happy?"

Sahra thanked her stars she'd attended the Saturday workshop. "Those happy memories may have been your way of giving yourself what you longed for—a good father and a good mother." She leaned forward and touched Phoebe barely, gently on the knee, nothing that could ever be used in court. "You deserved all that. Instead, you were mistreated, but take a bow, woman. You did your best to live, you've got a genius for living."

Phoebe wiped her cheek with her hand. "I can't go there."

"Where?"

"Home. For Christmas."

"You're quite right."

"They're . . . counting on me, though."

"You're thinking of them again. Think of yourself, Phoebe."

"Mom starts baking right after Thanksgiving."

"Quite a compensation, wouldn't you say? What's she making up for? Don't see them until you're ready to confront them. Are you strong enough to do that?"

"To what?"

"Confront them. That's the next step."

Phoebe's hands sought her hair. "You mean, *tell* them?"

"Yes, in order to heal."

"I can't tell them! They'll say it's my imagination!"

"Exactly. It didn't happen, that's the first thing they'll say. And then they'll grill you for details and for what they call proof. The 'proof' is sitting in front of me, a smart and gifted young woman who was so traumatized as a child that she can't get on in life."

Phoebe gave a laugh of sorts, tossed her head as Liz Tsui might do. "I'm scared."

"That's perfectly normal. When you're ready, you'll take charge and set up the ground rules for a new relationship with your family."

Phoebe barely heard Sahra. The whole past week of sleeplessness and confusion seemed to have put her brain under water. "I couldn't even work yesterday! I wrecked another bunch of letters!"

Sahra took a deep breath to ward off Phoebe's anxiety. "Okay, let's take one thing at a time. Don't go home. Tell them you've got the flu or something. Later, when you're ready, we'll confront them. Sooner or later they have to accept your knowledge as truth."

Phoebe stopped thinking about Mr. Reed and the mess at the office. Sahra was serious.

"Oh, they'll never do that."

"They'd better. They betrayed the trust of a small child."

Phoebe was puzzled. The chaos had expanded and it took her a second to understand how. "What's my mother got to do with it?"

"She must have known what your father was doing. Why didn't the woman protect you?"

"My mother didn't know!"

"She was married to the man! How could she not know?"

Phoebe's face took on volume as if it were filling with tears, but she said nothing.

"Your mother should have protected you, Phoebe, don't you think? I would have, if I were your mother."

Phoebe collapsed, protecting her chest with her arms. "This part can't be true."

"I know, dear. But that's how it is."

All the blessings were draining out of Phoebe.

With Phoebe crumpling in front of her eyes, Sahra recalled Carl's point about inertia. Cauterize it. Phoebe was too confused, too lost. That was clear. Phoebe needed something to hang on to, something to energize her. Sahra reached under her chair.

"Here's some samples of what to say when the day comes. I copied them from a workshop."

Phoebe didn't move. She didn't reach out for the papers even when Sahra placed them on her knees. A client can leave your office and jump off a bridge, Sahra knew. So she said, "Things being what they are, you really must begin to see me twice a week. Let's look at our schedules, Phoebe. How about Thursday at four?"

16

The girls were coming on the late train Monday, Christmas Eve, although Phoebe had the flu and might not make it. The fragrant boughs rested along the mantel. The tree stood in its pail of stones ready to be decorated. Red velvet throws were stacked for table and chairs. And on this Saturday before Christmas, there was one more batch of cookies to be spooned onto tins and slipped into the oven.

Claire could just see the girls years ago working over a gingerbread house. The one with red hair gathered the jelly beans willy-nilly in her fists, gazing intently at their various colors. The one with yellow hair cared more for the structure, its bare bones, how they fit together. Now they were grown, the faces fuller, the eyes drier, the fingers less supple, mature enough to reproduce themselves. Grown and gone, able to take care of themselves, you hope—even when they have the flu. At least Phoebe had roommates who would bring her orange juice.

This very week the daughter of her friend Lacey Quinn had telephoned at 4:00 A.M. from Paris, all alone, whispering over the wires, "Mom! I can't breathe." Lacey herself in that place of hers on Twentieth Street had stopped breathing. It had turned out all right, though, a Parisian flu.

Things turn out all right. Claire stuck the cookie sheets into the oven. Tidying up, she heard the mail fall through the slot onto the hall floor. There were heaps of it. She stooped to gather up the last-minute cards. And—what's this?—a letter from Phoebe! A Christmas card? Wonderful! She dropped the rest of the cards onto the kitchen counter and sat in the rocker to open Phoebe's.

"Dear Mother and Dad, I'm writing to tell you that I won't be coming to Philadelphia for Christmas but it's not because of the flu. I'm better. Quite a lot better. In the last few weeks with the help of a therapist I have remembered what happened to me as a child. I have remembered that Dad abused me sexually . . ."

What? Claire's heart beat in her throat. Were her eyes playing tricks? She went back to reread. ". . . Dad abused me sexually . . ."

Harvey abusing Phoebe? What was she talking about?

". . . Dad abused me sexually that summer we went camping in New Hampshire . . ."

What summer was that? She dragged up a foggy sense of nylon tents and constant mosquitoes.

". . . and then later at the lake . . ."

Oh, that lake! She'd never hear the end of that lake Harvey had dragged them to summer after summer! This is some kind of joke, but what? What?

". . . and then in the garden. This went on, as you both know . . ."

As we both know? Wait a minute! We do not both know anything. I don't anyway. And neither does your father. Unless he does. Does he? Oh God, Harvey?

". . . from the time I was eight to the time I was eleven, my father raped me . . ."

Raped her? Yes, that's what she means. Can she really mean that? She means incest. She can't mean that.

". . . while you, Mother, did nothing to help . . ."

Dear God, if I'd known anything about it, I'd have acted so fast!

"Therefore, I cannot come home for Christmas. We cannot enjoy family fellowship until you both go into therapy and remember what you've done to your daughter, a small child. Perhaps you can be forgiven, if you, too, were abused as children. Most abusers were themselves abused as children. Believe me, the burden of treatment will be far less heavy to you than the hidden situation has been to me. I live with the effects." The note was signed with a "sincerely" and a rapidly scratched "Phoebe."

Claire sat. She cannot have read such a letter. Her eyes moved along the edge of the refrigerator, noticing its pleasantly bland almond color, its hinges. How neatly her refrigerator was designed! She'd just sit here and look at it, for the rest of her life, which wouldn't be long, because it was somehow ending. Indeed, she had the odd sensation that she wasn't really located in her body anymore but was becoming a soul perched on her own shoulder, watching the large woman in the chair below her, waiting to see what she would do.

The woman stood. The woman placed the letter on the table. The woman walked to the hall and up a flight of stairs. The woman turned to the back of the house, to a so-called family room, where a man who was somehow related to her was watching a basketball game. The woman stopped at the threshold just before the peach-colored carpet: this wasn't a door the woman could go through. The woman's voice sounded remote, slow, and very strong. "Harvey, did you ever touch Phoebe sexually?"

The face of a lean man looked up from a screen, blue eyes examined her. "God, Claire, what do you mean?"

The woman's voice said, "She says you did. In the garden and out at the lake."

The man's face broke into lines. The man stood. "Of course not!"

"I didn't think so." The woman sounded so relieved. Yet not all of the woman believed the man. Some small part of this woman had turned skeptic and would remain an observer on the front lines here up in the air, full of suggestions to be relayed to the solid woman below. Look at his hands, the skeptic said. They're twitching. Look at his eyes. They're veiled.

"Something terrible is happening," the woman said to the man. "Come on down, read the letter." She sounded a little more normal.

The man came toward her, taller, bigger than she. "Claire, what is it?"

"Don't touch me!" she shouted. Then, "Harvey, Harvey! What happened? Did you do it? You have to tell me!"

He stood several feet away from the threshold and from his wife, his gaze meeting hers. She felt her eyes bulging.

"Claire, don't be crazy," he said quietly. "You know me. It's Harvey. You know me. I'm Harvey. You're Claire. We're not crazy. But you know me, don't you know me?"

Things fell back into place then. The soul snuck into Claire and she no longer felt that strange division. Here was Harvey, a fine, intelligent, good-hearted man. He'd never forced her sexually. Well, there'd been a few times where she was tired or impatient but she'd gone ahead anyway. He loved her. He brought flowers and paid the premiums on his life insurance. All the sudden-acquired strength went out of her body. She slumped against the threshold.

"God, Harvey. What's happened to her? Is she sick?"

"I don't know." Then he could approach her, put his arm around her. "Something's terribly wrong. Let's go downstairs. Let's call her up."

They walked downstairs side by side, though his arm felt slightly strange, his flesh repugnant past the slight protection of 50 percent wool, 50 percent polyester. They reached the table where the letter was and she handed it to him. He stood reading it. She stood waiting. The skeptic part was inside her now, behind her right eye. It noticed that the man did not cry out. He did not shout No! No! No! What he did was take a long time reading and then he said, "Phoebe's undergoing something. I don't know what."

"You think so?" she said coolly. "Let's call." She dialed from the wall phone in the galley and Harvey picked up the mantel phone. It rang once; it rang again. They stood there on opposite sides of the honey-colored kitchen with the bare undecorated tree, within the smell of pine while Christmas fell away and their daily lives along with it, their jobs, tomorrow, the future that had been theirs. Only this terrible thing, whatever it was, mattered, and Claire looked down at her feet. She knew there would be an outline of her feet on the floor right here forever. This is where I stood when we called Phoebe. The phone rang three times. It rang a fourth, short time. A female voice that wasn't Phoebe's answered and Harvey said, "May I speak with Phoebe Fairchild, please?"

"Phoebe doesn't live here anymore. She's moved."

"Where to?" Harvey said into his phone.

"Who's calling, please?"

"This is her father, Harvey Fairchild."

"Mr. Fairchild, Phoebe has instructed me not to give her new address or number to you. She has, I believe, some unfinished business with you."

"I've got to talk to her!"

"I am sorry, Mr. Fairchild."

"Give her a message then! Tell her to call home. Tell her we're coming up."

"You don't know where to find her, do you?"

"Listen, whoever you are, she's our daughter. We know where she works."

"School is on vacation, Mr. Fairchild. And besides, she's quit her job."

Claire spoke into her phone. "Is that you, Nora?"

"Yes."

"Nora, is she all right?"

"She is fine, Mrs. Fairchild. She's better than she's been in a long time. Now that she's remembered what her father—"

Claire heard a click and across the room Harvey was putting down the phone. As the young female voice went on, she hung up too.

Harvey went back to the table, sat down, and picked up the letter and read it again. Claire watched. He didn't look fierce. He looked the way he had when the tub at the lake overflowed and each time he screwed a pipe shut it made no difference. The water just kept flowing out over the top of the tub.

"Maybe she's having some kind of nightmare," Claire offered. "I mean like a dream, only when you're awake. Some kind of aberration. Why would she quit her job? Something is very wrong."

Harvey finished the letter, read it a third time, put his arms down on the table and then his head down on his arms.

Could this be an admission of guilt? Claire picked up her phone again and dialed Bess at the northern edge of Manhattan. A tape with some indistinguishable rock lyrics in the background announced that Cara had flown home to San Jose and Brooke to Shawnee Mission and that Bess was helping her sister move and was then working Christmas Eve until she left for Philadelphia. Claire was about to report this to Harvey when he cried out.

"Claire! I didn't do anything!"

"I know," the larger part of her said out loud, crossing the floor. She leaned down and put her arms around him and held him to her breast to comfort him in that great gesture of the female, saying, "I know. You'd never do a thing like that." The little voice inside had shrunk to almost nothing and only whispered, *How about that look of satisfaction coming in from a sail with Phoebe?* Don't be ridiculous. That's the same look he'd get at one of her plays. That's pride. That's the everyday amazement of parents. This is a good man. Good men don't fuck their daughters. I hope to God not. *I'll kill you if you did.*

17

Harvey lay in the dark with his head toward the North Pole because several years ago Claire had read that this orientation was best for sleeping, and now the idea seemed so sweet and harmless, a thought from an earlier life, before his daughter, his little girl, had accused him of the worst thing a man can do. His house had been invaded. He should be crouched downstairs in the kitchen with a rifle aimed at the invader. Except, somehow, the intruder was himself, with a stocking over his face. Phoebe had said so. He heaved up under the comforter and turned toward Claire's motionless, rounded shape.

Was Phoebe crazy? His amazing, lively girl? There was some manic depression on his father's side and Claire's family had a run of diabetes, but there was nothing mental. High-strung, his mother's family was, wired up. Phoebe had always squealed and stamped if you tied her shoelaces too tight. He could sympathize because he'd done the same. He stretched his legs and tried to relax them.

Could it be drugs? He remembered the time he'd taken LSD because their Village friends were doing it. Claire had refused, in case she might be a day or two pregnant. He'd swallowed the tab and gone for a walk and when he'd looked down he'd seen the sewer covers pulsating. Of course it was his own pupils and not the sewer lids expanding and contracting, but no one in the world could have persuaded him of that then. Drugs? Oh, Phoebe, poor Phoebe! He didn't know where to begin to help her if it was drugs. He turned away from Claire and toward the empty room.

He'd actually felt rather high at supper, full of crisis and plans. He'd solve this problem. There had to be some completely understandable mistake somewhere in here. He'd find it. *We'll get to the bottom of this, girl,* he'd written at the end of Claire's quick note to Phoebe. *Take good care of yourself.* Force himself upon his daughter? Christ! What kind of man would do that? He tried to relax his shoulders.

He'd always been especially careful with the girls, Bess in particular. Her body, when she stretched out on the kitchen couch, reading, had looked so like Claire's on their bed back on Cornelia Street, the same risings, the same indentations. Just looking at Bess like that from his reading chair under the soft light—he'd sometimes had to get up for coffee to disturb this unwonted concentration. Yet you can't not respond to them at all. "Tell her how beautiful she is," Claire had coaxed him when Bess had gone to her first dance in torn jeans and one of those artificially ripped and repinned blouses that had probably cost him thirty dollars. "She knows I think so!" he'd replied. Maybe that had even helped give Bess some of the confidence she had with boys.

Phoebe had always reminded him more of himself than of Claire. Had he treated her *too* much like a boy? Had that hurt her? It had been a tricky line to walk, Claire wanting the girls to hear that they could grow up to be president. Though a female White House in one generation had seemed unlikely, he'd understood the value of presenting the possibility. He'd shot baskets with both girls but Bess had enjoyed this more than Phoebe, or himself, for that matter. He turned over again.

Phoebe and he had loved climbing mountains and being out in the boat when it rained and they had always simultaneously removed the cheese from whatever cheeseburgers came their way as soon as they hit the table. They laughed at the same things, too: pratfalls of any kind, bops on the head. Yet Phoebe was subtler than he or even Claire. She had a poignant delicacy, almost a double awareness, divining what you were expecting of her and producing it as if it were a parody of what you meant. He thought of the night she'd come glowing offstage after playing the girl in *Our Town*. "You made this old fan of yours cry," he'd said with tears in his eyes. Maybe he should have told her she was beautiful. He felt dampness on his face, wiped away tears with the back of his hand. Clearly, he must have done something wrong. Or else that letter would never have arrived. Something Phoebe had misinterpreted? A hand on hip or breast, accidentally. Some sort of kid kiss delivered a couple of weeks too late, into puberty? He remembered once when he'd taken her hand on a mountain hike and for the first time realized hers was no longer a child's hand but a woman's. He'd felt sad. Proud, too. He'd let go as soon as he could do so discreetly.

It had been sad to lose his little girls. First Phoebe, then Bess. He missed his girls so much. Daddy! Daddy! Daddy! He saw them standing on the rocks that time at Cape Cod as the tide began to roll in ever so slowly. It's okay! he'd called back. Here I come! And he'd waded out to hand them both down into the shallow water. The baby first, Daddy! Daddy! Daddy! What a great feeling. Then Phoebe, he'd splashed back through the water to Phoebe, himself invincible, thinking this is the height, the peak of something, this is a wonderful life.

She'd told them to go into therapy. Why should he look into his own childhood? There'd been no incest there. His father had considered intimate contact to be a modest handshake and his mother an encouraging pat on the shoulder. Growing up on the flat fields of southern Jersey during the Depression, he'd had his major trouble from his sister, Phyllis, who at first, bigger and smarter, had casually and continually outwitted him. She'd always thought herself to be the best chocolate in the box. Of childhood, he could remember no significant sin.

Shame had arrived in basic training when he'd been scared on his belly with the bullets overhead, but everybody else had been scared, too. There was a little shoddy stuff early on at Sommers & Neugeboren, but only because he hadn't understood the business. That was ignorance, not sin. He turned over again.

Roxy.

He'd kept quiet about that evening after the Cornell Phone-a-thon. It all seemed so trite in the aftermath. But fun, God, yes. After ten years of marriage, to spend an evening as an anonymous man with an anonymous woman had been like traveling in a foreign country. He'd had no desire to repeat it. Well, yes, a small desire. But to really get going with Roxy seemed, well, not worth it. He'd hated having a secret from Claire, hated the distance that put between them. In the end, he preferred having a past and a future with the same woman. In the end he preferred Claire. Had his daughter somehow divined this small straying? Punished him for it?

There must be something he'd done. He'd find out, apologize, explain, and she'd say, "Oh, I get it now. Sorry, Dad." They'd handled all the other crises in their lives—Claire's two miscarriages, Bess's AIDS test, those times he'd had to borrow from his mother to meet the mortgage payments. They'd gotten through. They'd get through this. He rose up under the comforter and turned again.

Outside a car passed along the narrow street and came to a halt. A door slammed. This was hopeless. He would never sleep. Maybe he should get up, go down to the kitchen, warm up some milk, try a scotch.

Oh.

Suddenly he seemed to sink into the mattress. He could see himself years back walking downstairs in the dark, after some wedding, all that cheap champagne. It was summer, hot, and he had a terrible headache and nausea from drinking too much out of that melancholy boredom you get at weddings. He'd stood up, gone down to the kitchen for vitamin B or tomato juice, and then he'd come back up and stopped in the hallway of the third floor. He'd stood at their thresholds, Phoebe's, Bess's, wanting to go in, to warn them of marriage but at the same time to extol it. He'd wanted to explain to them that their husbands would not be gods, just guys, simple men, they wouldn't be perfect. Don't be afraid, don't expect too much. Jump in the water, swim. Give life a try. Maudlin, sloppy, he hadn't gone into either of their rooms.

Or had he?

Jesus, he had to remember. He squeezed his eyes tight but could see no more of that moment on the landing. It was all blackness, emptiness, and filled with the particular remorse of having had too much to drink in front of your children. He lay rigid and face up. If he had gone in that room and done something, he deserved to be jailed! He certainly did! And if he'd gone so far as to forget it, what else could he have forgotten? All those things she said he'd done? Jesus! Maybe he should see a therapist.

When a small gray light became visible behind the gauzy curtains, he slept.

In the morning he took the stairs with weary legs. The wedding was the Scatterbay girl's, he'd remembered that much more. Claire might know more about it, but she wasn't in the kitchen. No coffee was brewing in the white machine. No muffins.

"Claire?" he called out up the stairs, out the back door. *Dear Harvey, I've left you forever and you know why.* He scanned the counter for a note. Even if she'd left him, she'd be sure to provide all her reasons as well as a bunch of phone numbers. No note. He relaxed a little. It was now impossible to relax a lot. In every letting go of muscle, he came to the hard fact within: Phoebe had accused him.

He found juice in the refrigerator. He didn't know how to use the new coffeemaker. He stuck muffins in the toaster. He couldn't imagine life without Claire. To begin with, she remembered everything they'd done and been. That's the difference between male and female memory, she'd told him. She was full of strange little facts that seemed to make a lot of sense until you actually tried to work with them and then they sort of evaporated in your hands. But by then she usually had a new fact. It was endearing.

Where was she? The silence continued. Was the car out front or not? He hurried to the door and opened it. Gone. No car. And yes, on the hall table lay a bit of white paper. He picked it up, held it away. *Gone to New York to talk to Phoebe. Be back by late afternoon or will call. Sommers' at 6 p.m., if you still want to go.* He breathed out his relief. Of course she'd gone to New York. Of course she should talk with Phoebe, woman-to woman. Somehow or other, this was women's stuff.

18

In the cold dawn, the car motor had sounded isolate and significant. Claire made her way out of the low, flat city, past warehouses, heaps of red brick, tiles, dye works, water tanks, run-down Dutch-style houses in blue, light green, and maroon, lumberyards, huge ads for cigarettes, dead-car dumps. This morning she didn't think about all the work that needs to be done to keep the postindustrial world afloat in something other than its own debris. She thought about very little, in fact. She drove fast and didn't stop till the Walt Whitman Rest Area, where she bought coffee in a Styrofoam cup with lots of milk and sugar to comfort her. This was a business trip, unfinished business, family business.

Immediately after the next rest area, the car to her right in the slower lane veered crazily off the road and slapped itself against a post supporting a huge metal sign. The thud was substantial. Heart attack, she said to herself. In crisis one is calm. Almost immediately the sirens whined behind her. Help was arriving for that poor sucker. No help was appearing for this huge thud in her own life. She must be the help.

Getting into Manhattan was fairly simple, though Claire disliked the confines of the tunnel she'd always called Moby Dick. She and her family were lost now in the belly of some other whale. Spat out on the West Side, she dropped down to Fourteenth Street and made her way across the island to Second Avenue, pulling up many blocks to the south at a vacant meter. It wasn't even 9:00 A.M. She ought to have come here last week, the week before, this summer, but the last time she'd seen Phoebe at home, in the kitchen, there'd been no sign, no warning. Never mind, she should have come.

Scanning the shabby fronts and facades, she walked south to the number on the envelopes she'd been addressing to Phoebe. No wonder Phoebe hadn't urged them to visit! This was a terrible neighborhood.

Here.

Her heart's beating came to consciousness. What was she going to say? She reached over a hinged gate to a pair of rusty doorbells and pushed both. It was cold with the wind at her neck. She pushed the buttons again and looked up at the windows on the second and third floors. No sounds. She peered into the locked foyer at a set of newer buttons. Behind her the lights of the intersection clicked from one color to another. Young adults sleep late. She pushed the outside buttons again.

"Phoebe?" She called out, raising her head to the unyielding brick. The light at the intersection clicked again.

Okay, Plan B. Several dark-wrapped men were studying her. There must be drugs all around, on every corner. Harvey and she should subsidize Phoebe's rent and get her out of here. She walked to a coffee shop on the corner and pushed through the battered and graffitied door, out of the smell of garbage and car exhaust and into that of steam, Clorox, and onions. Choosing a stool, she turned sideways and acquired a view of Phoebe's apartment door. She was beginning to feel like a spy. Phoebe was moving this weekend. That could have meant yesterday, it could mean today. Bess would be helping her. She didn't want to see Bess. She needed Phoebe alone. Her coffee was set in front of her, in a white ceramic cup with a smear of lipstick on it. She wiped the lipstick off with her gloved hand and then asked for a new cup. The counterman was annoyed.

"There was lipstick on it."

"Where you say, lady!"

"There was. I wiped it off."

"Ach." He gave a shrug, grabbed the cup, dumped out the coffee, reached for another, filled it, and set it down, cursing her. The courteous world of her childhood had never existed here; her daughter's world was so different from her own.

This cup had a brown mark on the rim and she didn't complain. Sitting in an awkward twist, she watched someone coming out of Phoebe's door. A woman with a stroller! God, bringing a baby up here! The woman shoved the hinged gate so that it hung off as if broken. At ten, Claire ate a doughnut. At ten-thirty, she stood on the stoop trying the bell again. No answer.

Back at her car, she sat on the freezing plastic. She was tired now, having lain unmoving and awake as Harvey thrashed through the night. Come on, Phoebe! It hadn't been twenty-four hours since she'd read that letter, yet this part of her life seemed as long as the rest.

She'd failed as a mother.

There was the woman with the stroller again. She got out and followed her into a foul-smelling foyer with different, newer doorbells. She pressed 2B and there came an answering buzz and she opened an inner door and hurried toward the stairway.

A door down the hall opened and she called out, "I'm just going up to 2B."

"This is it," the man standing in the doorway said.

She walked toward him. Was that Daryl from Yale? He didn't look much like the senior she'd met in New Haven. "Number 2B?"

"You got it. I thought you were some friends of mine."

"Does Phoebe Fairchild live here?"

"Not anymore. She left yesterday."

"Where is she?"

"She's moved."

"Where to?"

"I believe that Phoebe wanted to keep her whereabouts private."

"I'm her mother."

"Exactly."

That came like a slap. She straightened up. "Phoebe is in trouble. I've come to help her. Please tell me where I can find her."

"Sorry. No can do."

"You have to tell me!"

"Why?"

"Because . . . I'm her mother." Her usual efficacy had fled. Nothing worked in this new world.

"As you said. We've met. Daryl here."

"Oh, it is you! You look so different, somehow."

"Look, Mrs. Fairchild, I can't have this talk. My loyalty is to Phoebe. So long now, I'm going to shut my door."

"Daryl! You can't. I . . . Please . . . please help me out. Phoebe seems to be suffering. She's my child. I have a right to see her."

"I'm going to shut the door now."

"Wait, stop it! Wait!" Claire raised her palm against the door that was closing on her life. "Call her. Tell her I'll wait for her in the coffee shop."

"I can't do that."

"What's wrong with you? Have you no compassion? No sense of right and wrong?"

"I may be gay, Mrs. Fairchild, but I am a man of principle."

The door closed.

19

Claire came home with a hypothesis: Maybe Phoebe was gay and unable to voice it, so she'd made up something else to tell them. This distracted Harvey and kept him from asking about the night of the Scatterbay wedding, or so he told himself. They moved about their bedroom changing into festive clothing, taking some small comfort in each other's physical presence—at least the other person in the room was predictable. He assured her that Phoebe wasn't gay, though that might be easier to accept than this. She said being gay might have been the thing that drove Phoebe into therapy. If not that, what? At least Phoebe had a therapist. That was a comfort.

Doug and Nancy Sommers lived over in Society Hill in a high-rise with a view of the Delaware—wide, dark, and forbidding below the picture window. Proper Nancy circled among the guests, proper Doug took coats. *Claire! Claire!* Someone was calling, waving. It was her old friend Lacey Quinn in black tights helping Junior Neugeboren serve up drinks at the bar. Claire had introduced this freewheeling artist to Junior after his wife left him. To her surprise, Lacey had found something loveable in a man whose major talent seemed to be keeping a plump wallet. Lacey's boy, Ezra, was gay. She'd know what to do in case. . . . No, she couldn't tell anyone anything about this! Especially Lacey! She waved back but didn't move toward the bar.

Floating from spot to spot in the faintly comforting superficiality, Claire paused and chewed on something cheesy while a man with a blond beard lectured her on the merits of Friends Select versus Girls High. That was the blond man's world. Claire no longer inhabited it.

By the piano, Harvey laughed at Doug's joke about the couple who'd waited till they were ninety-four to divorce but he didn't get the joke told by the young man from contracts.

"You don't know that case?" the young man said. "The guy out in California they say raped that little girl and killed her with a rock? You know, twenty years later his daughter remembered seeing him do it."

"What took her so long?"

"It was so stressful that she repressed it. That's the word, repressed it. A therapist hypnotized her and got at the truth."

"Fry the bastard," Doug said.

Later, in the car, Harvey and Claire talked about other possibilities.

"Could it have been someone else?" Claire asked. "A teacher of Phoebe's?"

"Those cases in the news," Harvey said. "They crop up all the time."

"There was that nursery school in California. And a day-care worker in New Jersey. I can't think of teachers it might be, though."

"How about that boy baby-sitter?"

"Nat? The druggy one? We never asked him back."

"What about that camp counselor, the one who taught tennis?"

"I've been wondering about the wallboard man who propositioned me."

At home what they felt was low, continual pain. What they wanted was painkillers. They each swallowed one of the last two capsules of Percodan left over from when Bess had her wisdom teeth pulled, then they lay in bed without touching. It was as if they'd been burned—the slightest pressure could peel off skin.

I can't ask her about the Scatterbay wedding now, Harvey reasoned with himself. She's too beat. So he said, "Today I got the feeling that this is like a fight of some kind. She's telling us not to cross a line she's drawn in the sand."

"Come on, this isn't one-upmanship. This isn't a fight between two boys."

"Is it a fight though? Some kind of female fight?"

"Maybe." Claire's voice drew into itself. "Maybe not. Maybe the fight's inside her. Remember that time at Cape Cod, when she wouldn't go into the water? I tried, you tried, we both tried. We gave up and sat under an umbrella with the baby and suddenly she was upon us with buckets and buckets of water, drenching us and screaming and screaming?"

"Sort of."

"I can just see her, in that little red bathing suit that rode up so high in the back. The fury in her!"

Their daughter had already lost her name, becoming She.

At dawn on the evening of our Savior's birth, Harvey moved toward the bathroom hopefully. Help might await him inside that small, warm room. No such luck. In the mirror he saw a middle-aged man puffy under the eyes, haggard around the mouth. Would you believe this unshaven man who says he did not rape his daughter?

"We've got to stay very calm," Claire began at breakfast, as he was about to bring up the Scatterbay girl's wedding. "Bess will help us. She'll have an angle."

Bess? My God, did Bess know about this? Oh, poor Bess. He closed his mouth.

"She'll know if Phoebe's on drugs. She'll know if Phoebe's gay. We'll be able to rule out those two possibilities."

He lost his car keys, cut himself on broken glass in the trash. Shortly before midnight, they drove up to the train station through a light snow. In the headlights individual flakes took on a starlike glow. What kind of man sleeps with his daughter? Why, this kind. See how he drives through the city? See how he puts on his left blinker? Abruptly, he pulled onto Market and nearly clipped a pedestrian.

Claire gasped but didn't criticize. Instead she said for the dozenth time,

"At least Bess will know if Phoebe's okay. Not crazy. Or mumbling. Or living in a cardboard box."

Harvey pictured Phoebe in a cardboard box on Fifth Avenue near the big, still lions she'd loved so much in front of the library. They'd gone up one Christmas to see the windows on Fifth decorated with trees and toys. She'd been as mesmerized by the little trains circling on their tracks as he. He could see all of them walking along Broadway imitating R2D2 after they'd seen *Star Wars* together. What a nice little family they'd made. The loss of it caused him to clear his throat. Had he gone into that room or not? No. Phoebe's lions had got loose in her head somehow instead, had assaulted her, had come down off their stone bases in one pounce and he could not ward them off, could not rescue her. Daddy, Daddy . . . Make a right! Jesus! He pulled into the parking strip—this is how he parks his car, like an idiot.

"Come on, honey." Claire was putting her hand through his arm. "Come on. Come on, now. Come on."

They walked like old, arthritic people across the marble floor to the escalator and down into the winter darkness alongside the track. They separated the way they usually did, so there'd be one parent at one end of the train and one at the other end. The train barreled in and steam hissed up from it, the smell of burning, hell's own fire. Harvey forced his shoulders down and tried to stand firmly on his feet. He scanned the opening doors, where uniformed men were bending to put the stepping platforms in place. *Baltimore, this way! Washington, that way!* Then he saw her, standing poised at the top of the platform, her sturdy look, her dark blond hair, her own scanning of the crowd, his daughter, his only daughter now, Bess. He moved toward her and stood waiting for the conductor to hand her down. He put his arms around her and realized that they were trembling.

20

Here they sat in the enormous kitchen with mulled cider before them just as Claire had wanted, trying for a semblance of normalcy by taking a few minutes to open up the one present Christmas Eve traditionally allowed. Normalcy wasn't working. Bess sat cool and removed on the lumpy couch. She'd just opened the crisp five-hundred-dollar bill Christmas had brought her every year since she turned eighteen, preferring to save the surprises for tomorrow. Maybe we've been too lenient, Claire advised herself. Maybe we've spoiled our children.

In one of the rockers, Harvey sat with eyes downcast but, thankfully for Claire, not wearing the red sweatband she'd given him for winter walks to work. Now it was her turn and Claire was kneeling to search beneath the tree for a likely choice. The starry lights sparkling on the dark, fragrant tree and the red-wrapped presents beneath it all seemed such a charade, such mockery. Where was Phoebe? She chose something flat that turned out to be a CD from Harvey, Billie Holiday in Paris. *We'll start here, then on to Crete,* he'd written on its wrapper. He must have done that before Phoebe's letter came, splitting their life into two parts, Normal and This. Claire gave up on normalcy and, though it was past one in the morning, said, "Bess, do you know anything about why Phoebe didn't come home?"

The shape on the couch did not move. "She had the flu."

Claire understood from the measured cadence that Bess did know. "That's not the real reason."

The shape on the couch adjusted itself. "She told you?"

"Yes, she wrote us a letter."

"What did she say?"

"You don't know?"

Bess swung her legs up on the couch. "She's got some funny ideas."

"She says that she was approached sexually by her father."

"God." Bess sighed, stretching out, fitting a pillow under her head. "So she told you."

"What do you know about it?"

"Not much." Bess appeared to undo a little, to relax, even to unravel. "It's all so strange. There's this roommate of hers, Nora. The first night I got there Nora was telling me how her mother had done gross things to her on her kitchen table. Now a couple of months later, Phoebe is saying that Dad . . ." Bess turned toward Harvey, who sat with the face of Abraham Lincoln in stone. "Excuse me, Dad, but it's what she's saying"—she turned back to Claire to deliver the actual words—"that Dad 'abused' her, as she puts it."

A choked voice from Harvey, who asked Claire, "Is that the girl we talked to? That Nora?"

Claire was alone, somehow, with each of them turned away from the other, toward her. "I think so."

"Don't worry, Dad," Bess said, looking into the couch this time. "I know you didn't do it."

Harvey's stiffness remained. "Thanks."

Bess glanced up at Claire to say, "Phoebe says her therapist wants to talk with me, but I told her I don't want any part of it."

"Why not? It might give us some insight into the whole thing."

"I don't want any more insights into anything! Hey, guys, I think we should just ignore it."

"How could we possibly ignore it?" Harvey's voice came a little easier.

"You know how she is. She gets carried away. Let her act it out—"

"But she's in pain, sweetie!" Claire interrupted. "She must be suffering. How does she look? Is she in danger?"

Bess veiled herself again. "She looks fine. I saw her Saturday. We moved her to . . . her new place. She needs a haircut."

Harvey snorted and his fluency of speech returned. "This is a serious accusation. It's serious business. Your sister could be in serious trouble. Does she look out of control?"

"Guys!" The shape on the couch filled with air. "Don't overreact. She looks fine. She didn't look crazy or anything."

Harvey took up another point. "Did I ever do anything to her that could have been misinterpreted? Anything you can remember?"

"How would I remember? I wouldn't have been there." Bess finally softened her voice. "No, Dad, I didn't see anything. She talked about a camping trip but it sounded dumb to me."

"What camping trip?"

"Well, didn't we go to New Hampshire once?"

"Tanworth, up around there? Yes."

"So what do you remember about it, Dad?"

"That beautiful lake. And the mountain. Your mother turned her ankle and you stayed halfway down with her while Phoebe and I climbed to the top."

Claire remembered that and added her own description. "It started to drizzle a little before you two got back and then I got my arms around everybody's shoulders and sort of hoisted myself up and we all walked back to the bottom."

"Sounds a bit on the dull side," Bess said. "Maybe that's why I don't remember it at all."

"What does Phoebe remember?" Harvey asked.

"She didn't really say. Something weird about a tent." Bess picked up her hot cider.

For a second Claire imagined Harvey and Phoebe alone on the mountain, his hand moving down her daughter's body . . . No, this is exactly what she must not, must not do! "Okay." Claire cut short her reverie. "No more presents tonight. It's one-thirty. Tomorrow morning, pecan rolls and the rest of the presents. You must be tired, Bess."

Claire climbed the stairs last and alone. Christmas in Iowa had never been the presents, but rather the dark, fragrant church, the people standing with their candles, the sense of being loved so much by God that he's sent you his very own baby to take care of. She'd always wanted to have a baby. When hers were born she'd understood why people would fashion a religion with a sacred day set aside for birth. Though she was of a generation that had moved out beyond this long-told tale into a void between tales, she did remember it warmly. How individual she'd felt, letting go of her faith. How emblematic of the times, she saw now, her one minuscule act. She was but a very small speck in a giant conglomerate. But oh, how she missed God tonight, because He saw into every heart and knew the truth. That's what they needed here.

The next day after not even mildly distracting presents, they sat at the dining room table, where Claire realized she'd made another mistake in the name of normalcy. Everything was so cold in here, so sterile, the white linen cloth, the red dishes—they looked like blood on a nun's wimple. Still, they'd always eaten Christmas dinner in the dining room. But of course, their own personal tradition no longer mattered. Their very history was history, gone.

Bess alternated between cool and relaxed. Claire could not get in as close to Bess as she wanted, and when she did, she remembered to remind herself that young women Bess's age need to feel less observed. Bess had shot down one possibility: Phoebe didn't do drugs—or nothing, as Bess put it, except the ordinary experimentation. She'd been so scornful at the query that Claire hadn't asked about homosexuality. Today at the table Claire found it to be herself who was turning her face away from both daughter and husband, toward the sweet potatoes, toward the beef, toward the green, buttered peas.

"How are you finding New York?" Harvey was asking.

"I don't know. It's awfully big. Adrianna Bender is coming home next month and wants to try Seattle or Portland. Me too."

"That's nice, sweetie, but—"

"The West, that's a good place but—"

"It's too far away? Is that what you're both going to say? Oh, you guys! Come on, it's still in the States. Think of James's parents. They don't even know if he's in China or the Khyber Pass."

"We have to have an address," Claire pointed out, feeling a rush of despair that she no longer had such a thing for Phoebe.

"I'll be on the road. And that brings me to my question. I'll need a van. And it might come as no surprise that at eight dollars an hour, I've hardly saved up for one."

Claire did see Harvey tensing up, and she sent the cranberry sauce around.

"So I was thinking," Bess continued. "If you could sport me to a van, I'd have the security of a safe place to sleep for the next ten years or so. The '91 vans run about twenty thousand and I know you wouldn't want me to get something so old it will break down in Missouri. An '88 or '87 goes for fifteen or so."

"Good Lord, honey," Harvey said in an aggrieved voice. "I don't have fifteen thousand extra dollars!"

"You don't have to pay for college this year," Bess returned. "That's about twenty thousand right there, isn't it?"

"But I'm paying back the loans at twelve thousand a year."

"Oh, I forgot that. You guys aren't pressed for money, though."

"We're comfortable, we're not rich."

Bess kept at it and a new tone appeared in her voice, a hurt tone, not something Claire associated with Bess. "You've got a house and a car and I've got nothing."

"You've got a college education, and rather a splendid one," Claire put in.

Harvey sounded dangerously patient: "We have to save for our retirement. With inflation you can never save enough."

"Times have changed, guys. It costs a bundle to live."

"It always did. The bundles get larger and larger but they buy only roughly the same thing."

"I know what inflation is, Dad. I'm living it. I'm paying six hundred dollars a month for a crummy room that doesn't even have a door! You guys pay five hundred a month for an entire house!"

"We pay five hundred twenty-five a month plus four hundred for taxes plus two hundred for heat plus one hundred for insurance. That's twelve hundred twenty-five dollars per month."

"Okay, okay. I'm wrong. But you make so much more than I do."

There was a silence and the sound of celery being crunched and the scraping of a serrated knife against a china plate. Then Harvey said, "You might find a reliable van of some sort for around eight thousand, 1985 or 1984, nothing earlier."

Claire was surprised. Harvey sounded afraid. What was he afraid of?

"Okay! Way to go, Dad! A very used van."

"But it has to be safe."

"Gotcha! It can't break down till after the Rockies."

"I can't just give the money to you, though," Harvey added. "It's not right. I could lend it to you interest-free. In five years you could start to repay the principal."

"Oh, thanks, Dad," Bess said with sarcasm. "For the generous loan. At fourteen thousand a year, though, I can't say just what decade I'll pay it back in."

The meanness in Bess's reply brought Claire up out of reverie. Her own father had lent her money at 3 percent for her first car out of his teacher retirement. She'd been grateful to get an affordable loan. Bess should be grateful for Harvey's offer, not full of attack. Maybe this was further evidence for one of her theories about Phoebe's attack: They had been too lenient. They'd spoiled their children. Given them too much. Claire was falling apart. She felt the self-control her own parents had insisted upon finally seep away and she heard herself blurt out, "Bess, where's Phoebe? Where has she moved to?"

Bess ladled cranberry sauce onto her plate and didn't look at either of them. "She wants to keep that private, Mom. I promised her I wouldn't tell. I know how you must feel but I know how she feels, too. So all I can do is tell you that if you want to get a message to her for an emergency or something, I'll relay it."

Claire stared at Bess's lowered head. Her family was gone. She wanted to stand up and throw dishes. Her parents had had God on their team. Speak softly, let Him carry the big stick. She didn't know what to do. Tears of helplessness came into her eyes.

In the silence, Bess turned to Harvey. "Her phone's going to be unlisted."

"Oh, is it?" Harvey said icily. "Just like that."

"I can't help it, Dad! It's not my fault! None of this is my fault!"

21

Exhausted from the day at home where the entire terrain seemed mined, Bess stood in line at the top of the escalator in the Thirtieth Street station. It rattled her, trying to please both sides, trying to avoid both angers. She hadn't known how much of Phoebe's life to go into with her parents. Phoebe'd seemed less frightened Saturday when they'd moved her stuff out of Second Avenue. She'd even inquired about Roger, which her mother certainly hadn't. In fact, nothing about her life seemed to matter to her parents anymore, only the tiniest little thing in Phoebe's life. And now she was cornered into running their errands to Phoebe—she had her sister's Christmas check in her pocket. She was nothing but a courier, running back and forth between them. And to top it off, she owed her parents practically eight thousand dollars! Never mind, if she could find a van, she'd buy it and get out of here. Point it west and not stop till the Pacific. Then maybe *she* would try an unlisted telephone, too.

But of course not, she couldn't. It would kill them. Her father already looked about ten years older. At his age men drop dead of heart attacks. And her mother—who was this minute coming toward her with the take-out espresso and a little white bakery bag—had acquired such a helpless look. She herself had somehow become the person who was holding everybody else upright.

"One other thing, Bess," her mother said as she handed over the coffee. "Is Phoebe gay?"

"What?"

"You can tell me. If it's true."

"No, she's not!"

"I just wondered. It could be connected."

"Oh, for God's sake, Mom! That's unbelievable! Something goes wrong and you people immediately think it's because someone is gay. I don't get it! And drugs! You think a little pot or something is so much worse than wine at dinner?"

Her mother looked too humbled. "It was just a thought. A possibility."

Bess tried to hang on until she reached the safety of the train. "Mom, how would being gay explain anything?"

"Not being able to tell us. Needing so much distance."

"She's not gay. Okay, listen, that's my train."

"Bess, one more thing?"

Bess tucked the bag tighter under her arm. "Shoot, Mom."

Her mother was reaching to embrace her. "Phoebe needs you. Keep watch over her. . . ." Her mother's voice died out.

"Sure, Mom," she murmured as they touched cheeks. "Love you. It'll be okay." The station master opened the train gate and the people behind Bess began to push forward.

"Say bye to Dad!" she called and grabbed the downward-moving rubber rail into the real world. Crowded, but she liked aisle seats best, anyway. Gee, half the kids at Wesleyan had cars their parents bought them. Hers seemed to think it was a crime to ask about a van! Westward ho with Adrianna, that was the answer. Raising goats might be good, in Oregon or Washington, maybe Montana. Everybody was heading for Missoula now. What did they have in Montana? Mining. Natural gas. Mormons. No, that was Utah.

Except her parents were relying on her. So was Phoebe.

She clicked back her seat and fetched the book of Phoebe's she'd been too tired to read on the train ride down. The book was for every woman, its authors, Ellen Bass and Laura Davis, assured her, even though they were both lesbians. It seemed like 80 percent of the world was gay lately! Actually, it was probably less than 2 percent, Professor Zolbrod had cautioned. She flipped through the pages, picking up occasional sentences, including some possible signs of abuse: "Do you feel crazy, invalidated, or depressed whenever you see your family?" Were they kidding? She had to laugh. Hey, join the little club that's called the human race.

She flipped on. "If children don't tell with words, they often tell through behavior. . . . They are terrified to go to sleep, and wake up screaming from nightmares. . . ." Whoa! What is this? Most kids go through a period like that, don't they? I did. Next thing these authors would be saying was that if you've got two eyes and two feet, you've probably been abused.

Where were their studies? Their evidence? Professor Zolbrod would be thumping his lectern. She read on and shut the book in disgust. In her mind's eye appeared the huge computer-printed banner he'd stretched around the lab: CORRELATION IS NOT CAUSALITY. CORRELATION IS NOT CAUSALITY. Leaning her head against the seat, she realized how tired she was—tired of this whole thing.

Back at her steaming hot apartment she found that Cara's cat had filled her box with unburied turds. Brooke had left a note in Magic Marker: *We're out of milk, butter, and eggs. Whose turn is it?* She flipped on her stereo, tucked in a little ska, pulled back the madras shield and pretended the whole apartment was hers. Roger would be coming over tonight. She'd missed him a little, actually. She moved round and round on the thin mat. Her mother had kept looking at her father. Did Mom suspect Dad? It wasn't *Dad* who'd asked her to stand by Phoebe. Her dancing slowed itself.

Maybe Dad was a much more complicated man than she had ever imagined.

Once when she'd walked into his office downtown he'd looked at her as a woman instead of a daughter. Then he'd recognized her and readjusted himself somehow.

She came to a total stop.

Why had he chosen Phoebe to love? Not her?

Oh, for God's sake, kid, see how easy it is? Don't get hooked into it like the rest of them! She flipped off the music and walked into the kitchen.

The red light of the answering machine was blinking and she heard Phoebe's voice dictating her new phone number, adding, "Please open any of the letters our mother or our father send you and scan them. If there's no confession in them, don't even bother to forward them."

"Fuck you!" she shouted at the machine. She picked up the loose roll of paper towels and hurled it at the steaming radiator that turned the kitchen into a hothouse. Better, that's better. She fell into a kitchen chair. She was so exhausted. Maybe she had the flu.

22

The Sunday after Christmas Phoebe woke in the closet-sized sleeping alcove of her loft high above Tribeca reciting the words from the letter that had come yesterday, forwarded by Daryl: "Phoebe, Phoebe, What's wrong? We love you. We want to help you. Your father says he definitely did not abuse you. Nothing happened, honey, not with Daddy. Maybe someone else did something? What incident do you have in your mind? Maybe it would help if you could give us a few details and that way we could try to figure out . . ." Exactly as Sahra had cautioned! Her parents had fallen into line totally and completely. And at the end from her father "We'll get to the bottom of this, girl." How disgusting! As if she were a child. She wasn't, not anymore; for the first time in her life she was not a child.

She threw back the comforter and rose to her knees to shuffle along her futon toward the small, low window. Bess had helped her get the futon in here. They'd struggled up the five flights, stopping every couple of minutes to get their breath and they'd laughed a lot, like kids—Bess in a funny way the older sister. That's good, it's good to be small now and then. Let someone take care of you. You can expect a little regression in the emergency phase. That's where she was now; her parents' denial confirmed everything. On her knees she reached the unfinished windowsill, yanked the quilt up around her shoulders, and lay her elbows on the rough splintery wood.

Those five flights of incredibly steep steel stairs were what she liked best about this place. Nobody who didn't care about her would bother to climb them. On the other hand, a stranger mustn't think there was a woman alone up here so instead of Phoebe Fairchild she'd written Fairchild & Company on the mailbox. An inch of snow covered the neighboring ledge across the airshaft where pigeons were speaking softly of their own emergencies. A siren raged below, far below, and she was safe up here above it all, a princess in a tower.

Dad looked half dead, Bess had told her midweek when she brought the check. A sign of his guilt, she'd figured. Now the letter with no confession, as Sahra said; he isn't willing to take responsibility, to be your father. She moved her elbows and acquired a splinter.

Dropping her quilt, she stood shivering as she worked her bare feet into slippers. The pipes were clanging below and a faint heat began to make its way to her mountaintop. Her mother had come to the city, Daryl said. That had seemed a good sign, too. And then the letter and she knew whose side her mother was really on. So they were gone. Take charge. Not everyone has loving parents. Become your own parent. For the first time, no tears came. Good. She must be making progress. Get active. Move around.

Today was painting day. Full of energy for the first time in weeks, she felt she could paint forever. She made her way out of what was essentially a closet into a small square area where sunlight fell gloriously, or at least semigloriously, through a dirt-encrusted skylight. She skirted the wicker chairs and the unpacked boxes. This place wouldn't be helter-skelter like all her others. Her old chaos—maybe it had been deliberate? Because of what she'd needed to hide? All that was over. She'd set herself free. Today was the first day of the rest of her life and pretty soon there'd be a whole new year beginning, her first as a real adult.

She passed through glass doors that the former tenant had installed to conduct light into the dark interior corridor where a kitchen had been cannily fitted. At the side of her pint-sized sink she opened a door into a makeshift bathroom, once nothing but attic floor and now encircled and closed off by flimsy wallboard. She looked into the mirror at the pale face with the long straggly red hair, took a breath, and recited the words: "I'm a survivor. I'm taking charge of my life." Then all the air came out of her.

It still came as a loathsome surprise. The daddy who had loved her, attended her, wrapped her in his old red sweater—he'd also used her? Maybe he'd just gotten carried away. She turned on the hot water and heard Sahra's voice: Watch out for your compassion, Phoebe. It can destroy you. Anger is what's appropriate. Get mad.

He did love me, she repeated silently, holding the bar of soap under the warm water. He came to every one of my plays with a bouquet of flowers until I finally told him it was just a little bit embarrassing. What about those poor girls who had to play the parts of trees? They didn't get any flowers from their fathers! Why should I have all the privileges? I'm not only a WASP, you know, I also have some Celtic blood. No, wait a minute, that wasn't the point. The point was what he'd done. And that her mother believed him instead of her.

She tossed her washcloth into the suds and washed her face, arms, hands. Oh, that felt good, the warmth of the water. What she wouldn't give for a hot bath! But you couldn't use the tub here. With even so little as three inches of water in it, the pipes leaked and ran out into the apartment below. That's how she'd spent Christmas morning, being shouted at by the huge man from downstairs. She'd spent the afternoon in Saint Patrick's, watching people dip their hands in holy water before she discovered the peace of the Lady Chapel behind the pulpits and stood for hours in front of the statue; pale pink and blue flowers ran around the hem of the robe of the Virgin. *Mater Omnia,* she'd whispered; be mine. Then she wasn't sure if *omnia* was the genitive case or not. *I'd like to talk with your therapist, what is her name?* Oh no, she wasn't letting her mother anywhere near Sahra.

She dried herself with a towel barely warmed by the radiator and looked in the mirror again. God, this hair. Got to get it cut. She pulled it behind her into a tight twist. It looked okay, in fact very grown-up, but more a valedictorian's than a ballerina's. She let go and what had once been a tousled mass fell past her shoulders more straight than crimped. It would take the entire decade before she could afford another permanent. She picked up her brush.

When Mr. Reed, the man in charge of her paycheck, the man who called her Felina, had come out from behind his glass door to complain about her work again, something in her had snapped. Mr. Reed, she mouthed into the mirror, brushing her hair up. I have just found out that I was abused by my father when I was a child. My mother did nothing. You cannot expect me to be able to concentrate under these conditions. She leaned her head back to brush her hair straight over the crown, obliterating the part. Wait, he'd said. Don't quit. It's not that important. It is very important to me, Mr. Reed.

She put the brush down and bent from her waist—a Degas girl—and gathered her hair loosely a couple of inches from her head, wrapped a hairband around it, and stood up. That's better, a ponytail of sorts, the sixties, a flower child's hair. God, she was glad to be out of that dandruff-filled office! Now her real life could begin. She dressed in old jeans and a couple of sweatshirts hanging from the bathroom hooks and went back into the kitchen, which seemed to have grown a bit warmer.

There were hardly any dishes in the cupboard over the sink. Treat this move as an opportunity to define yourself, Sahra had made clear. Find out what you yourself really like in life. I like the wicker birdcage over the sink. It makes an elegant home for my Swedish ivy. I like oranges in a white bowl. She took one and cut it in half. There were three left. She set a pan of water on a burner. She herself had been a copier, a sponge, sort of, like Mom. If she could define herself, maybe it would be a good example for Mom, that is, for Claire. Claire could learn to form her own opinions.

Reaching into the cookie tin for bread, she pulled out two of the last four slices. On her own, she was poor. She might get to be like those scholarship guys in New Haven who hardly washed their clothes. She wasn't going to touch a penny of her Christmas check for food, only to pay Sahra. That part they owed her. She set the narrow oven to broil and lay the bread on its rack. When you don't have a toaster, you improvise. She was a very resourceful young woman who had a lot to offer the world. Let go and lean on yourself, Sahra had said. I'll be there to catch you.

Your sister may laugh at *The Courage to Heal* because it threatens her. Half dead? You've been half dead far longer than your father has. Really, you must get your sister to come in and see me. Or find a new friend. Someone who won't deny your feelings. In the emergency phase, safety is the important thing. She opened the refrigerator on which she'd hung her safety list of phone numbers: Sahra at work and at home; Bess at work and at home; Ibrahim at work and at home. How could she forget her own number on Second Avenue? You might in an emergency, Sahra had cautioned. Write it down. We don't want anything to happen to you. We want you among the living.

And last on the list, the Warburg Clinic. That was there in case she couldn't reach anybody else when the veil of the world fell away and the dark pictures reeled in, engulfing her. To her relief, it hadn't happened here, not yet. Maybe it wouldn't, especially if she could make everything white, white, white.

She removed half a bar of butter from the refrigerator. Slow down, simplify. You won't be so capable in this emergency phase. Take it easy painting, you're such an overachiever. You were violated by those who nurtured you. Nurture yourself.

After breakfast, she filled a mug with coffee and, in the studio room, opened a can of real old-fashioned oil paint. What a lovely, thick white liquid lapped itself into the pan. She ran her roller in it and stood on her stool to reach the top of the first wall. The FM from her boom box tossed out words: Bush, Kuwait, Bush, savings and loans, Bush, deficit, Bush, debt, Bush says there's no problem with the economy.

By the time she moved her stool to the second wall, Bach had replaced Bush. Here was music thumpy and juicy, so reassuring. She leaned her head way back to reach the top of the wall. Oh, she didn't want to get any memories here. She wanted to be safe. Sahra had given her a workbook full of questions. *Have you ever felt safe? Where?* At home in her room over the garden with its two leaded windows giving that shaded light and the rain running off the roof and down over the panes because Dad didn't believe in gutters. She'd felt safe in her room and in the kitchen, with Mom scrambling eggs in her big slippers with the lamb faces. That had been safe. But, of course, it wasn't safe at all. She'd been fooled! Totally fooled!

That kitchen was a mirage she'd put up to hide the wicked things that existed beyond the scrim.

Don't think about it.

I'm safe up here in my loft. Except, could this be a mirage, too? Am I this very minute repressing something that's happening here? In the alcove? In the bathroom?

Stay calm. Stay easy. She moved her chair to the next wall. Okay, Dad had denied it. But Mom? Oh, my God, Phoebe, if I'd only known! I'm divorcing your father!

Hah.

Leaning still further back, she felt dizzy but not nauseous. Nausea meant a new memory was coming on. It must be the paint fumes making her dizzy. But it was too cold to open the window. The phone rang and her whole body tensed.

Harvey! Claire!

Could Bess have given them her number? She let it ring four times, until her own recorded voice came on, speaking in the empty flat, and that gave her the creepiest feeling, like looking too long at your own eyes in a mirror. Then a man began to speak and she went cold all over.

It was only Ibrahim: "New Year's Eve party at work, angel. Join me? It would be politic of you to show up looking smart and ravishing at the studio. The whole crew will be on deck and you can fish for compliments, and jobs."

Whew! She stayed up on her stool.

Maybe she should get out of here today, go see another film at the Modern. It's smart to structure weekends. But it was so cozy now that it was finally warming up and if she stopped painting, she'd never finish. By late afternoon she'd painted the sleeping alcove, the kitchen, and the bathroom and was beginning to put softly colored paper globes up over the bulbs and to position just a few bits of bright cloth, three scarves, no more, and some huge palm fans. No posters in this place. No more Andrew. He'd been an illusion, too. There was one last, new object to unveil: a large ceramic vase. She placed it carefully in the square room by the glass doors, and then from a paper-wrapped package in her dish drain she undid a bunch of tall dried grasses and settled them into the vase.

I like tall grasses.

She stood up to find that it was coming on, the nausea. Oh no! Not here where it was so white! Not now! Darkness collected in the corners of the white room, and straight ahead at the glass door she could see her father holding out his hand and then he was lifting her and he was settling her with her legs around his waist, only it wasn't his waist he was settling her on. . . . Then she was running into the kitchen, to the list on the refrigerator, and dialing. A voice said: *This is Sahra Meehan! Your call is important to me. If this is an emergency, call the Warburg Clinic.* Shaking and heaving, Phoebe listened to the voice till it was done. Brushing back her hair with a hand that left paint on her forehead, she dialed the number again. There you are, Sahra. There you are. Oh, Sahra, they've found me here, the memories. Keep talking. Keep talking. Keep talking.

23

Rachel North-Neiman and Leonard Neiman invited them over for New Year's Eve and Claire accepted with relief. They'd seen no one, spoken of nothing but the accusation, and made no progress except to find confirmed from a secretary at the Hinckley School that Phoebe Fairchild had indeed left her job. New Year's Eve they drove over to the Mexican place on Lancaster Avenue to have dinner beforehand and the sight of its twinkling lights raised Claire's spirits a little. She ordered wine. Harvey did not. He hadn't been drinking anything lately. She opened her menu and studied the options with cilantro and without. They ordered chili.

"Claire," her husband said in his new, narrowed voice. "Do you remember the Scatterbay girl's wedding?"

"When Nan married her boss? Sure."

"What do you remember?"

"You drank too much. It was hot."

"Anything else?"

She looked up to find his face less tight but more focused than in the last few days. "It was six or seven years ago, wasn't it? The wedding was terribly sad somehow. Everyone wanted Nan to be marrying someone fresh instead of a forty-year-old with kids. Except you, you went on about how no man is perfect. When you finally got home, you fell into bed. I'd never seen you drunk like that."

"Then what?"

"Isn't that enough? Well, let's see. You got up, I think."

He nodded.

She was enjoying this diversion from the all-consuming topic. "Yes, I was afraid you'd fall down the stairs. And I got up to see if you were okay. There you were, on the third-floor landing, passed out."

He looked around and said in a softer voice, "Did I go into Phoebe's room?"

"Oh, God, Harvey!" She finally got it. "Did you?"

He lowered his voice still further. "I don't think so. But I've been trying to go back over it. When things are very stressful, apparently, we can sort of forget them. They call it repression."

"Harvey! Did you?"

"Shhh! I told you, I don't know. That's what I'm trying to figure out."

She kept on breathing, the way you do when the sky is falling.

"Let's look at the time element," he went on. "Do you remember anything about how long you waited upstairs?"

Normally, it made Claire resistant to have Harvey tell her in public to lower her voice, but this time she complied. "Not really."

"Try."

"It's all faded."

"Start with when I get up."

She leaned over the table and spoke a bit above a whisper. "You get up. I lie there in bed. Maybe I was listening for a fall. Okay, enough time goes by for you to get to the kitchen and back—"

"Only that long? To the kitchen and back?"

"Come on, how do I know? I don't really remember. I can't say for sure. But about that long, maybe. I get up. . . . Oh, look, I'm making half of this up! Don't count on this as truth."

"Go on."

"I start down the stairs. I can't tell exactly how long. I do know that I found you passed out on the third-floor landing."

"Go on."

"I do have a clear picture of that. It stuck in my mind because you looked so very young, surprisingly young, defenseless, lying there, splayed. I can see you now."

"Was I wearing my pajamas?"

"No. An undershirt and shorts."

He unfolded his hands. He looked relieved and spoke in a normal voice. "Then I would never have gone in."

"What do you mean?"

"I wouldn't have gone into either girl's room just wearing shorts."

Her sudden laugh brought eyes to their table. "You mean you might have raped her, but not in shorts?"

"Shhh!"

"All right!"

Now he leaned across the table. "Do you think I went in there?"

"I don't know! How can I know if you don't know yourself?"

He sighed and tightened his hands. "I had to tell you, Claire. It was killing me."

Oh, poor little boy—anger swept over her. She understood that he was giving her complete power over him and she didn't want it. Yet she knew how absolutely wretched he was and said, "It would be totally out of character for you to touch your daughter that way."

He didn't look hopeful. "But if I did?"

Her lip twisted and the reality of the conversation took hold of her. "Then it's all over."

"Claire."

"I can't help it."

"Me neither. I had to tell you."

"You haven't told me a goddamned thing."

"Shhh! I don't know anymore! How can I find out?"

"Ask your daughter."

"Ask if I came into her room?"

"Oh, for Pete's sake, Harvey, get hold of yourself. I'm not your mother. Yes. Ask her." Claire put her hand to her forehead. She needed a rock and Harvey was turning into water. This was like the end of her mother's cancer when she'd had to tell her father what to eat and whether to wear a sweater.

"How can I? Where is she?"

Deflated, she said, "You've got a point."

The waiter came with their chili. Harvey looked at his food and didn't eat. "Here's a new idea," he said, not meeting her in the eye. "What if I lie? I tell Bess I did do it. She tells Phoebe. And then Phoebe will talk to us."

The very question proved his innocence to her: he would do this for his daughter, how Harveyish. She was very firm. "If you lie now, this family will never again know the truth."

"Come on, honey," he said, leaning over the table suddenly, "let's skip supper. Let's skip the Neimans. We'll go home. I'll put you to bed. You look awful. We'll get some sleep."

New Year's Eve they usually made love. Was he referring to that?

"No, I promised Rachel."

She needed to see someone, a friend, anyone but Harvey. Lacey was out of the question. Rachel, smarter, if less original, was the one to talk to, and Rachel *was* a social worker. She would know of a therapist. Therapy, that was the way to get to Phoebe, not lies.

So after supper they drove to the sedate little residential section off Seventeenth North and took an elevator to a spacious flat where heaps of coats hung on a rented rack outside the apartment door. Inside were twenty or thirty people, including an art student playing tunes on an Irish harp. They were greeted by Leonard Neiman, a handsome, bearded man who always helped you off with your coat. When Claire kissed Leonard, it felt good; he exuded a sexual confidence that had stripped itself from Harvey in the last week. The living room was full of noise, champagne, scrambled eggs, and Leonard's psychoanalyst colleagues mingling somewhat uncomfortably with Rachel's social workers. Claire followed her nose to the kitchen, where Rachel was pulling scores of cheese dollars out of the oven, one thousand grams of butter on a cookie tin. Thirty years ago they'd taken psychology together; Rachel had shown Harvey and her around Philadelphia when they'd first moved down. Rachel stood, straightened her spare, carefully exercised body.

"Hey, Monroe. You know why they called us by our last names at school? That's how you address domestics."

They talked a bit and then Claire said, "Let's get together soon. I've got a question for you."

At home in bed, Harvey moved hesitantly toward Claire for the first time since the letter, and she found she could not respond. Images of a red-haired girl in a seersucker nightgown appeared before her. She pulled away from him and jammed her fists between the railings of the headboard.

"I can't. Sorry. Just can't."

"Okay. Take it easy. Get some sleep."

He was just as glad. Though buoyed by Claire's account of Nan Scatterbay's wedding, he didn't know if he could have followed through either. It wasn't Claire he needed. It was a big voice booming out for all the world to hear, You're Innocent.

24

1991

Claire was insisting they try therapy. He didn't want to. It hadn't helped his sister, Phyllis, and she'd about given her life to it. Besides, the money for Bess's van had put him way behind on the college loans and a therapy bill would further slow him down. They'd argued: silence; it's a draw; think about it. So they had begun to treasure daytime, when each could leave the house and get away from the other.

During January thaw Harvey stood on a crusty hill west of the city in quiet old Pottstown looking out over the dried grass that stuck up through granulated snow. A new developer wanted to put up eighteen capes and colonials here—moderately priced at a hundred and fifty thousand each. Perfect for older women—his mother would have loved one. A not insignificant number of middle-class women lived in eastern Pennsylvania and they'd been left enough cash to die within their own walls, surrounded by their own trophies, loved by golden retrievers or chocolate Labs, visited reproachfully by sons. Build now, be ready when the recession is over. He turned downhill, crunching through crust. Self-doubt had rolled over him. "It'll wash," he would have assured Doug a couple of months ago. But now he wasn't sure it would. Our most treasured asset is our reputation, old buddy. Fry the bastard.

He reached the ice-covered puddles of the side road and got into his car, slamming the door hard. Junior had looked at him funny in the men's room, making him wonder if Claire had told Lacey. Lacey was a weak spot in the line of defense. He turned the key and looked back over his shoulder—danger can come from behind you. Was it a good investment? Who the hell knew!

On the wooded road, he snapped on the radio. *Loving you, loving you, you left me,* that was always the refrain of men singing with guitars. He snapped the radio off. The sun glinted on the damp tar and off the back of the pickup truck ahead of him. Everybody seemed to think of him as not to be trusted, so why not? Impulsively, he pulled out and passed the pickup, even though he couldn't see around the coming curve. The snout of a jeep rounded the curve at him, close up, and they both swerved, the jeep driver shouting, Bastard! Freaking bastard! He felt good. Justice restored. He'd deserved *that* name-calling.

He hadn't gone into Phoebe's bedroom, but maybe he'd been a lousy model of a male. He seldom went out with buddies. He didn't play squash or racquetball. That could have had its effect. He didn't need a therapist to tell him that, though. There was only one thing that would get him to a therapist: if they had some way to do a CAT scan on his memory, something like hypnosis.

Back at his office, he shut the door and dialed his brother-in-law in Minneapolis. Ben was a doctor. He would know what was doable. Prepared to give a message to a secretary, he was instantly connected.

"Dr. Hanson here."

"Ben? It's Harvey."

"Hiya. Everything okay?"

"Sure. Fine. Got a question for you. You know anything about hypnosis?"

"As a painkiller, novocaine beats the hell out of it."

"Can it bring back memory?"

"I doubt that." Ben's voice took on scorn. "People want to believe in miracles, Harvey. They want magic. Tell them that at the age of eight they were pricked by a briar and they're thrilled. That way, they can pull the briar out and find happiness. Hypnosis is in, it's resurfacing, it's New Age. But it's tricky stuff. That guy in California was just sentenced to life in prison on some so-called memory his daughter dragged up twenty years later while under hypnosis."

Harvey swung his chair toward the great window and inquired nonchalantly, "Who's that?"

"You know, that guy who's supposed to have hit the little girl with a rock. Jesus, don't you Easterners watch the news?"

"How about drinking too much—you drink too much and you can't remember. What's that all about?"

"You mean blackout? That's when the brain is numbed by alcohol, it no longer records what's happening. Nothing gets coded into memory. The AA people could tell you more about it than I could."

"Hypnosis couldn't bring it back?"

"Nothing could bring it back. Just what are you talking about, Harvey?"

"A legal question here, one of my clients."

"Maybe he needs a lawyer."

"That's what I'll tell him. My best to Phyllis."

"And to Claire."

At lunch he strode into the stock exchange building past the sunken gardens to the New York Deli. That settled it. He wouldn't do therapy, period. He wouldn't let Phoebe or Claire or Phyllis tell him what to do. Carrying a Styrofoam dish full of meatballs, he sat among other men on stools in front of a window, through which he could see pedestrians unwrapping their scarves and opening their coats in the thaw. Behind them came the ping of the cashier, the naming of numbers, prices, the sound of plastic dish on plastic tray, the smell of melting slush on the floor. He was glad to be among men. His sister used to goad him till he started swinging and then his mother would blame him. The way of women, that little smile of theirs, stronger than a fist! Christ! It wasn't fair. The whole thing wasn't fair.

25

Surrounded by those endless cakes, those endless doughnuts, and all the beautiful work from the Dutch Republic when men suddenly felt free—free of their Spanish overlords, free of the pope, free to read Holy Writ in their own language—Claire felt imprisoned. Phoebe had control of her life. Winnie's daughter had control of Winnie's, too; at seventeen little Cathy was pregnant.

Winnie slammed down the phone.

"More bad news?" Claire asked.

"I say abortion. She says single mother. I say stay on track. She says the track is wrong. I say feminism. She says that's for women who hate men."

"All we worked for?"

"What did we get—a dozen execs and a couple million single mothers."

"Don't forget the TV anchors."

Before lunch Claire spoke to the face over the sink in the ladies' room: Mirror, mirror on the wall, who's the wickedest of us all?

I am, the mother. I failed.

Mother, go into therapy. Search your own memory.

There's nothing to remember, Phoebe. He couldn't have raped you without my knowing it.

We can't enjoy fellowship as a family, until you remember . . .

Stop it! Stop it! She wanted to shout. Oh, sometimes she wanted to shake her daughter until her teeth rattled and she spit out the bitter apple stuck in her throat! Immediately she swung to the opposite pole: Oh, my baby, my baby. What's wrong? The oscillation paralyzed her.

Downstairs she charged out a couple of sandwiches from a young cashier with short hair in yellow spikes. Carrying the bag past docents and tourists, she reached the outside and climbed into the waiting car, which the carefully coiffed Rachel drove to a niche over the Schuylkill. Claire leaned against the passenger door and Rachel unwrapped her sandwich.

"Brie. Good."

"Can you recommend a therapist?"

"What kind?"

"I don't know."

"We come in brands. A doctor can do drugs, a clinical psychologist sounds like laboratory but isn't, and a psychotherapist can be an MSW or a doctor of education or divinity—which means everything from great to lousy, though not necessarily in that order. It's not a science, you know. It's an art. What's the problem?"

"It's got to be confidential."

"Shoot. I can do marriage, career, and kids, but I can't cook. It's safe with me."

"Absolutely?"

"Wild horses."

Claire took a breath. "It's Phoebe. She says Harvey abused her as a child."

"Oh, my God, our Harvey?"

Claire nodded.

"I've heard of this but it doesn't sound like Harvey."

Lightness filled Claire's chest. "You don't think so?"

"Not the Harvey I know."

Tears came up at this small comfort. "It's so horrible, Rachel. And I'm so mad at Phoebe and scared for her at the same time."

"It sucks."

"Oh, Rachel, what'll I do?"

Rachel put her hand on Claire's arm. "Hang on. I'll help you. We'll figure out what to do."

Tears rolled over Claire's eyelids. "She won't even talk to us."

"That won't kill you," Rachel said matter-of-factly. "For a while, anyway."

"Do you think she's crazy?"

"She's never seemed unstable. She must be suffering from something."

"What?"

"I don't know. She needs to talk to someone."

"She's seeing a therapist."

"Who?"

"Someone in New York. I don't get any information."

"It's good she's seeing someone."

"Yes, that keeps me calm at two A.M. Harvey is very depressed."

"I shouldn't wonder."

"He won't go into therapy."

"He could use some support." Rachel wrapped up her papers, shoved them into her empty coffee cup. "You, too."

"That's what Phoebe wants us to do. Do you know someone?"

"If you're only doing it to get to Phoebe, you'd better start by asking for a recommendation from her therapist. Can you find out who that is?"

"Bess won't tell me."

"Find out. A lot of the younger therapists have been talking about abuse lately, with all those cases in the news. They probably have a whole new theory I've failed to notice. I don't keep up the way I did. We in the geriatric field have our own peculiar slant on sex. I'll ask Leonard—"

"Don't tell Leonard!"

Rachel handed Claire her cup. "Don't worry, I'll keep it general. There is new theory on Freud, for sure, feminist theory, at last."

"What's that?" Claire wiped her fingers on her napkin.

Rachel turned the key in the ignition. "They say he made up the Oedipus complex to clear fathers of incest charges because one of the fathers was a friend of his. Ho for our side! Incest exists, Claire. I've seen it. I've heard about it. And I'm overjoyed that we can finally talk about it."

"Of course," Claire said in a small voice. "Me, too. When it's real."

"It's sure hard for me to think of Harvey in that context. Maybe he did something else that Phoebe reads that way? Or something way back that went wrong somehow?"

"We've been trying to think of things."

Rachel pulled up behind the museum. "Okay, it sucks. Call me anytime. I'll get back to you in a few days."

"Thanks, Rachel. Some days I think I'll just drop dead."

"Don't. I'd miss you. And our elegant lunches."

Claire felt funny about telling Rachel. Was it her imagination or had Rachel implied they'd really done something wrong, too? What? Not being able to pinpoint the crucial mistake had already caused them to suspect every move, every decision, every emotion. And not being able to get angry at Phoebe for fear that she was too fragile, too elusive, made them angry at each other, made things break down around existing fissures.

"Any news?" Harvey didn't mean Desert Storm.

Claire gave her nightly head shake. "But I told Rachel."

"Rachel? I wish you hadn't." Harvey got out crackers and cheese. "What did she say?"

"We should find out who Phoebe's therapist is. She's asking around about things in general and she'll talk to Leonard."

"Leonard!"

"Just in general, about what goes on in a young woman's head. Not mentioning Phoebe, or you or me."

Harvey set the plate on the counter and poured them each a glass of red wine. It had taken him a month to decide that a glass of wine before supper was okay.

"Well," Harvey said, "I talked to Ben."

"What for?"

"I asked him if hypnosis could help a person remember something forgotten after too much drink."

"God, Harvey, he'll see through that!"

"No quicker than your friend Leonard."

"What did Ben say?"

"No."

"So it's final then? You won't go into therapy? Is that what you're telling me?"

"That's right."

"I'm going into therapy then, alone."

"What for?"

"Well, I could use some, some support, Rachel thought. And because it's what Phoebe asked us to do."

"We're the parents, not the children. You're falling into the same trap I almost fell into. I even wanted to confess to get to Phoebe. To lie about it. Now you want to do therapy to get to Phoebe."

She gave that awful little smile. "What if she needs me, Harvey? What if she's scared?"

"Scared?"

Daddy! Daddy! Daddy! He heard their voices again, full of confidence in him, and of desire. An innocent desire, just for him to come, to save them. Of course Phoebe was scared. Oh, Claire was so much smarter than he was, so much stronger, so much steadier, and so much like his sister, with that little smile. He was beginning to hate her.

"She's afraid of something," Claire went on. "I can tell."

"You're going into therapy to find out what's wrong with your daughter?"

"Maybe it's something I did."

"Oh, Claire, you always think it's your fault!"

"And you never think it's yours!"

"For Christ's sake, I've thought of nothing else lately but what I might have done wrong!"

Something drove her to say it, to give over to him what had bothered her since lunch. "Rachel did say there might be something we did or didn't do when Phoebe was little."

"We did it all! We did the whole damn thing! We did every fucking thing there was, and you know it! We gave them everything. They never lacked for nothing. Our girls had it easy! Our girls never heard of hard times!"

"That's not their fault."

"Or mine either!"

"Harvey, you're shouting at me."

"Fucking right, I'm shouting. I'm fucking shouting!"

"It doesn't help."

"And you won't even open your mouth, of course. You won't even object."

"I'm objecting right now."

"You know what I thought today? Maybe I should die. If I died, she'd come back to you!"

"Oh, stuff the self-pity, will you!"

"Self-pity? For Christ's sake, my daughter is accusing me of rape. She's not accusing you. What do you want me to do!"

"I fucking want you to do something! I want you to figure it out! I want you to stop whimpering! I want you to—"

"Shit!" He grabbed his scarf and cap and ran out the front door. He hadn't run in years. Maybe he should take up jogging. He could feel the blood pumping in his legs, too slow, an old man's legs. He'd never liked Rachel North, a stiff and a half, if you asked him. His life had come to this, a bull with a ring in his nose led round and round by women.

26

Emerging from the subway at Seventy-second and Broadway on a bitter February day, Bess hugged her coat close. Adrianna was back in Philadelphia but her mother was having a biopsy and she couldn't leave for the West till May 1, if then. "Wait till June," Roger had urged her, "and I'll hitch a ride to the Coast with you." Maybe she ought to. Was Roger the one? Usually she didn't settle for solid and, let's admit it, somewhat boring, but the mess with Phoebe had made her value reliability. And after all, she'd taken him from Phoebe and maybe that's why Phoebe . . . Whoa! She hadn't taken Roger from Phoebe. She always felt so responsible lately, so guilty about everything! And so boxed in.

"Please, Bess," Phoebe had said over the phone. "Sahra thinks you're an important link. Please come." Okay, okay. This wasn't her Phoebe; her Phoebe gave orders, her Phoebe didn't plead. This Phoebe needed her. Ahead Bess could see Central Park glittery under its ice and then she turned and climbed up the steps of the middle of three connected brownstones and into the Warburg Clinic for Women.

A noiseless elevator left her on the second floor, where she found herself in a newly renovated hallway that smelled of fresh paint. Where was room 211? A dozen women came swarming out of room 202, looking flushed and absent. She scanned them for Phoebe's face but, thank God, her sister wasn't among them. No, that was Phoebe, at the end of the hall, looking worse than last time.

"Thanks for coming, Bess. It's really good to see you."

"Who were they? The Girl Scouts?"

"Oh, a support group, I guess."

"They all looked sort of white, middle-class, and depressed."

Phoebe smiled just a little. "They were screaming earlier. I could hear them." She pressed open a pneumatic door into the next brownstone.

"Screaming? That's what you do here?"

"Letting out their—how you say it, comrade?—rage. How come you don't look tortured? We look tortured here. You're from another planet, that's why—the Planet of the Untortured."

The old repartee pleased Bess, but not the content.

"They're nuts," Phoebe continued, with one of her real smiles, wry, loaded with mockery of mockery of mockery. "I belong among nuts. Everybody here is, like, living on Oprah or something."

Bess laughed. "You're not a nut. How are you, really?"

"In pain. You have to feel the pain as you break each abscess. And I've gotten confused. What happened when? Who knew what? I mean really confused. Sahra says you're a link. You grew up in the same house. You can give me pieces of the puzzle." Phoebe slowed down, lowering her voice. "Sometimes it's tricky talking to Sahra. Don't laugh at her, promise? She doesn't always get the joke, you know. Irony is not her forte. But she's a genius on the main point. So let her ask you whatever she wants, okay? Be nice. No high-handed shit. She's human. Come on in. It's in here." They entered a bare room containing an orange table at which sat a clean-looking woman in dark balloon pants.

She is beautiful, but so's Phoebe, Sahra reasoned. What's her role, this Bess? In these cases, the whole family is dysfunctional. Start with an offending father and you'll find an offending mother and siblings who take various roles. Was Bess abused, too? She stood and offered her hand.

"I'm Sah-ra Meehan. Please call me Sahra."

Bess registered the well-pitched voice as she took the hand with the long, cool fingers. "I'm Bess."

"I'm so glad you've come. Sit down. This isn't where Phoebe and I usually meet, Bess, but since we're here today as a little family group, we're using the Warburg. Did you have any trouble finding us?"

Bess slid her backpack off its shoulder strap and let it rest on the floor. "Nope."

"We had some trouble getting you here!" Sahra said with a laugh. "Bess, in cases like Phoebe's—"

"What kinds of cases are those, anyway?"

"Where there's a history of family sexual abuse," Sahra replied matter-of-factly. "Your father penetrated your sister vaginally from the summer of what now seems to be her third or fourth year until the summer of her eleventh."

Bess felt a sudden repugnance. "You know, Sahra, I just don't believe any of this."

Sahra smiled. "These things are hard to believe. We all want our mothers and fathers to have loved us. Sometimes we want this so much that we make up a whole video of pretty memories through which we peer at our childhoods. But the pretty scenes aren't always the truth."

"Our parents did love us and it's not fair, what's happening to them."

"Let's get this straight. It wasn't fair what happened to your sister." Sahra paused. "Bess, do you want to help your sister?"

"Yes."

"Then you mustn't downplay or minimize what she's saying or make her feel guilty. You must accept what she says."

"But she already knows I don't."

"That's okay. She didn't remember it herself at first. Did your father ever act strange around her?"

"No."

"Did he ever seem to be aware of Phoebe's presence in a room, for instance?"

"Of course. But not in a sexual way, if that's what you mean."

"Or of your presence?"

Bess delayed, remembering that time she'd walked into Dad's office unexpectedly, before he'd realized she wasn't a coworker. "No."

"Did your father ever make verbal remarks about Phoebe's sexuality?" Sahra paused, reproducing Bess's delay to the minisecond. "Or yours?"

Sahra was mirroring her, somehow, Bess decided, shadowboxing. She took emotion out of her words, so as to give herself protection from this scrutiny. "He encouraged us to be girls, if that's what you mean."

"How?"

"He told us we were beautiful. I mean, he told us we were beautiful and talented and smart." Everything she said began to seem wrong. "The way a father should."

"Did he approach you sexually, Bess?"

"Absolutely not."

"You seem remarkably sure on that. Why so?"

"Because he didn't!"

Sahra laced her fingers over her knee and looked at Bess a long time. "Bess, you know how it is in a concentration camp? Some people survive and some don't? The ones who survive often feel guilty. They don't know why they feel so guilty. They just do, all their lives. Do you feel guilty about anything?"

Startled at this insightful perception, Bess replied, "About what?"

"Oh, I don't know, maybe about not being able to protect your sister?"

"There was nothing to protect her from!"

"Maybe you did notice some small thing that was wrong and you tried to tell someone about it—your mother, a teacher, someone. They didn't listen, and you felt guilty because you couldn't make them listen."

"That didn't happen!"

"Does Phoebe speaking out about your father make you feel threatened in some way?"

"When did you stop beating your wife, sir?"

"What? I don't understand, Bess."

Phoebe slumped in her chair as if she were very tired and Bess said, "It's a joke. It means that if I answered your question the way it was worded, I would have incriminated myself or my father."

"Incriminated your father? That's interesting you chose him, Bess."

Bess felt a blush pass over her face. What a cheap shot!

"What's causing you such embarrassment?" Sahra asked softly.

Bess demurred. "I don't know."

"Now, Bess," Sahra continued, "I'm going to suggest something to you and I want you to stay open. Don't get analytical on us. Life isn't a laboratory. Use your whole mind, your deepest intuition. Life is a leap of faith, Bess, not a lesson in logic. Let your subconscious speak for you. Once more, does Phoebe's recollection cause you to remember your own abuse?"

"That's bullshit!"

"I like your directness, Bess. But are you angry at Phoebe?"

"No."

"Why can't you look at her?"

Bess looked at Phoebe then, and a coldness passed between them. All the warmth, all the real Phoebe from the hallway was lost. "Okay, I'm a little angry."

"Who at?"

"It's not a who. It's everything." Bess tried to continue being honest with this woman who twisted her words so. "I've lost my sister. I've lost my parents. And yet I'm somehow stuck in the middle. I want my own life."

"Of course you do. And you deserve to have it." Sahra unfolded her hands. She couldn't help Bess, not today anyway. It would take a lot of individual work—maybe with Dr. Phillips?—before Bess would be able to feel entitled to remember. She put her entire focus on Phoebe's needs. "Can you try a little harder for us, Bess? Can you give Phoebe a gift? She's confused. Can you think of some small detail that would validate her story? What comes to mind?"

"Our parents were good to us."

"Oh, Bess, there's that fantasy again. Dr. Phillips is writing a book on that very topic, *Alice in the Garden of Eden*—"

Suddenly Phoebe reached out a hand across the table, too cool, too moist. And in that strangely pleading voice she said, "It's exactly because our parents were also good to us that this is such a rough trip, Bess. I know. But start slowly, in the dark places where you don't remember. . . ." Just as suddenly, Phoebe seemed to lose heart and let go of Bess's hand.

Sahra followed. "Phoebe's right. Do you have any uncomfortable spots in your memory, Bess? Places where there's a sense of strangeness?"

Bess couldn't believe this. How could her straight-A sister have fallen for this? It was so much like the stuff in the book Phoebe had given her.

She watched as Phoebe put her hands over her face and let her head drop to the table. Her red hair and the orange plastic didn't mix. As steadily as she could, Bess replied. "There are large parts of my childhood I don't remember but neither does anybody else remember ordinary days. My parents did not do these things to me. If they had, I would remember something about it."

Instead of defeat, Sahra's voice held a kind of pleasure. "Like your sister, you've got a wonderful ability to express yourself. So I know you'll understand what I'm about to say next. Sometimes you have two statements or two"—here Sahra raised her fingers to make quotation marks in the air—" 'facts.' " She jiggled her fingers again as she said, " 'He did' and 'I did not.' That's what we have in your family's case."

Bess didn't blink. "Those statements are not facts. They're opinions."

"Exactly! Your sister has 'an opinion' "—Sahra jiggled her fingers—"and your father has 'an opinion,' " and jiggled again. "Now, when opinions differ, how is the truth, as you call it, to be arrived at? I'll tell you how. By its effects. By what happens when you pour the contents of the test tube onto the powder in the dish. If it explodes, you know what it was. And your sister has exploded, in a way . . ."

Bess pressed her palms together: How do you argue with such reasoning without Professor Zolbrod at your side?

". . . because here she is—a bright, talented, educated young woman, such as yourself, who nonetheless thinks of herself as incapable. She can't find a good job or a good relationship, she's depressed and she doesn't sleep. That, Bess, is the very explosion you get when you've been sexually abused as a child."

Bess did her best. "I don't like my job either and I don't have the perfect guy myself. And *I* wasn't abused." She dared a glance toward Phoebe and saw tears gathering on the table under her cheek.

Sahra felt a denseness, a steeliness, in Bess, so different from the light-filled crystal that was her client Phoebe. "If nothing else," Sahra said, "there are larger considerations. When people begin to remember sexual abuse, they always need our support. If they don't get it, there can be serious consequences, very serious. Do you understand me?"

"No."

"Your sister is passing through an emergency stage." Sahra's eyes moistened. "You must make a real attempt to accept and believe her story. Otherwise, we can't be sure that she won't lose control and do some kind of harm to herself."

Bess could hear the traffic out on Amsterdam. Did Sahra mean suicide?

Sahra's voice softened further. "It would be safest, Bess, if you would simply follow Phoebe's lead in this. Do what she does. If Phoebe is not in communication with your parents, neither should you be. If Phoebe suspects them of wrongdoing, you might at least investigate her allegations. You want a sister, after all." Sahra touched Bess lightly on the cuff of her sweater. "I've had your sister put on antidepressants. And I've given her a list of precautions that I hope will anchor her. I'll sit here a minute with your sister, Bess. You may leave now."

Bess stood up. She wasn't trapped in the middle any longer. It was worse—she had to take a step one way or the other.

27

To mask her inactivity, Claire turned the unchanging letters on her computer screen into floating cats—cats of all colors, postmodern cats, cats among whom there are no absolutes.

On her own mind's screen she was someplace else, in New York, standing by the lions in front of the public library. It was snowing and she was scanning the faces coming up Fifth Avenue. There were no young women with red hair. She turned and there was such a person coming along the sidewalk but it was only a small schoolgirl, carrying books, and plump. She turned again and there came a whole crowd of people, walking fast to make the light. And yes, in the middle, Phoebe, in a black coat, narrow, her face pinched with cold. The light turned green and Phoebe came on, toward her, toward where she stood with open arms. "Oh, Mom," Phoebe whispered, "I knew you would come. . . ."

"Hey, you okay?" Winnie's voice at the next desk interrupted a tearful reunion.

"Fine, fine." Good Lord, it showed, her complete preoccupation. Trying to look busier, Claire grabbed the Yellow Pages and opened to Psychiatrists, scanning their somber listings. She turned next to

Psychologists, who were far more numerous and, to her surprise, ran display ads: DEPRESSION AND ANXIETY, SELF-ESTEEM AND STRESS, EATING DISORDERS, MOST INSURANCE ACCEPTED. Since when did professionals run ads? Next she turned to Psychotherapists and they had twice as many listings and ads with red letters for emphasis: TRAUMA AND PATTERNS, ACOAS AND CODEPENDENTS, ADDICTIONS, DECISION MAKING, PAIN, TRANSITIONS, PMS, SPIRITUAL, HYPNOSIS, and there it was—SURVIVORS OF SEXUAL ABUSE. She hadn't known it was a specialty. Should she start with a specialist? Would that lead the quickest to Phoebe?

She couldn't decide. With the endless search for their mistakes, all her strengths had begun to appear to her as weaknesses: her willingness to let go, her reasonableness, her tolerance, her own need of space, her long fuse and the corresponding delay in forgiving. The more shortcomings she named, the more the whole thing began to feel like her fault. She'd best do nothing further.

At home the phone was ringing. "Sit back and wait," Rachel's voice advised her. "Leonard thinks it's probably a separation thing—a young woman's identity crisis writ large."

"It doesn't make sense, Rachel. I haven't been clinging. It's okay with me if she separates. I'm ready."

"Maybe *she's* not. Sometimes a girl has to come back to Mum after a bad start in the big world."

Claire tucked that away and returned to their mistakes. "Did you mention that old closeness of theirs, Harvey and Phoebe's? He never paid any attention to Bess at first."

"Pairings are normal, if they're flexible."

"Okay."

"Think, Claire. What has Phoebe accomplished by this?"

"She's destroying us."

"No, no, for herself."

"She's got away."

"I rest my case, I mean Leonard's case. Don't go after her. Sit back, way back, and wait."

"Why would she want to get away so much if at the same time she wants to come back?"

"Fear of what returning could mean. She might have to stay a kid, forever, and never separate."

Fear. Somehow Claire had known it was fear.

They didn't talk much at supper. Harvey didn't want her suggesting things anymore. He was mad and getting madder day by day. He wanted an apology from Phoebe. He wanted truth. He wanted justice. He was terribly restless. They went to the movies every other night now simply to get away from it. While he was upstairs changing out of his suit, Claire dialed Bess, who needed attention, too, she reminded herself.

"You got a card, from your friend James. We couldn't make it out, but I forwarded it."

"Could you read any of the words?"

"Something about a mountain pass and a lambskin coat. He hasn't lost his originality. I'm so sorry to hear about Adrianna's mother. How is she?"

"They're doing the surgery in a couple of weeks."

"Here's hoping. How's . . . everything?"

"I saw Phoebe Wednesday, if that's what you mean."

"Bess, about the name of her therapist—"

"Don't press me, Mom! I told you I can't tell you her name! Listen, this stuff is killing me! Don't you understand?"

Me too, she wanted to say, but she was the mother. "All right, honey. I do understand. I'll write to Phoebe myself and ask."

"Don't bother. She doesn't see your letters. She told me to toss them if there's no confession."

Although Claire had lost her instinctive response to the larger issues, she still possessed immediate clarity on the smaller ones: "You mean you read my letters to Phoebe? That's not right! Where are they?"

"In my laundry basket."

"You kept them?"

"Of course."

Pleasure at this somehow loyal act broke through to Claire. "Thanks, sweetie." Somewhere there was trust and sanity. "But please don't open my letters. Just forward them to Phoebe. If she throws them out, okay. It's her decision."

"Mom, please! I've got to stop talking to you about Phoebe!"

"How else would we get news of her?"

"I'll call you if there's an emergency."

"What kind of emergency?"

"Oh, you know, anything."

An emergency. She couldn't just sit back and wait. But what should she do?

They saw *Undercover:* cops, drugs. Claire held the popcorn and the napkins. Harvey cracked his knuckles. Harvey swung his foot. Harvey got up to walk around. It didn't seem fair that all the white men in the movies were wimpy and wicked and all the black men kindly and good. He returned to his seat. "But it was the other way around for so long," Claire whispered, her voice tight. "Poetic justice. This is only fair."

"That's crazy," he said in a voice audible enough to make the people in front of them turn around. "It wasn't fair before and it isn't fair now!"

She wondered whether she'd be able to help Phoebe more if she could get away from Harvey. That way, she wouldn't be losing half her brain waves comforting him. Emergencies were developing. Time could be running out. But what? What to do? Where to go? Baltimore was out. She'd talked to Amy Broderick. Her leaving the collector had nothing to do with Amy's lack of knowledge in history. The collector wasn't an honest man; he fudged his attributions. If only she could find something like what Lacey Quinn had won, a stay at the American Academy in Rome. A research project, in New York, near Phoebe? If only she weren't too dispirited to collect herself.

The days passed, moving as if in rusty cogwheels, in dirty software, in polluted synapses. Spring came and one day Claire walked out of the museum in her low heels to find there was still light in the sky. The sky itself, however, had lowered. It sat on her shoulders. The heavens of her Iowa girlhood had formed a high beneficent dome from which goodwill shone down, blessing all below. This lowered sky oozed malice. The sky has fallen. You mean a sort of dropped-ceiling effect? her brain rushed in to query in its relentless efforts toward cheer. She couldn't laugh. The heart is the arbiter of taste.

At home, she spotted an envelope on the floor with Phoebe's handwriting, and she snatched it up, holding it away from her body as if it might contain more poison. Thank God Harvey wasn't here or she'd have to vanish into comfort mode and handle his feelings as well as her own. "Dear Claire and Harvey, Your Christmas check covered my first $500 for therapy this year. I must discharge the next $1060 myself. Of course I can't afford to. And since my problems stem from childhood, I'm passing the enclosed bill along to you. Phoebe."

Claire read it again. Well, at least Phoebe was alive. She'd even asked them for help. It wasn't so bad. It was good news, very good news. And, wait! Here it is, on the bill, the name of the therapist, SAHRA MEEHAN, M.S.W., PSYCHOTHERAPIST, AN ASSOCIATE OF THE WARBURG CLINIC. And the number, the therapist's phone number!

Claire assembled supper. Now they'd move forward. They'd telephone at 6:55. Rachel and Leonard always joked about five of the hour being the time to reach a therapist. If this Sahra—what kind of name was that?—Meehan weren't in her office that late, they'd leave a message. Sooner or later they'd get through. A therapist would be objective and professional and would tell them what was wrong and what to do. They were under way! Toward Phoebe.

She didn't go upstairs to change out of her heels; this was no call to make in your sneakers. When Harvey came home, she nodded yes instead of no and indicated the note. Stand by, he may throw a fit about the money—no dollars for Phoebe's therapy until she comes to her senses. He reached into his pocket for his glasses and, like her, read the note standing up.

"Well," he said lightly, "this part we can do."

She smiled and nodded. Okay, all bluster, no storm. He sat on a stool and reached into his pocket for his checkbook and wrote a check right there at the counter, saying, "I want this therapist to know that Phoebe Fairchild has parents. We'll pay and we'll hold this . . . this Meehan person responsible for our girl."

Claire filled the plates, set one before Harvey. The good news broke the silence that had collected above their nightly meal. It didn't matter who said what; they spoke as one again, having new hope.

"Phoebe is sick. If she's sick, she can get well."

"We'll get her diagnosis."

"You think she's mentally ill, I mean really bad?"

Chilling words: *schizophrenic, shock treatment.* "Do you?"

"No," Harvey said. "She's just in trouble."

She couldn't be pregnant, Claire caught herself thinking, she has a diaphragm. At least I didn't fail her there. Still wearing the black pumps, Claire cleaned up the sink. It was crazy that heels should give a person confidence. What does *crazy* mean? Crazy is when one's idea of the truth isn't the same as most people's idea of the truth. Aren't all truths equal? Absolutely not, my dear. All truths are not equal. That is a postmodern error. There is an absolute truth. There *is* a history. A thing has happened or it has not happened. Opinion has nothing to do with it.

At 6:55 Harvey sat down in the rocker. Claire stood by the counter and dialed; she cleared her throat and heard a voice, a nice strong voice, assured, forthright.

"Sahra Meehan here."

"This is Claire Fairchild. I'm calling about my daughter Phoebe, a patient of yours."

"A client," the voice, suddenly cold, corrected her.

"A client." Claire proceeded, taking correction in order to demonstrate her flexibility. "I'm very worried about her. Is she all right?"

"Mrs. Fairchild, your daughter is an adult. I do not discuss my clients with anyone."

"But she's in trouble! I need to know how she is!"

"Ask your daughter how she is, Mrs. Fairchild. I can tell you this, your daughter is finally getting the attention she needs."

"Could we . . . could I see you in some sort of joint session?"

"If you two can admit to what you've done, I'll happily see both or either one of you with Phoebe. Otherwise, no."

"But . . . but we didn't . . . he didn't . . . nothing happened."

"If you are still in denial, Mrs. Fairchild, I can recommend a family therapist at the Warburg Clinic. He can help you and your husband look back into your own childhoods. So often abusers have been abused themselves as children." Here the voice grew less confrontational. "That is the only understandable reason why this tragic cycle goes on and on unbroken. So I can recommend Dr. Carl Mundiger at the Warburg Clinic. He is superb, a family therapist. See him, and then perhaps we'll have a joint session."

"I was not abused!"

"Dr. Mundiger can be reached at the Warburg Clinic. I can tell you nothing more until we get to the bottom of this—as you know—criminal act of your husband's." The phone clicked.

Claire stood there holding the dead phone. Harvey jumped up to take it from her hands.

"Is Phoebe all right?"

Claire didn't answer, only stared at him without expression.

"She isn't dead or anything?"

Claire shook her head slowly, saying, "There's something terribly wrong with her." Then, seeing Harvey's face, she added, "Not with Phoebe. With the therapist."

28

An April Fool's wind worked at the door of the flower shop, opened it, stretched it, slammed it shut. Bess handed a dozen long-stemmed roses to the man with white hair and a ruddy face like Dad's. *She'd walked into Dad's office that time and he'd looked at her as if she were any woman, a stranger. "Come on in," he'd said, in a suggestive way, taking off his jacket, too slowly. "Have a seat," he'd said, sitting and patting the couch beside him. . . .*

A young woman came in for one red rose, her eyes full of love. Bess handed it to her, careful of thorns. She herself was glad to be free of love. Roger had given up on her, to her great relief. She'd almost begun to share his fantasies of Jeremiah and Tess. And James was in Nepal:

Nations fade away
The tribes return
But I am hostage
To the draft of peace.

She was free to travel. The van was bought and parked out on Long Island till the first of May. Adrianna wouldn't be joining her, though. Mrs.

Bender was starting chemo. Bess closed the shop and set out along upper Broadway. The only thing holding her here was Phoebe. With Roger gone, her whole life revolved around Phoebe. She'd been trying to eat supper with her once a week but Phoebe'd canceled last week's get-together. Was she worse? Garish with neon, the puddles shimmered and fled as she stepped through their surfaces. Her friends were gravitating west. Bloomer Gates was in Seattle. He was sure to know a lot of people by now, not to mention Cat Benz. Cat was waiting tables and singing in a band. But if Phoebe were worse? Hostage, she was held hostage by her sister.

There ahead was the glowing red of the Indian restaurant and standing outside, Phoebe, looking . . . you've got to be kidding! . . . terrific. You couldn't keep up with Phoebe! Her collar was up, her neck swathed in a scarf, and she looked like an ad, holding her scarf like that, scanning the street for someone, a lover, probably—nothing so boring as a sister.

"Hiya." Bess pulled up beside her. "Happy twenty-five."

"Is this Connecticut? It's so far north. You live in the suburbs or something?"

Under Sahra's edict to remain noncritical, Bess could think of no rejoinder. They went inside to take the last two remaining seats in the restaurant, which happened to be at a table in the front window, where it was extremely drafty. They kept their coats on and ordered their food hot instead of mild.

"My treat," Bess said. "This is your birthday present, in advance."

"Yum!" Phoebe took off her scarf and she looked better than when she played Emily in *Our Town*.

"You in love or something?"

"I've got a job. I'm working in Queens at a TV studio, Ibrahim's, remember? They do documentaries. We do documentaries!"

"Terrific! What exactly do you do?"

"I'm a researcher. I bring up the facts for the story line. But I want to move into camera work, producing, directing, the whole thing. I love it!"

"Your hair, it's your hair!"

"I had it cut and shaped the day before I started work. You like?" Phoebe moved her head from profile to profile and the red hair was straight, knotted low and loose on the nape of the neck, with tendrils about the face. It gave her sister an elegance that Bess did not remember.

Phoebe was going to be okay. Bess felt the bonds of childhood pull close: my sister, Phoebe. Lately Phoebe had seemed raw, unfinished, kidlike, and now she looked grown-up, and beautifully composed.

"You look straight out of the Tweeds catalog."

"Ugh. Glad you like it."

"Exactly how do you find facts?"

"At the library, and I'll be learning how to go online. We've got Internet." Phoebe poured them each tea. "They encourage us to learn. They pay half of any course you take. I've signed up at NYU to learn camera work. I mean, it's really thrilling. Oh, Bessie, this is what I've always wanted to do."

"That's terrific, Feeb. That's wonderful."

They ate their bread, warm, pungent. Now she could go west. Her parents could relax . . . well, no. She wouldn't even be able to tell them this. Within the largeness of her relief, Bess began to feel a spasm of irritation, not to mention a queer jealousy. Things were shifting back. No longer taking care of Phoebe, she was shrinking to the little sister again, soon to be unhoused, unemployed, and unloved. She warmed her hands over her tiny teacup. "Thanks for driving the van to Long Island."

"No problem."

"Mr. Kaplan thanks you, too. He really needed me there on Saint Patrick's Day."

"Thank Nora. It was her idea. Their driveway fits four cars."

"It seems so strange. Sure it's okay?"

"Nora's mother was as good as her word. She grilled me on Nora, of course, but I don't know diddly about Nora's new place." Phoebe's face grew somber. "Have you tried, Bess, to remember?"

"I did try! I told you."

"Sahra's so worried about you. Me, too. Anything more on that stuff at Dad's office?"

"I told you that stuff is not for real. It just comes into my head now whenever I think of Dad, thanks to you and Sahra. I meant it as an example of how—"

"Nobody makes this stuff up, Bess."

"I know, I know. But my pictures are white elephants. I mean, remember that game of Mom's? Stand in a Corner and Don't Think of a White Elephant?" Phoebe made a face and Bess appended an apology. "I'm sorry. It's not a criticism. It's just that that's the way my pictures are for me, white elephants. Not for you, I know. Guess what I did remember, though."

"What?"

"Don't get excited. It was just about how we used to lie in bed at the lake and read all those books Mom said weren't fit for a real house but were perfect for a guest room at a cottage?"

Phoebe's eyes went wide. "Well, what is it?"

"It's just that. That's what popped into my mind somehow, when nothing else did." Actually, it had been their parents' old copy of *The Joy of Sex* that she'd remembered, the one with the paintings that pulled you into them. Somehow it had seemed to fit into this discussion but Bess could see it would only rile Phoebe up.

Phoebe balanced her chin on a hand. "Are you still calling Claire and Harvey?"

"Not for weeks."

"Thanks. Tell me something, anything, about how we grew up. It's all gone out of my head."

"We had enough to eat. We went on vacations. We had educated parents who tried to explain things to us. Mom taught us music and art and all that Walt Whitman. Dad taught us basketball. He took us on separate trips, you to the theater, me to the symphony. He taught us swimming. And, as we both recall with a certain amount of pain, he tried to teach us about money—"

"You're making Dad sound like Mr. Rogers. What he taught me was how to be a wife."

Bess kept on eating. She heard the clamor of utensils, voices, a baby at a far table. "You can tell me in general, okay? But spare the details."

"Afraid you'll remember something?"

"I'm afraid for you, Feeb."

"For me?" Phoebe's face took on a look of concern, if not exactly compassion. "Well, I'm afraid for you. And for Harvey and Claire. They were probably abused themselves as kids. You know, Bess, Sahra says my speaking out could break the cycle for them. They could get some help."

Sadness engulfed Bess. "Phoebe, don't you remember anything good about them anymore?"

"Those pretty pictures were a screen. Sahra explained that to you."

"How about Dad's pancakes? How about Mom's Guess-This-Painter suppers? We had fun, Phoebe. Don't you remember?"

"You heard what Sahra said. That good stuff was just a fantasy we made up to cover the bad."

"You can't have forgotten everything. That was real!"

"So's the bad. It wipes away the good. You know what? Sahra says you can repress things even while they're happening! It's called a 'screen of immediate repression.' Isn't that wild? Like now. I could be repressing this very sentence as I speak it!"

"I wish I were."

Phoebe didn't laugh. "Think of it this way. Dad may have had the same stuff done to him by Mama or Papa Fairchild. What do you remember about Papa?"

"He was tall."

"Was he creepy?"

"I don't think so."

"Did he look at us funny?"

"I don't remember. I wasn't very old when he died."

"Me neither."

"I don't think he was gay. So why would he abuse a little boy?"

"Maybe he abused Aunt Phyllis?"

"What difference would that make?"

"We have to try everything, Bess! Look at every symptom, like a scientist. For instance, I'm not at all interested in men now. The sight of a man sort of terrifies me. There's this guy at work, Fitz? He invited me for coffee. There I was sitting in the coffee shop, hoping he'd like me because I actually do like him, sort of, but all I could see was Harvey Fairchild taking my hand and saying, 'Honey, this will hurt just a little, but—' "

"Stop it!"

"Okay, no details. But how can I ever find a lover? With a sexual past like mine?"

"You found a job. You've already lost one symptom."

"Bess! I found that job because I'm beginning to recover!"

"Cripes, you can't have it both ways! Have you ever heard of logic? It's too simple, what you're saying! It's like those movies where the woman wears glasses in the beginning and the man kisses her midway and after that she doesn't need her glasses anymore."

"Sylvester Stallone, Rocky. Something with Bogart, she's a librarian? I forget who played the librarian."

"That isn't the point! The point is, sex doesn't cure nearsightedness! And it doesn't cause it either."

"Oh, forget it! You can never take me seriously! How about Grandpa Monroe. Could he have been an abuser?"

"Not a chance. He loved little girls."

"Well, exactly!"

Keep low, don't react. Bess dodged the Endless Topic and tried something of her own, something that suddenly visited her as beautiful—and why shouldn't she have something beautiful? Why shouldn't she have a life of her own? "Grandpa Monroe took us to the zoo, remember? He showed us those monkeys that walk on two legs on the grass. Remember them? They were standing up and using their front legs just like arms so delicate and sensitive right out on the grass behind the monkey house. It was late in the afternoon. I'll never forget them. They were so beautiful. They weren't in cages and they weren't swinging on some dumb tire. They were standing there, one in front and one behind, and the one in front just reached back and touched the one behind ever so slightly on its wrist to draw its attention to the sound Grandpa was making, sort of a rustling sound with a paper bag. . . ."

"I don't remember that. I remember the white lions. They were the main attraction. You know, Bess, because of me, Sahra's going to specialize in this field." Phoebe pressed on. "She says Claire and Harvey are totally typical in their denial."

"Oh, does she? And what does Sahra say about me?" The instant Bess asked, she was sorry.

"She doesn't know which third you fit in. In a third of these cases, all the children in the family have been abused. In another third, nothing happened to the other children. They were not the object. . . ."

Not the object, Bess repeated the words to herself. The other children didn't count or something? That did it. That just did it. Phoebe could take care of herself. Not one more minute would she take care of this sister who never even listened to her. She chewed on some peanuts in the middle of whatever she was eating and bided her time.

"And in the last third," Phoebe continued, "you just don't know. There simply haven't been enough studies yet."

"That's the first we've heard here of the scientific method."

"So tell me, which one are you?"

"I am the one who is moving to Seattle on May first."

Phoebe contracted a little. "You're really leaving?"

"Yeah, hey, I'm ready."

When Phoebe spoke it was the listless Phoebe again. "Harvey and Claire may be seeing Dr. Mundiger in New York. He's an expert on cases like mine and he won't be fooled by them."

"Mom's not going to him."

"She's not? Then you've been talking to her!"

"Well, she does call me. They have to talk to somebody. Don't you ever think about what you're doing to them? You're killing them!"

Phoebe seemed to fade a little more and they concentrated on eating. Bess paid and, feeling remorseful for having spoken out so abruptly, walked Phoebe into her side of the subway station. They stood together on the downtown platform, where Phoebe leaned dangerously over the track, peering down the tunnel at an approaching light. When she turned to Bess, her eyes were darker somehow, fear-filled, and her pale face luminescent. "Be my family, Bessie. Sahra's putting me in group so I'll have a family, but you're my family, aren't you?"

Bess flung her arms around her sister as the train barreled in, rattling and shaking and screaming on its rails. Yes, yes, I am. I am your family. When they pulled apart, Phoebe looked blank. The door opened and she boarded the train.

Fighting tears and the desire to take the next train after her, Bess crossed to the uptown platform. Grandpa Monroe had taken them to the Mutter Museum, too. He'd shown them the plaster model of Chang and Eng, the original Siamese twins who'd been joined together forever by their shared liver. Eng was a well-formed and cheerful man, as the caption put it. The smaller Chang was given to depression, which may have been due to the fact that he was less comfortably hitched to his brother. No matter how he moved, it hurt.

29

"It isn't like you, Harvey," Doug had said. "Why'd you back Nicols and Black?" Harvey'd explained as best he could. "An indoor playground. It's the coming thing." But the fact is that two young women, Anne Nicols and Michelle Black, had looked at him with trust. So he'd given them a loan. It was as simple as that.

He'd begun to divide the world into those who trusted him and those who didn't. Where once he'd brushed aside his clients' emotionality and gone straight to their paperwork, he now looked into their faces, listened to their flattery, and luxuriated in any respect tossed his way. And now Nicols and Black had gone bust.

"Anything wrong at home?" Doug had asked. He might have told Doug, *We've had a health scare,* by which Doug would have taken him to mean Claire, some menopausal thing. But he still had his honor, didn't he? Some of it? "Poor judgment," he'd told Doug. "No excuses." If only Doug had fired him, he'd be free to take Claire and flee to Alaska. Instead, he sat at his desk and punched up all his recent loans to see who else might have suckered him.

"It's only twice a week," Lacey in her black tights and sweater explained to Claire at the museum cafeteria. Soup and salad, the cheapest lunch; Lacey never had money. "Ezzy was going to do it but now he's got this chance to work for Disney, so of course I had to let him off the hook."

"Of course," Claire said. She'd gotten through the reports of children—Bess driving west, Phoebe in New York—without revealing anything.

"And I can't ask Junior. He's allergic to cats. He's a great guy but we all have our limits." Lacey smiled, her hair perfectly darkened, her lips reddened again in the current fashion, her silver bracelets colliding pleasantly with each other.

Claire knew that this immaculate packaging of Lacey's protected a very vulnerable girl from the Bronx. "Starting when?"

"Wednesday. What's wrong, Claire? You don't look yourself."

Claire slid away. "Midlife crisis, I guess."

"Can I help?"

"Maybe if I do the cats, I could stay a night or two at your apartment? It's walkable from the museum, isn't it?"

"By day, not by night. Be my guest. It's Harvey, then, is it?"

"It's general restlessness. You artists take it out in paint, the rest of us travel."

"To North Twentieth? Doesn't seem far enough! I won't press you, Claire. Remember, it's a fairly rough area. Get to know your neighbors. You'll feel safer."

"It's middle-class, isn't it?"

"It's mixed. Two blocks up and it's drugs and guns."

"Are you safe?"

"I keep my pocketbook under my coat."

That kind of neighborhood would bring her nearer to Phoebe.

Discussing it with Harvey didn't work. Absolutely not, he'd said. It was dangerous, wrong. And so it blew up, out of proportion, and they'd each said things they couldn't take back. And somewhere in there Claire had decided she had to do it. This was the way to salvation. Phoebe needed her. Phoebe wanted to come home to her mother and maybe she couldn't do that while her mother was with her father. She'd leave Harvey, just for a while. Then Phoebe would come.

"It's only temporary. Please, Harvey. It makes a lot of sense."

"Your leaving me to live in North Philadelphia makes sense?"

"It's not a divorce. It's something we're trying, for Phoebe."

"Get the wicked old man off the scene, and she'll come home?"

"You're not wicked and you're not the one who's clearing out. I am. You'll be holding the fort here, home base. It's just for a few months."

"Think it over, Claire. Think it over very carefully. I don't like it."

They talked about it more and once or twice he seemed to say okay, then back to no. It wasn't his decision though, she finally pointed out; he shouldn't be telling her what to do. It ought to be something they both wanted. He agreed to that, and he didn't want it.

She suspected he was right. It might not be the perfect move but at least it was a move. She felt as if the boat of family had capsized and that she and Bess were both afloat while Harvey and Phoebe were going under for the third time. It was the old question they used to ask themselves in the dormitories at Smith: Which one would you save? And the answer she'd always given was the child.

After work on the day Lacey flew to Rome, Claire stood on the central porch of the great complex of Greek temples that formed the museum on the hill. She could see over the parkway and the esplanade to the low-buildinged city. Men of the Reformation had built the old city, and their sons and grandsons of the Enlightenment had peopled it to forty thousand—the largest city in the New World and home to a constitution. Out of this sky Benjamin Franklin had coaxed electricity, and not far to the north Thomas Edison had charmed its current through filaments that would turn night into day the world around. We can act. We can decide. We can do.

Benjamin Franklin had had a Tory son, whom he found it hard to keep on loving. Mary of Nazareth had had a radical son and been obliged to stand there helplessly while soldiers hammered nails through his tender wrists. She had to do something. Harvey could take care of himself.

At home she readied the suitcase and was walking downstairs with it when he came in from work and stood pathetically at the base of the stairs.

"Don't go, Claire."

"I've got to, I've just got to. I'll call you in a few days."

"You're my wife! It's not right!"

"I'm her mother. What's right anymore anyway?" She passed him, did not embrace him, reached the door. "There's no right left in the world."

"You're right about that!" he called at the closing door. "Absolutely right!" He nodded to emphasize his agreement. Why bother? She was the smart one. She thought she knew everything. His opinion was worthless. He stormed into the kitchen. He supposed he'd open the freezer now and find a whole row of little packages for his supper marked Monday, Tuesday, Wednesday, as if he were an idiot.

The first couple of days, he watched television on the second floor, taking his food up there. He left the set on all night, wanting to feel someone in the house. He ate his meals on the peach-colored sofa and took his dishes down to pile them in the sink before heading quickly back up to the television. Mostly he watched the science programs, the segments on animals, sheep, wolves, whales, birds. He found the birds boring, but the woolly things were agreeable. He wanted to bury his face in their fur. Big brown bears, a mother bear grooming her cub, a bear teaching her cub to fish in the chilled waters of the arctic. The claw moving in the frothy tide, the quick blood, the white landscape behind. He put his face into his hands and cried.

He stayed up past one, two, dozing on the stiff sofa. By three it was okay. He could handle the walk up the higher two flights, the falling into bed at the top of the house, covers over his head. He woke and showered. Good. Hot shower. That was the single pleasure of the day, to stand beneath the needles of hot sweet comfort. Then downstairs in rumpled clothes to the sinkful of despair: bits of tomato and egg on plates. He'd forgotten the routine of washing dishes, of taking clothes to the dry cleaner. He'd forgotten all that.

You're not supposed to eat eggs, Claire had insisted. But he remembered how to make eggs—you scramble them. So he did that. And toast. He did that. Coffee he picked up at the deli, then on to his office, where he could shut the door and put his head down on his desk and sleep. Or later at a site, he'd sleep in the parked car, where no one knew him, where he was unidentified, unaccused.

On Saturday when everyone else was sweating over their tax forms, there was nothing to do. He'd mailed his forms off ahead of time. The stairway creaked under his steep descent. If only they'd bought a house in the suburbs, they could have stretched their arms out, run in wider and wider circles. He didn't feel the anger until he came into the kitchen and then the emptiness hit, an insult. No movement, no voices, no sounds but the endless refrigerator.

Not only had right left the world, so had cause and effect. Nothing he'd done had led to this. *A* did not lead to *B* anymore. *B* did not lead to *C*. Chaos had flowed into his life in all those mysterious formulas that ought to apply to waterfalls and not to a man's days. He made eggs. He raked away a few sodden leaves. The phone rang.

"Bessie? That you? . . . I'm okay."

"What's wrong?"

"Your mother has gone to live at Lacey's."

"You mean you guys are separating!"

"No, she's taking a little break." Then he remembered that Bess was supposed to pass this along to Phoebe. "Who knows? We'll see. She's sorting things out."

"No!"

A lifelong loyalty surfaced. "Your mother is a free human being, Bess."

Of course Bess needed money. Eight hundred dollars for the van insurance. "I lent you eight thousand dollars! That's all I can do."

"Dad, I can't go on my trip without insurance!"

"What about your own money?"

"I wouldn't ask you if I had the money!"

"Bess. Come on home. I want to see you before you leave." He felt as if he were bribing her.

"I can't. Especially now. Which one of you would I visit?"

Right. Good. He wouldn't put her on the spot. He didn't want to talk about Claire's leaving him, anyway. Who knew if it was true?

"Okay, bon voyage. I'll call you before you start off. Now, we talked about insurance at Christmas. You know that. I'll send an additional hundred dollars to add to your loan. You can buy a month's insurance with that."

"Okay, okay. Listen, Dad, keep calm, okay?"

He tried breathing slowly, deliberately. "I'm a little rattled, I guess."

After the call, there was still the afternoon to contend with. Up on the second floor, he played his way through old records, mostly cello, a bad choice. He ate a hamburger in silence. After lunch he put on horns and oboes and walked back and forth in the adjoining parlor, over the Chinese rug. Maybe he'd sell this place. There was too much sorrow here now, stale and palpitating. When his women came home, the house would be gone. They'd see what they'd done to him. No, he could never sell it, there was too much joy here.

That made him sob and he put his head in his hands. He made another hamburger. Time for television? Maybe he should kill himself. Get a gun and shoot himself the sure way, the barrel right into the open mouth. Claire would find him. She'd have to clean up. Blood. Urine. Feces. She wouldn't think highly of him. She'd think, "What did I marry that jerk for?" You can place plastic over the rug. You can lie down on the plastic. When the back of your head blows off, it doesn't go anywhere. It's pretty neat actually. But even on plastic it would be an ugly sight. He could call the police station beforehand. Tell them to show up in ten minutes, clean him up. There's a fake rock in the patio, the key . . .

They'd want to know why. What is the motive? My wife left me. My daughter wants money. My other daughter says I raped her.

This guy kills himself? He must be guilty.

And then he began to think about the $1,060 he'd put into the hands of Sahra Meehan and the $540 due soon for April. Follow the money, his father had always advised him in his rare discussions of politics: *cherchez* the buck. His own industry, insurance, must be paying out millions to therapists. Ten million? A hundred million? Therapy was in some respects a business like any other. How many therapists were there? What kinds? How much did they make? Off how many patients? And how much per patient? And how did a therapist keep patients coming? Did he cure any of them? How many patients did a therapist need to break even? What kinds of compromises might a therapist find himself making to keep a patient? Monday he'd get to his computer. He'd call up some figures. He'd find out where Phoebe stood in the numbers. There was always something to learn from the numbers.

30

In Lacey's kitchen the faucet dripped and the curtains moved in a constant draft; the cats had finally come out of hiding and slept comfortably now, one gray, one yellow, on the chairs at the round oak table. What pleasure Lacey took in common objects: a vase of tree twigs suggesting attenuation to a myriad of points, a jar of spoons, faded palms from a Sunday service. On the walls hung photographs of Anya and Ezzie from years back in Rittenhouse Square, before the divorce. All that in the far end of the huge kitchen. From the studio end, a glow of yellows, pinks, and aquas—decorator colors but in abstract shapes possessing power and will. Claire sat herself at the round table.

"Sunday, April 14, 1991, Dear Phoebe, I'm on my own now, staying at the address above. Love, Mom." Should she say "temporarily?" No. Keep it simple. The postcards themselves were an inspiration—Phoebe could hardly avoid reading the words on them. "Dear Bess, Of course I meant that. You've done your part in New York, sail on. See you noon Sunday at that trattoria near Grand Central Station. Love, Mom."

The bedroom was up a narrow stair and occupied almost the whole top of the duplex snugged into the front of an old brownstone. Lacey's double bed about filled the bedroom. The curtains were filmy, to let in light from the street. Could people see in? On the mirror in the adjoining bathroom Claire taped a snapshot of Phoebe at Yale in cap and gown. That's where she'd start. Her family was broken into four separate people now. She'd begin one by one to reclaim them. Alert in the wide bed, she did feel closer to Phoebe.

Here I am.

Lacey Quinn had eaten pot-filled brownies when her kids were teenagers, in order to try to understand them. And here she herself was on North Twentieth Street trying to get to Phoebe.

Where are you?

Only prayer helped with the fear she felt for her daughter. She'd discovered something: Prayer is obsession turned inside out—you focus on the good outcome and thereby block out the bad images that come upon you in the night: Phoebe mugged in New York, Phoebe stepping off a subway platform onto the third rail.

The shouting began after midnight. It got worse on the weekend. Twice there were gunshots, followed by the converging of sirens a few blocks to the north. One night a woman screamed over and over, "William! William! Oh, my God, William!" and no sirens came.

In morning's brightness, she walked the mile to the museum, nodding good morning at the children, who looked far too wary. As a kid, she'd trusted practically everybody, indeed, right up until Phoebe's letter. How naïve of her. These children knew better than that. They knew more than they should have to know. She'd better learn it.

As she neared the museum the neighborhood became more prosperous and eventually quite grand, but inside in the elevator she didn't forget North Twentieth. No one at the museum knew what she'd done. She worked late and ate over in the university area or on the way back to Lacey's at the Eden, where a mixed black and white clientele downed an international cuisine of hummus, mozzarella, and barbecued turkey wings and she could imagine harmony. On Lacey's block she walked fast and kept her vision broad and loose for sudden movements, all the while trying to appear as if she were not doing that. Everything required such delicate balance. Unlocking Lacey's door, she held her breath until she was inside with the bolt in place.

Rachel met her for a movie Leonard didn't want to see and they talked before the house lights dimmed.

"We had a nice informal chat last night, Leonard and I," Rachel began. "He was thrilled to talk about psychoanalysis. Hardly anybody does anymore, you know. The poor guy has spent his whole life in a field that's being pulled right out from under him. I asked what brings on visions or hallucinations."

"Like Phoebe's memories? What'd he say?"

"There's a couple of things. Drugs, even one-time pot use can do it to the susceptible brain. Hypnagogic sleep is another. That's when you've just gone to bed and suddenly you're falling from the top of the Empire State Building—"

"When you sort of jerk awake?"

"That's it. Those visions seem completely real and even when you open your eyes, you can still see them. Then there's sleep deprivation. If you don't get much sleep, you can slip into little microsleeps and have little microdreams that are so short you think you're awake, so you think the dreams have to be real."

"My God, could that be it?"

"Any of these could be it. There's also that eerie feeling you can get when you're really anxious or depressed. It's called depersonalization. The world doesn't seem real. Buildings go flat. You're not even sure that your own hand is yours. Reality just drains out of things—all the world's a stage."

"That's what I felt when I got the letter."

"Exactly, extreme anxiety. And then there's schizophrenia."

That word. "I thought you said she didn't have that."

"I don't think she does. But it does present with hallucination."

"It's the mother's fault, isn't it? Schizophrenia? The schizophreniagenic mother, cold and distant? Remember Psych 101?"

"That's what they said when we were in school but no more. She's gone. Now it's a biological disease. Psychiatry doesn't help it, only drugs. It's drugs now for everything major. That's one reason psychotherapists are scrambling around for new theories, to keep the talking cure alive."

"I'm thinking of all those mothers of schizophrenics who were told they were the cause!"

"Me too. I've got one old lady at a nursing home who is still taking the blame for her fifty-year-old psychotic son."

The lights went down and the huge screen delivered yet another kind of dream, after which Rachel drove Claire to Twentieth Street and refused to drive off until Claire was safe inside.

Bess woke up on Long Island. Nora's mother had been so nice, last night, so welcoming, saying by all means, dear, use Nora's room. So, instead of testing out the big gray van in the driveway, she'd climbed with relief into the four-poster beneath the low ranch-house ceiling. She raised the blind, looked along the drive to an extensive backyard with hammock, picnic table, and swimming pool. Inviting, except for the image from Nora's stories of Mrs. Mercer calling her from the pool to the kitchen for a session on the table. Dressed in elasticized jeans and a cotton top from Thailand, Bess moved along the carpeted hall for breakfast.

"Good morning," Mrs. Mercer said, putting down her *New York Times* and looking perhaps too eagerly in Bess's direction. Apparently, she'd been spooning out the last bits of melon from what must have been a diet breakfast. She was a small Southern woman with a barrel chest and a head of hair dyed black. "Now, sit right down. Do you want eggs?"

"Oh, no thanks. I don't do eggs. Toast or a muffin is fine." Bess slipped into the white-petaled and winged metal breakfast chair. Sunshine lay across the Mercers' floor, illuminating an expensive linoleum. Studying Mrs. Mercer, she tried to appear nonchalant and to refrain from peering past the dining alcove into the kitchen to see if it was still painted entirely in green as Nora had said and to determine where Mrs. Mercer had stood while tying Nora to the table or to something on the table—Nora's legs, somehow, to a curtain rod? She hadn't quite understood the technicalities of Nora's stories last summer.

Mrs. Mercer passed her a basket of English muffins. Those short-fingered hands had touched Nora in a way gross past belief. The red nail polish was thick on the long nails. Long nails would hurt inside you, especially if you were a little girl. Or if they were holding a spoon.

"Harry's gone to the office, but he was so eager to meet you, Bess. We've always enjoyed your sister Phoebe. Why, since the girls were first-year students together! Anything we can do for Nora's friends is a pleasure."

What kind of person am I? Bess asked herself. Here I am accepting a free driveway and a muffin from a woman who abused her child on her own kitchen table under a hanging lamp. The fact is, Mrs. Mercer didn't look much different from anyone else's mother. Bess had to admit her immediate thought when she'd gazed on Mrs. Mercer last night: This woman would never do what Nora had said.

Mrs. Mercer encouraged a muffin into an elegant toaster and sent it down to the fiery furnace. Bess could see Mrs. Mercer's knees through the glass tabletop. Had Mrs. Mercer made Nora do anything to her, between those two huge knees? They looked like regular old-lady knees.

"Marmalade," she answered dryly in response to Mrs. Mercer's offer. "No thanks. One is enough. I've got to stay in shape to drive this baby three thousand miles."

After breakfast, she climbed into the cab and pulled out. She made it to the George Washington Bridge, up to Albany, and out onto the endless westward-spilling interstate. If only Adrianna were here, but she was standing by her mother. *That* family stays together, she'd told Mom on Sunday. She'd so wanted to talk to her mother, really talk, about Phoebe, but Sahra's threat stilled her. At least her mother had looked better than at Christmas. Some strengths you get by hitching things together, her mother had replied, and some strengths you get by taking things apart. Go, I'll be here for Phoebe. Call me or your father every two weeks.

James could make a clean good-bye, and in honor of him she didn't turn on the radio. Be where you are, he always said: she drove for hours silently past rivers and hills and the very rise of land where Joseph Smith had found the golden tablets of the Mormons—suspiciously similar in description to some Spanish plate the local natives had acquired from trading. You can't believe everything you hear. Can you believe anyone? *Let's go out and play some tricks at Watergate, said Mr. Nix.*

Half an hour after dark, she pulled off at Geneva and parked at a McDonald's. She ordered practically all the nonmeat selections, washed her hands, brushed her teeth, and climbed back into the van. Gee, but she was going to need a nice hot shower pretty soon. She found a church on a quiet street and pulled into its empty parking lot. Locking the cab, she climbed over the seat into the back and crawled into her sleeping bag. It wasn't dark enough—too many street lights nearby.

She got up on her knees and fashioned some curtains out of her sheets. Then she lay down again. Were her parents separating or not? She couldn't tell. In some ways, she didn't want to know. If only she could talk to someone reasonable about all this, someone brilliant. Wherever you are, James, I'm here. It's Geneva, NY, Exit 42. My parents have separated, maybe, maybe not. There is no rule of life that works in every direction, James. Don't tell me it's to stay detached! Not to love! That hurts too. We're all moving away from each other. We're alone. It's what you call the centrifugal force of love. It is on that force, on one great spiraling arm of that force that I send you this message of . . . Oh, bullshit, James. There's no such thing. I don't believe in you either.

31

Inconstant images filled the monitors lining the walls in the editing studio in Queens where a red-haired woman sat at one of the keyboards practicing a simple letter arrangement of CHANNEL 62, AMERICA'S NEIGHBORHOODS. Blue letters, outlined in red? Yes. Good. Simple and dignified. All she was supposed to do was practice with the vertical and horizontal knob and then run it through scroll and practice scrolling. Ah, it worked. Nice. If only she could stay here working. She felt so good here. She looked over at Fitz, the man with the dark hair and five o'clock shadow at the desk near the editing-room door. She felt so good here with Fitz.

"Long lunch," she called to him. "Gotta go into Midtown." She liked Fitz to know where she was, even though their friendship never actually seemed to develop. It's because of his daughter, she told herself. Then she was out the door of a one-story concrete building into low-lying Queens, long legs in sandals, black tee under black jumper. Briskly she made her way to the subway, past drugstores and liquor stores, past rows of houses that gave between them a slotted view of small green gardens. She and Fitz had done a research job for a TV spot about the entire route of the A train. He'd ridden the route with her. They hadn't held hands or anything but somehow it was such a pleasure. Her mother would have liked Fitz. You're not killing your mother, Phoebe. It's not as if she stepped in to save you, is it? No, it's not. But that was her old family. Today she'd meet her new family.

She'd had an okay talk with Bess before Bess left—until she'd mentioned the new memory, in which she was small and standing by the roses looking down at two big shoes, men's shoes planted on the ground in front of her. That's all. She hadn't dared look up from those shoes. Bess had laughed. Laughter is your sister's defense; it pushes the fear away.

Before she knew it, Phoebe was on the Upper West Side in the jarringly new interior of the Warburg, standing in the upstairs corridor outside a room and looking in at a circle of women in plastic chairs. This was too big a family. And it was all women. "Are you Phoebe?" the woman who must be the famous Dr. Phillips asked. She nodded, swallowed, felt the blood rush to her face.

"Come on in, Phoebe. There's nothing to be afraid of. Here's a seat for you."

"Hi," they all said, turning their faces toward her. Reluctantly, she took her place. Half of them were her age—the one with the sweatshirt that said I'M A SURVIVOR and the one with big hips. Half were older, quite a lot older. It wasn't easy to tell age because so many seemed to be partly out of it on medication. The sound level lowered as Dr. Phillips spoke across the circle. She was short and full of energy, like a gym instructor.

"Hi, guys," she began, looking slowly around the circle to make eye contact with each of them, skipping over Phoebe very fast and leaving her feeling like nobody even though here she was, her own client Nora Mercer's former roommate. "I'm Dr. Phillips, but you can call me Donna. This is session one of the ten we'll do. Let me run over the ground rules of this Warburg Survivor Workshop. One, you must listen to, accept, and believe in each other. It's forbidden to doubt what anyone says. Two, you must be kind to each other. It's forbidden to criticize, because this is a safe place. You are each other's new family. Okay? Got that?"

There were nods and murmurs of agreement.

"Now, some of you have discovered that if you tell your families what happened to you, they don't believe you. Let's play a game. What do they say, your families?" She gestured with her wiggling fingers to bring in comments, which came quickly:

"You're crazy."

"I don't believe you."

"That was so long ago!"

Phoebe didn't open her mouth, but then a couple of the women in the circle were looking at her expectantly and she said the first thing that came into her mind: "That didn't happen." Nobody seemed to have heard her. But blessedly, nobody was staring at her anymore, either.

She was sweating under the arms. The others were calling out answers now, shouting. It was noisy, hot.

"Forget it!"

"I'd of killed the bastard if I'd of known!"

"Exactly what did he do to you?"

This brought laughter and a slew of lewdly enunciated additions.

"Exactly how did he do it?"

"Exactly where did he do it?"

"Exactly—"

"You got it." Donna Phillips calmed them with a broad hand. "And you guys know how this makes you feel. You start to wonder if what happened to you really did happen. You start to wonder if you really are crazy. Listen, you guys must believe in yourselves. And if you aren't sure about every last detail, so what? Just act as if you are, and get it under your belt. It'll come easier after a while. Okay? You'll feel surer. This is like Native American rights or gay rights or Black Power or people with disabilities. You walk in those moccasins and you see if they work for you. Okay?"

"Okay," replied scattered voices.

Really, Sahra was much more . . . no, *elegant* was hardly the word. Approachable? Responsive? This Donna was vulgar, almost. There was no connection to be made with her. She simply made pronouncements.

"So here's how we reinforce our own truths. We speak out. We tell each other. Okay? The more often you tell, the surer you'll be. We'll have two or three go-rounds now."

Phoebe braced herself.

"Let's start here at my left." Donna turned to the witty-looking person with the big hips and said, "Just go over your tale for us. Keep it short, a couple of sentences. Okay?"

"Okay." The woman, who was her own age, looked around the circle. "You know how your dad keeps kissing you a little too long? Holding you a little too close? Mine had such trouble keeping control of himself and then one night out in the garage he lost it. We'd driven home from somewhere and I'd fallen asleep in the car and when I woke up he was moving his hand over my skirt, over my left hip . . ."

Phoebe shuddered. God, that would be terrible. They had no garage in the city but up at the lake there'd been a dilapidated barn where you could see light coming in through the slats. Nothing had happened there, had it?

A woman who was impeccably dressed managed to speak a few quiet words: "I'm still not sure if this counts because it only happened once—"

"It counts!" Donna Phillips interrupted emphatically. "Does it count, guys?"

"It counts!" they all shouted. Phoebe didn't catch on quick enough to join in on time and came in half a beat late. She'd been too intent on what to say when her turn came. You had to say something to stay alive in here. What? The two-part memory she called The Lake had been fading lately so maybe she'd try the newer picture, Rosebushes. Only, really, all it was was muddy shoes . . . okay, shit, her neighbor was finishing up.

". . . Then he's pulling my head toward him, forcing his penis into my mouth, a little girl's mouth, and that's it. You know the rest."

Phoebe felt flushed and sweaty all over. Good, maybe something new would come. She opened her mouth. "Okay . . ." And there they were, the shoes, the muddy shoes. She could really see them! They were in front of her, sort of, and she was small, trying to look up. "I'm about three years old and I'm out in the backyard by the rosebushes and suddenly I see before me two huge men's shoes and they are covered with mud. I look up . . . and there it is. I see a man's pants and they are unzipped and there's this thing hanging out. It's the first time I've seen one. It's hanging out. And he says to me, 'Little girl, you want to taste something good?' and I . . . I shake my head and I don't know what he's talking about but I know everything is wrong, very wrong, and then, you know, he shows me what he means." Phoebe sat back, trying to hold on to the picture. What was so odd was that when she'd been in the picture just now and looked up past the strange dangling skin to the shirt, which was blue and black checked, it hadn't been her father's face she'd seen. It was a man with brown hair and a brown beard and nice brown eyes. She felt hot all over. Who was it? Too young a man for Grandpa Monroe or even for Mr. Scatterbay next door. Was it Mr. Jencks, the other neighbor? With a beard? She tried to get into the picture again but it was gone.

Dr. Phillips was speaking, responding to someone. "Yes, that's it. Get angry! Get angry at that mother of yours, not at yourself! Don't ever take your anger out on yourself! You're a good person. Now, I'm glad you brought that up. In session one we do try to talk a bit about our mothers. Look, there are two ways to think of mothers. Some therapists—even some who are here at the clinic—say that it's wrong to blame the mother for anything. When things go wrong in our society, they say, the nearest woman gets the blame. I can see what they mean, but guys, I side with the other therapists. And you know why? There's a real pattern in the families of abused children. Yes, surprised? It's this. The father is overworked and underrewarded. He may have a low-paying job, he may work long hours. He may drink too much because in that kind of situation, people turn to alcohol as a way out. The mother is turned off to the father. She's afraid of him maybe because when he drinks, he gets mean to her. He calls her overweight or a lousy cook or a bad mother. Sound familiar?"

Her father had been drunk at Nan Scatterbay's wedding.

"So their sexual life vanishes. The man is frustrated. He turns to the daughter. The mother sees what's happening, or hints of it. But she's kind of relieved, you know? She's free of him."

Her mother did seem happiest when she was off for the museum.

"So your mother doesn't protect you. She lets it happen to you! And what do I say? I say get angry at that mother! But at the same time, remember she didn't do the actual abuse. It was your father who used you to get off on. But this time, for this go-round, let's concentrate on our moms. Let's get that anger out so it doesn't fester inside us and make us want to kill ourselves, which so many of us want to do when we finally meet all the anger stored inside us. Okay, start again."

"My mom didn't see. She would have died if I told her, so I didn't. But I'm really mad! She was the grown-up! She should have seen!"

"My mom *was* the abuser and I'm already plenty mad! She'd bring popcorn upstairs and we'd watch TV on her bed and then she'd go down on me."

"I am out of my mind mad at mine because she'd rather stay there in that marriage being codependent with that fat, disgusting slob than listen to me and get a divorce."

My mother, my mother, my mother—there was nothing left to say, everything had been taken. And she didn't want to say anything, she didn't want to kill her mother. The answers came round closer and closer and everything was used up. Phoebe felt hot and cold at the same time, and her head began to pound. Even though she didn't have any picture, she had a feeling, a visceral feeling—those count, they do count. And then it was her turn. She opened her mouth: "A grown person did this to a little girl, that's what blows my mind. Get out of that bathing suit, the woman says. So I take out one leg and then the other. Here's a towel, she says. I'm going to show you how to rub yourself to get the sand out. Like this, she says. Yes . . . I can feel her touching me!" The nausea was coming now and she might throw up. Good God, did that mean it was real? Nausea meant real. But this couldn't be true. She'd ask Sahra. Sahra actually listened to you!

When the go-round was finished, Donna Phillips instructed them to hold hands and to feel one another's lives beating in their palms. Phoebe couldn't feel anything much. Under the luminescent lights, they let go hands and Donna asked for a final go-round, in which each should tell how therapy or group had been helpful. One of the younger women nearby started it up.

"Therapy has taught me that the human mind is marvelously designed. It protects you. I'm not going to be able to remember the most horrible details of how my father incested me until I'm strong enough to handle them."

Only two away from her: "The group shows that there's help out there for everyone. I watch the news and there's a new case practically every night. Priests, day-care workers, ordinary people. Abuse is all around us! Knowing there's help makes me cry. And that makes me feel better, releasing so much emotion."

The woman next to her: "It's like having company, here in group. My friends are all so busy. And they've got their own problems. Quite a few of them have been abused, I think, but they don't know it yet."

"Here I'm not alone," Phoebe said, because that's what Sahra had promised her, and then she couldn't go on. She started to cry, real tears because she actually felt more alone than ever. She started to sob. Those around her said, "That's right, honey, get it out. That's right, Phoebe, express it. You're doing fine, Phoebe. You're doing great. Hey, everybody! Three cheers for Phoebe!" The two closest to her put their arms around her. And then the tears and sobs ended. She couldn't believe it. And she'd thought the tears were real! Oh, she was losing her mind! But at least the nausea was gone. The circle moved on past her.

"I can't get close to people out in the world but I know my therapist will never leave me, or you guys, either. Thanks."

"My friends talk about sex and I can't have that till I'm healed and I want to get healed. . . ."

"Here, everyone knows why I can't get anything going. . . ."

"You need supporters when so many men are rapists, especially fathers."

"I'm changing. I'm feeling stronger, more sure of myself, more able."

"There," Donna Phillips said. "That's where we end, and a good end note it is. Because if you want proof that you were abused, I'll tell you where that proof is. Look around, it's in you. If your behavior has changed even slightly, even one little bit since you confronted your parents, that's your proof right there. Now, let's remember that from session five on, we will be seeking outside evidence of what happened to us—journals, photographs, marks on the body."

Phoebe stood up. Her head was reeling. If only she'd never left the studio. She'd felt so much better there. The tears were coming back. A different kind of tears, tears of rage. She felt like weeping and weeping. She did not know what could have overcome her so. She felt angry, so angry. She wanted to hit things, kick things, throw chairs around, bite things. Pissed, she said to herself. I'm pissed! I'm really totally totally pissed!

32

Harvey picked the two postcards off the hall floor. "Dear Mom, Country wide, Dakota flat. Love, Bess." "Dear Dad, Country wide, Dakota flat. Love, Bess." It discouraged him. They could be a demonstration of Bess's neutrality or maybe she'd simply lost Claire's new address. He called Claire to read her the cards. Now that he wasn't so mad anymore, he liked to hear her voice.

"Hey, you want to join me?" he added after his report. "Just thought I'd run down to Chinatown for some of those terrific eggrolls."

"No, thanks. I brought dinner in."

He hung up before he could get mad, forgetting to tell her that he was going away. His sister was turning sixty and Ben had summoned him for a surprise party.

Looking down over the coastal green from thirty thousand feet, Harvey could see the juncture of the Ohio and the Mississippi. It dwarfed such things as human age and human sorrow or even human profit-seeking. Some 20 million Americans try therapy every year, he'd discovered, twice as many women as men. They consult some 300,000 health professionals. That might be 35,000 psychiatrists, 65,000 psychologists, and maybe 200,000 masters and doctors of various specialties, including medical doctors and some completely uncredentialed counselors. It's big business. It's growing. Professionals have doubled in numbers since 1975. They pass through examining boards of varying rigor and once they're licensed, there's only continuing education demanded of them and very little regulation. How many are helpful, life-improving guides? How many are phrenologists selling sugar water? In this profit-based culture of ours, what sells is what we have been made to believe in or to crave.

How much money changes hands? About $19 billion had been spent the year before on mental health, but he didn't know how much of it went to the therapeutic hour. Those 300,000 give an hour or two a week to the 20 million at prices ranging from $15 to $200 per hour. He took a stab at $2 billion. Who pays it? Private wallets like his? HMOs? Insurance companies? But who pays for the insurance? Employers? Individuals? Taxpayers? And how much do they pay? Do the 20 million get what they need?

After the plane circled down to the Twin Cities, as the descendants of Swedes and Norwegians in neighboring seats stood and their heads almost touched the ceiling, Harvey felt short by comparison. At the end of the roped-off pathway, his brother-in-law, Ben, stood in doctor tweeds, rounder and balder than at either of his daughters' weddings.

"Hi, there!" Harvey stuck out his hand.

"Great timing. She doesn't know a thing."

Ben attempted to take Harvey's bag but Harvey held on to it. "This a big affair?"

"No, just family, just you. But I knew you'd be the biggest treat I could deliver. No Claire?"

"Like I said, she's a little overwhelmed. A new project."

They walked side by side toward a station wagon. Ben drove them under the huge sky of the plains and then they moved into the curves of the suburbs where the forsythia had faded to green. Harvey remembered when this whole area had been a new cut in the ground without a tree or bush. Indeed, he'd brought Phyllis a check for a dogwood tree. Ben pulled past fir trees into a garage and the two of them entered the back door of a split-level with a pristine kitchen and there was small, neat Phyllis, putting her arms around the younger brother she'd corrected so frequently as a child.

"Harvey! My gosh, Harvey!"

He embraced her with reserve. "Happy birthday!"

"You're so thin!"

He let go of her.

"Where's Claire?"

"Couldn't come. Sends her love."

"Uncle Harvey!" The nieces rolled in from the den. They were bigger, fleshier women than their mother and not quite so authoritative.

"Abby! Georgia!"

Abby was pregnant. Their husbands stood up from easy chairs in the den, where they'd been watching the news. Then they were all piling into station wagons and heading for Phyllis's favorite little Italian restaurant at a mall not far away. They sat around a wide table and Harvey's monthlong loneliness subsided a little.

"How's Bessie?"

"Ought to be in Seattle by now."

"She came by for a night, you know."

"She did? I . . . we didn't know!"

"Just here for a hot shower," Ben reported, looking suddenly at his menu.

Phyllis said, "Any news from Phoebe?"

"Not much," he told them. "Still in the Big Apple. How's Mother?"

"The same. We'll see her Sunday," Phyllis replied, consulting her own menu. "If you want to call it Mother."

Ben laughed. "Well, it's remarkable how the basic personality survives, even when the brain goes."

"Ben means she's still thoughtful," Phyllis explained, "even though she can't think."

They all laughed, the younger ones because they couldn't imagine losing their memories and the older because they could. The talk eased away from family. The younger ones were wild with anger about the oil spill off Alaska and worried about the Kurdish refugees making their way into the hills after the Gulf War. Despite the distressing subject matter, Harvey enjoyed their intermingling voices, the sheer bulk of them. It was peaceful here. His sister's children seemed to be from another time.

The food came and Abby instructed them in what pregnant mothers may eat, as if she'd been born without benefit of belly button herself—straight from the starry void. Georgia was delaying pregnancy until she'd logged up seven years in the public school system and paid off half the mortgage on their house in the suburbs. Wise planning, but wasn't Georgia too young for such caution? No, his sister's girls were as they should be. Their expressions were not clouded. They evinced no rage. They didn't ask for money. They made no accusations. And they were sitting here in the same room with their parents and actually talking with them. He tried to think of subjects far from the domestic front and recalled from Georgia's wedding that her husband, a lawyer now, had been a student volunteer for Minnesota's Walter Mondale during his '84 presidential campaign. He'd always liked the way Mondale had faced up to the deficit and the debt, and Claire had been so thrilled when Mondale chose Geraldine Ferraro for a running mate.

"Mondale? He's left a lasting mark," the young lawyer replied. "With the '74 Mondale Act."

"What's that?"

"Oh, you know, Uncle Harvey. It's the Act for the Prevention and Treatment of Child Abuse. The one where if you're a teacher and suspect a child of yours is being abused at home, you've got to report it or you can be prosecuted." The rest of the table grew silent as Georgia's husband explained the law in a tone that began to sound more and more significant to Harvey. "It isn't just teachers who have to report sexual abuse or violence. It's doctors, psychologists, or any professionals who work with children."

"That's a good act." Harvey made clear his approval. "And needed, I bet." Then against his better judgment, he went on, "But what if they're wrong?"

"Oh, the people who report have immunity. If the accusations turn out to be wrong, nothing happens."

Nothing happens! Harvey turned to his veal to silence himself.

Abby, a social worker, threw in a little more information. "That's how my agency got started, Uncle Harvey, from the Mondale Act. And lots of other agencies, too."

"How's that?" he asked, wondering why he was the only person at the table who'd never heard of this act.

"The Mondale Act established federal funding for treatment centers for people who abuse children."

"And what's the treatment?" he asked, struggling for levity. "Eye for an eye? Tooth for a tooth?"

"Oh, Uncle Harvey! It's therapy, of course."

"Ah, yes, your line of work." The footing was so treacherous that he hardly heard the little firings in his brain: funding, money, how many thousands? Millions? How many new treatment centers, each with salaried staff?

"Our clinic has pioneered lots of therapy programs. Most of our clients come to us direct from the court or the police."

"Here's to Walter Mondale!" he raised his wineglass in an attempt to close the topic.

"A child is the most precious thing in the world, Uncle Harvey," Abby went on, patting her rounded belly. "When a child is abused, it's up to all of us to step in."

Tiny cups of espresso arrived, and Harvey gave them his report on the recession on both coasts. Eventually, to his relief, Ben lifted a big plastic bag onto the table and Phyllis opened her presents—including one from Claire, who'd carried through on the family obligations without his even reminding her, which pleased and relaxed him. He'd give Phyllis and Ben the dogwood at Christmas.

Saturday they visited his mother at the nursing home. Phyllis went upstairs to drop off some new nightgowns. Inside the crowded dayroom with its faint smell of overdone broccoli and dried urine, Harvey spotted quite a few of the old bodies scattered about in slumped postures with the television blaring around them. He finally distinguished his mother from the other quite similar shapes and crossed the room toward the woman who had taught him that you reap what you sow. He wasn't so sure about that anymore. But this woman in the wheelchair had run beside his bicycle, steadying the handlebars. She had corrected his homework and told him to slow down because being right mattered more than being first. And she had watched him completely, even if she sometimes got him wrong. You can get your children wrong, both of them: he'd learned that. He pulled up a chair and sat down beside her.

"Hello, Mother."

The blue eyes were absent of him. In that brain, he no longer existed.

"Hi, there." She smiled, shifting her wrinkled skin into a pattern of puzzlement.

"It's good to see you."

"Oh, you too!" She took his hand. Her bones felt small, birdy, crackable.

"I've come to tell you about the girls," he said. "They're fine. Absolutely fine."

"The girls," she repeated, smiling again. She was studying his face, looking for clues as to who those girls might be.

"I thought you might be worrying about Phoebe. I know Bess sends you a card now and then. But Phoebe is very busy. She said to tell you that she misses you." He could not believe what was coming over him but it felt so good to spend a moment where the truth is what we want it to be. He went on. "Phoebe's engaged and Bess has a boyfriend who's going into bank finance with the hope that he can provide money to young people who want to climb out of poverty." Oh, this was such a relief, this world of lies. "And I've retired. Can you believe it? Claire and I are leaving tomorrow for the Caribbean. Actually, the minute I leave here. She's meeting me at the airport. It's the start of a long tour in summery climes."

She smiled again and nodded. They held hands and listened to the TV keyed loud enough to enter so many ancient ears. The light of understanding finally came into his mother's eyes. "I did enjoy the pot roast," she said, squeezing his hand. "It was lovely of you to put it on the menu. I know you do get so many contrary requests."

In the quiet of Sunday morning, Harvey sat on the deck with Phyllis. A breeze moved the just-budding leaves of the birch trees, and the smell of the grassy earth wafted through the curving landscape. There was coffee on the table, an airplane overhead, the sounds of children on the cul-de-sac beyond his sister's house, a dog's barking. This is the sort of house he'd craved for his own family. It wasn't damp here. It wasn't dark. It wasn't narrow or steep. And there were people in it.

"Harvey," Phyllis said in a voice that put him on instant alert but even that was not fast enough. "Bess told us that Claire has left you."

"Claire hasn't left me."

"She's not living away from the house?"

He stood up. He wanted to be taller than his sister. "It's just one of those temporary things, an experiment. Women at fifty, you know." He walked to the railing, took in a breath of the fragrant air.

"Bess told us about Phoebe, too." His sister's voice pierced his back at kidney level.

Betrayed by Bess. Now all his women had betrayed him. There was one woman left. Could he trust Phyllis?

She spoke. "Did you do it?"

He turned around; his big sister could be comforting, if you were hurt, really hurt. "Of course not."

She fingered the coffeepot. "Ben said you called him a while back. You had a question about drunkenness, blackout."

Ah! The kicker. But an understandable question. "And?"

"Are you drinking or something, Harvey? Is that why she's left? Is that what happened with Phoebe?"

"Nothing happened with Phoebe, Phyllis. Would I do that sort of thing?"

"Well," she said, casting her judgmental eye upon him. "I never would have thought it . . ."

That felt good. He walked back toward his chair.

"But there's so much of it out there and sometimes people can't help themselves, Abby says—"

Thoughts of comfort vanished. "Did you discuss this with Abby?"

"Well, yes. This is her field, after all. They do such wonderful things in therapy, you know."

"Phyllis, you can't let Abby or Georgia or Ben discuss this with a living soul!" He stood by the table. "It could get back East and I'd lose my job. I'd never get another job!"

She pushed the coffeepot away. "I just thought maybe I could help, Harvey. There are these twelve-step programs, you know. Abby says—"

"Drinking isn't my problem, Phyllis." He sank down into his chair. "A glass of wine at supper is actually recommended."

"You know, Harvey, if you hadn't left the church—"

"For God's sake, Phyllis! My problems don't have a lot to do with the church."

"They don't?" She smiled the smile of the righteous. "What are they, then, your problems? How did you get yourself into this spot? You must have done *something*, you know. What?"

He didn't attempt to answer; his sister's surprise birthday had been a ruse so they could get him out here and correct him.

On the way to the airport Ben took a parting shot. "Phyllis told me she'd talked to you. If you did it, you need help. Abby says there's lots of counseling out there for men who do this sort of thing and don't even remember it."

He wanted to kill. He wanted to put his hands around Ben's neck and squeeze the air out. But Ben mustn't know the power they had over him. "Nice to see you," he said outside the terminal, shaking Ben's hand. "Bye to Phyllis."

33

With Rachel suggesting that their thirtieth college reunion might take Claire's mind off things, they flew to New England and rented a car for an early-evening drive up an ancient river valley exquisite with the half-leafed trees of mid-May. Eons ago glacial ice had filled the whole valley: what did it matter on that scale of time if a single daughter were lost?

In Massachusetts, the town of Northampton seemed bigger and brighter than in 1961, if less indigenous. Its streets and storefronts might be in Pennsylvania or Michigan or simply on TV as the typical college town. Up the hill they pulled into a lot near white-pillared Capen House and hung their clothes in the closets of adjoining rooms. Outside they passed a bulletin board announcing a series of talks on gender politics, and a flyer offering rape counseling. In their day, the flyers had concerned Amherst mixers. On the main campus not all the faces were white as they'd once been. And on the lower quad two young women were holding hands. Changes; things in historic time transform themselves as well as they do in geologic periods. They turned under trees past the statue given in memory of a twenty-one-year-old student by her parents. Thirty years ago Claire had felt anguish for this lost girl; now she felt it for the parents.

"Feeling better?" Rachel inquired.

Twilight darkened the perennial garden, and the petals of white flowers assumed a contrary glow. Bullfrogs near the plant house played cello in their throats. The two women crossed the road and stood above a silent pond that held itself motionless against the wooden steps of a boathouse. Here they were thirty years later, their biological mission completed. What remained?

"It's good to be here," Claire said. "Thanks for insisting."

They walked to a low white building that resonated with the noise of a hundred conversations and headed down crowded stairs past the '66 buffet to '61's. In line for drinks and hors d'oeuvres, Claire finally did begin to lose track of her preoccupations as they were quickly approached by women peering first at their name tags and then into their faces.

"Claire Monroe?"

"Emily? Emily Turner Bernstein, you're looking great."

Emily had four grown kids and volunteered for American Cancer. Sarah Ross White was hoping for early retirement from the public school system of Cincinnati. Kathy Banner's husband had left her twenty-five years ago with two small children and in desperation she'd moonlighted a phonics text, which had been adopted by Texas and still provided substantial royalties. Mary Tillinghast, however, had been caught out in the real estate market in New Hampshire; never mind, she was selling off her antiques and taking a computer course. Janice Wills couldn't come, she was this minute in Cleveland having her breast cut off.

It braced Claire to hear that these women had met disaster and kept on going. Feminism, they agreed at her dinner table, had liberated them all. Yet their daughters seemed to have new kinds of restrictions on their lives, as did their sons. Claire didn't join in much. After dinner, when Rachel went off with social worker friends, Claire grabbed at the chance to be alone. She wanted to get closer to the hopeful person she'd been when she last walked these paths. Intrigued by an astronomy open house on the roof of McConnell, she climbed the stairs to the top of that building and stood quietly in the balmy darkness waiting for a free telescope. The pain of her life began to seem more and more paltry. There were billions of people on earth today, more humans than had lived in the entire history of the species. Some were at war, some hungry, some born weighing a single pound, some about to die after suffering months of pain or immobility or constant itching. Looked at from that perspective, she was sort of lucky.

A telescope was freed up and she took it, locating the moon, huge and white in its lens. It moved so quickly out of focus that, leaning with it, she nearly fell against an older woman at the next telescope.

"So fast! Isn't it?"

"Wild!"

She found the moon again. She found stars. She found a great black emptiness. That was the future. By the time the world reached that future, there'd be no Claire and no Phoebe, and maybe not even any Earth. She let go of her telescope and walked down the stairs with her neighbor.

"Great night, isn't it? I'm Connie, '51."

"Claire, '61."

Outside, maintenance men were stretching wire at shoulder height.

"I bet they're for the lanterns!"

"It's tomorrow night."

"Il-lum-i-na-tion." Connie drew out the world.

"I could use some!" Then Claire fell silent, having said too much.

"Me too," Connie replied. "You know, you're lucky, to be born when you were. We were already middle-aged when the great changes came."

"You mean civil rights? Feminism? Computers?"

"Feminism, mostly. What happened to it, anyway? Out in Kansas City, it seems to have turned into something about hating men."

"I never hated men."

"Me neither."

Connie paused at a juncture in the path. "Want to drop in on the Shakespeare thing?"

Still wanting solitude, Claire declined and moved along a grassy arc above the pond. On her own graduation night several thousand paper lanterns had circled the campus, each containing a candle that cast a pastel-tinged light into the dreamy darkness. Good-bye, they'd said to each other, good luck. They'd left without once hearing the name of Susan B. Anthony or realizing that they were the first fruits of the Nineteenth Amendment. Yet somehow, by osmosis, they'd dared more than their mothers. Only now the things that had strengthened them, or some of the things, seemed to have gotten out of control and overshot the mark.

At a spot on the dark circumference of the pond, Claire noticed a set of unfamiliar stepping stones that moved dimly up a slope to a small structure. Following the stones, she reached an open-air platform under a roof. It was a small pagoda and as in the Buddha room at the museum, she instantly became aware of breath, her own, and this time not that of the Buddhas' but of the earth's, the pond's. She sat and looked out over the still water where distant lights from the boathouse gleamed. Where are you, Phoebe? Tell me you are breathing. Will you ever come back? We living things cool down, you know. Don't wait until I've cooled down too far. Until I'm too angry. Until I can't forgive you. Then suddenly she was crying out over the dark water, "I want to go on loving her!"

On the ride to the airport, Rachel said, "Something's going on. I met a psychologist from Berkeley named Brodie Sellars. She does intelligence testing. She's got friends, though, who treat clients. Lately, she says, a couple of them have been telling her about helping clients remember sexual abuse. She'll ask around. She'll get back to me."

Back in Lacey's drafty kitchen on North Twentieth, Claire dialed Harvey to report. He wasn't home. Surveying Lacey's bowl of wooden spoons, she listened to her own voice ask her for her name and phone number.

She was alone. Phoebe was alone. Bess was alone. Harvey was alone.

Or maybe he wasn't?

34

Sahra Meehan had fourteen clients now, all young adults and most suffering from anxiety. Her newest, Andrea, might be a multiple personality but she hoped not. Donna Phillips said that MPD work took so long. Of course, Andrea might be an incest survivor, like Phoebe, her favorite client. And Phoebe? Carl always asked at the end of the weekly review. Oh, Phoebe likes her job but she keeps on doubting herself and she doesn't have many friends or a boyfriend. She might be resting on a plateau, he'd suggested, before she delves down into those memories again. When they don't get completely better, it can mean there's more to recover. Recovery, Sahra really liked memory-recovery work. She would put the abuse question to Andrea this week. But today, Phoebe: Donna had alerted her that Phoebe was skipping group. She began with that.

"Yes," Phoebe admitted. "I didn't go because I don't have any corroboration about my father. And I hate group, anyway. Especially the older women, they're off the wall. Half the people in the group make up what they say."

Sahra loved to see this phase of therapy in a client, when they looked right at you and spoke with conviction. That was growth. But she'd learned so much at the Warburg's continuing education workshops on sexual abuse that she knew her first job was to challenge resistance.

"Who would make up horrible things like this?"

"Me. I did. That stuff about my mother touching me between the legs with a towel? That wasn't my mother," Phoebe said with more authority than usual. "I don't even know who it was. Or if it happened."

"Phoebe Fairchild, you've got the Rolls-Royce of repressors! See what you're doing? You dig a little deeper, you find a new memory, you bring it up to light. And then you slap yourself on the hand and tell yourself it wasn't true." Phoebe glared and didn't speak, a sign of resistance, Sahra knew. "I'll tell you what," she went on. "If you feel so unsure about the towel memory, let's sit back and relax a little. We'll go over it together." Sahra waited while Phoebe shut her eyes and placed her hands, palm up, in her lap.

How she loved it when a client sat with eyes shut and face totally open and available like that. It was a sacred trust that she'd never betray. "Ten, nine, eight"—Sahra actually went into a count, something she didn't usually bother with— "Raise your hand when you're in the cottage at the lake."

When Phoebe's hand went up, Sahra said softly, "Where are you?"

"In the bedroom."

"Hear anything?"

"The lake, at the shoreline, and maybe a radio is playing."

"See anything?"

"She bends down."

"Who?"

"A baby-sitter, maybe."

"What does she look like? Her hair?"

"Blond."

"Eyes?"

"Brown."

"What's she doing with the towel?"

"She brushes at the sand."

"Who is it?"

"It's the baby-sitter, Stephanie. Stephanie someone."

"It's not your mother?"

"I told you, no."

After a few more questions, Phoebe was sitting with open eyes. "Congratulations, Phoebe! You're working hard again. You've found someone else. Don't slap her down. Think about Stephanie this week." Sahra interlaced her fingers and leaned her head against them, stretching. "One day, Phoebe, you'll have all your memories, even the ones that lie so deep you hardly dare begin the search. Sooner or later, you'll relax and invite them. 'I relax and invite my soul.' Someone said that."

The blue eyes flicked. "Walt Whitman."

"I can sure count on you, Phoebe! Now, let's get back to group. What is everybody else doing to find corroboration about their abusers?"

With the entire country behind her Bess finally felt free. Her family lived on the small green waters of the Atlantic while she stood alone on the high cliffs of Oregon claiming for herself the immense blue of the Pacific. She hadn't once called home; she'd meant to but somehow, after Minneapolis, she couldn't. Soon she was down the cliff and wading into water with her legs going numb from cold. This is my baptism, she told herself. I got here. I'm me. Birds flew over her; the smell of seaweed entered her nose.

The great but triumphant aloneness of crossing the country ended when Bess parked the van on a street outside a split-level in the northeast quadrant of Portland, where Doreen, a gamelan major she'd never been crazy about, lived. Inside, the rooms were clean and painted white and there were bare floors and low ceilings, which worked fine because the furniture was mostly colorful pillows cast about the floor, and futons. The only wooden furniture, a table and chairs, stood in the kitchen. Doreen made coffee and explained the house. "Mike works nights and weekends at McDonald's and is getting a master's in philosophy so he doesn't have to start paying back his loans. He sleeps till noon. Tanya is a home health aide and works all funny hours; she's in and out. Neil's working at the Copyquik from ten to eight. I'm the only nine to five and I shower around seven-thirty."

They agreed that Bess would pay fifty dollars a week for the privilege of using the bathroom and parking the van out front, plus a cup of coffee in the morning. The bathroom was painted pink and the tiles were beginning to crack on the floor near the tub; the whole room smelled of mold and dirty clothes.

"Great," Bess said.

There was a basement room where the TV sat. Doreen explained that the set was broken but that the VCR worked. Mike was a video freak and brought films home almost every night. "It's kind of a kitty arrangement," Doreen said, leading the way back up the short flight of stairs. "You put a buck in the jar if you want to watch."

"Great," Bess said.

She was perfectly happy in her van but you can't get by without a bathroom. She picked up a slice of pizza and drove off for a laundromat, where she studied a map of Portland while her underwear leapt through suds. She was hungry but already over budget because she'd never caught up from the fourteen dollars she'd laid out in Seattle on new sunglasses. When she got back to the house, nobody was there. On the kitchen counter, she spotted somebody's jar of peanut butter and somebody's bread. She didn't want to get off on the wrong foot by eating somebody else's stuff. When you're feeling low, her mother always said, it's a good time to tackle something you've been putting off. Mom? Dad? Or Phoebe? She picked up the phone.

"Ho, Bess," Phoebe said. "How's Hollywood?"

"Pretty far south. I'm in Portland. How's everything?"

"Okay, except for group."

"How're the zombies?"

"They're all such losers. There's this contagion and sometimes I wonder if they say things just to have something to say."

Bess took a chance. "Do you? And do you do that, make things up, Phoebe?"

"It's not that simple," Phoebe's voice closed a little, although not entirely. "You know, I saw his face? The face of the guy in the rosebushes. I did. It came right up in a memory. He has a brown beard and brown eyes and brown hair. He's real and I'm absolutely sure of how he looks. But then, in group, I've got him saying things to me that I don't quite trust, you see how complicated—"

"You're telling me you made stuff up?"

"I'm saying I'm worried! These are legitimate questions! How do I tell what from what? Confusion is normal for stuff you've repressed. I've told Sahra and she says not to worry, everything will sort out later."

"I bet she did."

"Okay, forget it, Bess." Now Phoebe's voice closed entirely. "Has Mom left Dad or something?"

"Beats me, Phoebe. The whole thing beats me."

"What's she doing at Lacey Quinn's?"

"Lacey's gone to Rome on a grant." Bess's courage seeped away as Phoebe talked about that man at work. When she hung up, there was no energy left for calling her parents. Stretched out in her tepee-on-wheels, she heard occasional traffic. A dog barked nearby. This was civilization.

In the morning she carried her clothes into the bathroom, which was still damp and fuzzy from Doreen's shower. Today she was hitting the temporary agencies and it wasn't going to be easy. People her age were flocking here, too. They'd been lining the streets in Seattle, all applying for the same jobs. Bloomer Gates had been laid off and Cat Benz was thinking of grad school. She moved quietly about in the low-ceilinged galley kitchen, pouring the single cup of coffee Doreen allowed. She would blow her day's food money in a quick rice shop at lunch. That was cheaper than cooking for yourself—if you count in the fact that a stove means you're paying rent somewhere. She could get by on $200 a week, or $800 a month, which would allow her $200 for housing, $300 food, and $70 for the van insurance and maybe $75 for buses and $20 for laundry and maybe $100 for unpredictables like when she ran over her sunglasses outside a Wendy's in Walla Walla. A certain bounciness in the van's brakes worried her, but forget that. Yes, something like $200 take-home per week would be comfortable enough. She boarded a bus for Portland's low, beige downtown.

They weren't hiring at Starbucks and you need an Oregon license to drive a pizza-delivery van. She stopped next at a great barn of a bookstore with concrete walls and rows and rows of shelves filled with books like so many wholesale tires. At the front desk she inquired about the job in the paper.

"Somebody else in there now," a bald man with granny glasses told her. "Hang around. He'll be free in twenty minutes."

Bess walked the aisles, stopped near Women's Studies, where a table display of books seemed to be about sexual abuse. She quit that in a hurry and in the front of the store reached a display of the new edition of *The Joy of Sex*. Now, that's more like it! Good old-fashioned sex. She picked up a copy to see the paintings she and Phoebe had always loved. They'd pored over them out at the lake, sneaking the book from the bedside table in the cottage out into the old barn. But these weren't the same illustrations! How disappointing. How off-putting these photographs and pastels seemed compared to the old drawings and paintings of that nice-looking man with the brown beard and brown hair and brown eyes—whoa!

Where could she get her hands on that old edition?

"Ms. Fairchild?" The bald man was calling from the end of the long aisle. "Mr. Pratt will see you now."

During the interview she tried to keep her mind on the short white proprietor with the Afro. "We pay five dollars and eighty cents an hour," he was telling her.

"What's the medical plan?"

"There isn't any. This is part-time, thirty-five hours per week. No bennies."

"I'm interested," she told him. It would only come to $175 a week take-home.

"I'll let you know in a few days."

Armed with good news, she finally called her mother at the museum. Her mother was not in a fun mood.

"Good God, Bess! It's been over a month!"

"Sorry, Mom."

"Where are you?"

"Portland."

"We thought you were in Seattle."

"By 'we' do you mean Dad and you?"

"Of course."

"Are you together again? It's hard to keep up!"

"We talk, you know. And we're getting together after work next week. Are you eating? Have you got a safe place to stay?"

"Sure. I've got a job."

"Oh, great, great. Wonderful. What doing?"

"Bookstore. Selling books. Now both your daughters are in the media."

"Phoebe has a job? In a bookstore?"

"Oh, screw it! I forgot. I'm out of practice as a channel. She's at a TV studio, been there awhile. That's all I can tell you. Gotta go."

"Thanks, Bess. Thanks. Call in two weeks. Good luck on your job."

"I'll call Dad now."

"He's very upset, Bess. About Aunt Phyllis and Uncle Ben . . ."

Bess had been hanging up and she just kept on moving the receiver closer and closer to its base until she could no longer hear the voices from the East. No wonder she hadn't called home sooner. Uncle Ben was a doctor, after all, and objective. He'd asked how everybody was. She'd needed somebody objective to talk to, and now she'd blown it.

35

On a warm evening Claire and Harvey strolled the channeled Delaware with the lights of the Ben Franklin Bridge green in the distance. Claire gave Harvey the latest of Rachel's findings from Brodie Sellars: There are schools of social work that turn out therapists who specialize in treating sexual abuse. These specially trained therapists work with clients to recall a memory of abuse, even though the client may not come in with any such memory. Certain clinics—and Brodie suggested they look into the Warburg—report a very high percentage of these recalled-memory cases.

"Sounds like a muffler shop," Harvey said. "You take your car there and they tell you you have a muffler problem."

"Except the muffler people know they're conning you. Sexual-abuse specialists believe in what they're doing. They believe that one hundred percent of recovered memories are true."

"One hundred percent? That's a muffler shop, all right."

Their shoulders brushed and each moved slightly away. Claire went on. "Brodie says there seems to be a pattern typical to abuse that has been recalled only after therapy. It's this: The client tends to remember more and more abuse as the therapy continues. She tends to remember events from when she was younger and younger or older and older, and she may remember more and more abusers."

"It's not just the muffler, it's the entire exhaust system."

"When clients simply come in and report abuse on their own, Brodie says, the pattern tends to go like this: The father has started in with the daughter when she was around eight, usually without penetration. He wasn't violent but persuaded his daughter by his authority. Sometimes he used bribes—candy, privileges."

Harvey made a noise in his throat. "You mean 'Do this and you can have a Hershey bar'?"

"Sort of. The girls are emotionally repulsed but physiologically aroused. The arousal makes them feel terribly guilty. And that guilt gives them trouble in their adult sexual lives."

"I should think. Which is Phoebe?"

"How would we know?"

They came to the end of a paved section of walk and stopped, turned back toward the ferry and Penn's Landing. It was Harvey's turn and he had an idea.

"Let's not pay Meehan anymore."

"We can't leave Phoebe out in the cold."

"Cut her free, see what happens."

"She needs a therapist. She needs support."

"Outside the muffler shop, she might come to her senses."

"Or lose them entirely."

"Come on, Claire, you're crazy. Doesn't it gall you to finance an operation that may be intent on destroying us!"

She stopped in her place. "Don't call me crazy!"

"I don't mean really crazy."

"Don't call me crazy."

"Okay. Don't tell me what to do, either."

They resumed walking, farther apart. Harvey tried again. "This begins to sound more and more like Moonie stuff. We could kidnap her and get her deprogrammed."

"Did that work with Daphne Jencks?"

"Okay, score. What's your plan?"

"Rachel says all we can do is keep calm and steady."

"She's been saying that for six months! It's time to cut off the money."

"No, that's us taking the lead."

"What's wrong with that?"

"I told you! If the basic problem is separation, then Phoebe leads and we follow. We don't manipulate her."

The first meeting didn't go the way Harvey wanted but he was glad they'd agreed to meet every week. And Claire was pleased she'd held her ground.

The phone rang when Claire was spooning pasta out of the kettle in Lacey's kitchen and she picked it up with a wet hand. Hello? There was silence on the other end but somebody was there. Hello? She felt cold around her shoulders and glanced at the screened and barred windows whose curtains she'd pushed aside to let in air. Someone in back of the row houses could be watching her. Hello? The line went dead and she slammed down the phone.

She checked the bolts on the front door and when she went up to bed lay listening to the sirens, which came now as a comfort. They weren't for her; the violence hadn't yet collected in her own bedroom. Then somehow she began to think of those times before a performance when Phoebe's face would turn pale and drain of color as she fought off the precurtain nausea. Often she'd come into the kitchen, where Claire was working at supper or laundry, to repeat her lines out loud. It was always most comforting to Phoebe, Claire remembered, if she kept on calmly loading the dishwasher or ironing, as if everything would be fine.

When the phone rang again several nights later, Claire was eating a sweet potato. She picked up the phone, said hello, took a breath and continued into the silence. "Hi, Phoebe. It's Mom."

"Mom?"

Her voice, Phoebe's voice! Claire's body warmed but she did her best to remain matter-of-fact. "Yup, I'm here. Great to hear you."

"Well, I . . . " Phoebe's voice faltered.

"Things are okay here."

"They are? You're okay? Oh, good! Why are you living up there?"

"Taking some space for myself. How are you, honey?"

"Could we . . . could we get together? You and me?"

"Sure thing. When?"

"Sunday the thirtieth."

"Fine. Where?"

"I was thinking . . . you know that slanty path that goes from the Plaza into Central Park where the benches are, before the zoo?"

"Central Park. Slanty path. Sure do."

"Two o'clock is good."

"Two on the thirtieth. Got it." Claire used all her powers not to go on, not to say more. She waited.

"Oh," the voice finally said. "And will you bring something with you?"

"What's that?"

"The photo album with the flags in front."

"The flags? Okay." The strain of it finally led Claire to lose control. She made a joke. "I'll be wearing a straw hat and carrying a photo album."

Phoebe didn't laugh. She said good-bye and the line went dead.

The great pleasure, the great relief, ended abruptly when she told Rachel, who warned her of something else: These therapists sometimes send their clients home to look for corroborating evidence. Sometimes it's prior to instituting a lawsuit.

Steady for so long, Claire suddenly lost it and rang up Harvey.

"Claire, take it easy, sweetheart. It's okay."

"A lawsuit! Her own father!"

"She's not suing us yet. Take it easy."

"I can't."

"Look, she called you. She's alive. She's talking to you. You'll be seeing her in a week and a half. I'll bring the album right over, okay?"

He delivered it and sat at Lacey's kitchen table studying his wife, who looked so ravaged. He got up and made her a cup of tea. Of course their daughter might be suing him. Anything could happen. But it didn't seem so important to Harvey tonight. His wife had turned to him. She had sought him out, relied on him. That was enough. If he could have his wife back, somehow the girls would come too, part of the package. That was enough for him. Simply to sit here, simply to know that one person in the world trusted him. That was enough.

Together they looked at the album laid out on the table. It ran from Phoebe's first day in the Greenfield kindergarten to the trip to New Hampshire and the lake in the mountains he'd so loved that he'd come home and sought out another lake in New Jersey for the girls to grow up by, summer after summer. On the table before them was their family again, the sweet girls, red-haired Harvey, slim Claire, a campfire with a great black frying pan and four perfect eggs in it.

"We may never have her again," Claire said, the tears gathering in her eyes. "Only this." She lay her palm flat on the album. "We'll be like the Jenckses, part dead. We'll have infinite patience, the kind of patience you learn when your child is stolen by the Moonies. Or has cerebral palsy or is retarded or permanently paralyzed in a car accident."

"Get some sleep," he told her, placing his hand on top of hers. He knew he mustn't push it. Mustn't even lecture her on her safety here below the bottom tip of North Philadelphia. It would be a simple blessing if the car hadn't been broken into when he got back outside.

The great dank heat of a Philadelphia summer rose off the streets, and even Penn's Landing was steaming when Harvey spotted Claire the next time, buying food off a kiosk cart and stuffing it into her string bag. He took the wide steps down the amphitheater with pleasure—at seeing her looking better, and at the good news he carried in his pocket. He reached her and took up the string bag. In twilight, they boarded the ferry and stood at the railing of a squarish boat as it set out across the water toward Camden. He looked at her there, leaning on the railing, and said, "Hey, I got a great thing in the mail." He pulled out the crumpled paper napkin and unwrapped it to show her the five-dollar bill.

"What is it?"

"From Bess," he said, as he smoothed out the soft paper and read the ballpoint message. "Happy Advance Birthday, Dad. Token payment on the van, only 1599 more to go. Private B."

They laughed, touched hands, kissed.

36

Claire held the album to her breast as she strode up the slanted path from the Plaza. She mustn't let her anxiety lead her astray again into witticisms or accusations, she must stay matter-of-fact throughout the visit. That's what worked best with Phoebe when she was scared. Too restless to sit, she stood looking first toward the zoo, where men were selling peanuts and hot dogs, and then toward Fifty-ninth Street, where the drivers of horse-drawn wagons stood in nineteenth-century dress waiting for twentieth-century customers. And there walking came a young red-haired woman clothed in rayon with her feet in sandals, crisp, grown, citified.

"Phoebe!" she called out, waved.

Phoebe approached the blond woman with caution. In the last few weeks with group and all, everything had grown so much harder to understand. The whole world, this park, these pretzel carts might not be here. Or they might be a mirage for some other reality behind them, something evil, a force of darkness. You can't be sure. You can never be sure what lies behind an image.

They stopped short of each other and did not embrace. Children cried out from the playground.

"Hello, honey," Claire said, tightening her arms around the photo album rather than around the young woman who looked as if she did not wish to be hugged.

"Hello, Claire." Phoebe tried to shake off the sense of illusion. She imagined a boundary around herself, the way Sahra had instructed. I'm here, she's there. Which mother was this? The good one who'd helped her or the bad who had not? Her mother's features altered slightly. Her mother was saying something. What was she saying?

"You Phoebe, me Claire."

"What?" This mother might not even be real!

"Sorry, sorry, Phoebe," Claire said. "I got carried away. It's an old joke that came to me because I'm nervous. Tarzan and Jane. You probably don't remember Tarzan and Jane. They were in the jungle."

This mother was dangerous. "Only you're Tarzan, right?"

Claire pulled the album tighter, overwhelmed at whatever she'd done to make her daughter shrink from her. She started over. "Sorry, I'm sorry, Phoebe. I'm not Tarzan. It was just something about seeing you out here in the park with the zoo nearby and of course I've missed you . . ." No, that was wrong, too. She must wait, must follow Phoebe.

This mother was playing the guilt card and Phoebe said coldly, "You didn't hear from me, that's right, you didn't, and for good reason."

Claire started a third time, took an arm off the album and—not actually touching Phoebe—encircled her and led her toward the bench. "Shall we sit?"

They sat. The sun shone upon them. Claire debated her options.

Phoebe moved a little farther from the woman with the brown eyes and the small hands who was sitting so quietly on the bench. Were those the hands on The Towel? She must get to her questions. "Claire, I'd like to talk with you about some aspects of this case."

Claire lowered her eyelids against the sun. "Here I am."

"I'm wondering if you're ready to tell me more about Harvey."

How strangely calm Claire felt here in the warmth of the sun so long as she kept her eyes half closed. This was the ultimate luxury, to be here in the sun with her daughter beside her. She had the right note now. She would not lose her calm again. "I'll tell you anything you want to know."

"Did he ever keep a diary?"

When you give birth, the connection does not end. The child is always out there at a distance from your nerve ends. You wait for reconnection. And today she had it. "A diary? No, not that I know of."

"Did you?"

"No. Occasional notes, when you were born. Bess, born."

"You gave me a diary once at Christmas."

Claire smiled. "Yes. Red leather."

"I never wrote in it."

"That's right, honey. You said you didn't want to keep a diary."

"So who wrote in it?"

"Nobody. Not that I know of. It was in your room."

"Didn't I give it back to you?"

"Did you? I don't remember."

"Dad didn't write in it?"

"Not that I know of. Why?"

"For my group. In case he wrote about what he did."

If Claire were not so relieved to be here, the heaviness of that—more evidence for court—would have sunk her. She did her best with it. "You're in a group?"

"Yes. For survivors."

"What's it like?"

"I don't like it much."

Through her narrowed eyes, Claire saw a less wary look pass over Phoebe's face and for that glimpse of her daughter, she was very thankful. She lifted the album from her lap.

"Here's the album."

"Thanks."

Phoebe took the album. It was such a natural gesture from her mother, handing it to her, that some of the new strangeness of things fell away. She wanted to reach out and touch her mother. This was Mom! But she must not break the boundary. That would be the temptation, she'd been warned.

"I hope it helps you, honey. Don't ever lose it."

Oh, she was so close to reaching out. This was the mother she'd been wanting so much, to be alone with her, the two of them together, her mother telling her the secrets, how to live, how to die, how to love, now that she'd discovered how hard life really is. Even though Sahra had warned her against it, she leaned the littlest bit forward and said what came to her. "Mom, you must have seen what Dad did to me!"

"I didn't see him do anything."

"Where were you, then?"

"Right there."

"Why didn't you see?"

"Because it didn't happen."

Drawn past the boundary now, Phoebe was unable to resist the pull and said, "You've always been so . . . so afraid of Dad! Of course you couldn't admit what he did!"

"Afraid of Dad? No, I haven't been afraid of Dad. There's nothing scary about Dad."

"Are you kidding? He's such a manipulator!"

"How?"

"He says what will be done and those around him do it!"

"But he's your father, he's my husband."

"That's what I mean. Being a husband shouldn't make him a dictator!"

"He doesn't dictate."

"Oh, Mom. He made you climb all those mountains you didn't want to climb."

"But I wanted to be where the rest of you were. That's compromise."

"You wanted to live in New York! His job took him to Philadelphia! So you went to Philadelphia! Is that what you call compromise?"

"He wanted to live in Willow Grove. I wanted to live in the city. We live in the city."

That was the truth, what her mother was saying—not what she herself was saying. Phoebe couldn't stop herself, although she did turn back to Sahra for language.

"Oh, don't you see what a codependent you are!"

"When people live together, everybody has to give up something."

"But you're married to a man who drinks."

"Dad isn't an alcoholic."

"Remember Nan Scatterbay's wedding? Bess and I were so embarrassed!"

That wedding! Still, Claire stuck to the facts. "That's just about the only time I ever saw him drunk."

"Why does he drink at all?"

"Our generation drinks, Phoebe. Yours uses drugs."

"I don't." Phoebe knew she'd lost herself, that she was growing smaller and smaller, and that soon she'd be entirely obliterated. She wanted to throw herself into her mother's lap, be gathered home. Get out! Get away! Quick, get the information first!

"Did we have a baby-sitter named Stephanie?"

"Yes, out at the lake. Stephanie Murray."

"Did she abuse me?"

Other abusers, another abuser—Claire registered this as belonging to Brodie's pattern of recalled abuse. She went on. "Oh, I don't think so, honey. She was a country girl and perfectly fine."

"What did she look like?"

"Stephanie? Let's see. Brown hair, medium size, she had a great gap between her front teeth. She chewed gum. And she could twirl a baton. I could help you look her up."

"I may not need to."

"What do you mean?"

"I don't think it was her, after all." Phoebe straightened up. "I don't want to talk about it." The woman who had held the towel did not have brown hair, she had blond hair and brown eyes. Her mother, this mother.

"Okay."

Sahra was right: Each time you found another part of yourself, you felt stronger, abler, even sympathetic toward others. "I could forgive you for being in denial because I know it happened to you, too. Didn't it, Mom?"

Claire was confused by the change of direction. "What is denial, anyway? Is that the same as repression?"

"Not quite."

"I don't believe I'm denying anything." Claire tried to figure out where they were. "And I don't think I've repressed anything in my life. Except maybe the pain of childbirth and I had painkillers to help with that."

"You're avoiding the question. Did your mother or father abuse you?"

"Oh, no! I already told your therapist that."

"You know, there are ways to tell if a person has been abused. Did you have trouble with sex, for instance?"

"No."

"Even the first time?"

"Well, it hurt, and it was bloody. But other than that, no problem."

Phoebe thought of the blood she'd found on her underpants when she got home from the back of Vince Lamberra's car. It had been shocking, more shocking somehow than the pain, which she'd hardly felt. A child on a tricycle pedaled by their bench. Something was wrong with this picture. If there's blood, it comes from a hymen that's been broken through. How could she have had a hymen then? If Dad had been penetrating her all those years? She could hear Sahra's voice saying, "Stand up, Phoebe. Get away from her now!"

She stood up. "Thanks for the album."

"Oh, honey, wait!" Claire called out and stopped herself. Phoebe was striding away. And it had been going so well!

Phoebe crossed Fifth, turned a corner, and leaned, breathless, against an apartment building. She felt like throwing up. She felt dizzy. Oh, what was wrong? A tide carried her to sea and turned her about and about and she couldn't tell where she was, which was the sky, which the water. If she couldn't have her mother, she had to have Sahra. She had to have someone. Then she was fumbling in her shoulder bag, trying to find a quarter. There had to be a quarter here! Sahra had told her this would happen if she wasn't careful of the boundaries. Call me if it's really bad, I'll be here for you. If only she could find a quarter! Sahra would tell her that she hadn't made any of it up, that it was all true, of course it was. It was!

"Part of the hymen can always be left, Phoebe," Sahra said, but there was no relief on the young face in the chair across from her and so she went on. "It sounds like your mother really rocked you."

"I got the album but there's nothing in it," Phoebe said mechanically. "I brought you these." She handed over some color snapshots. "This is my father and me sailing in a mist. We're just sailing."

Sahra felt distanced by the deadness in Phoebe's voice.

"And here's one of New Hampshire where we went camping. There were two tents, one for them and one for me and my sister."

For the first time, Sahra felt she couldn't reach Phoebe at all.

"And here's one of the four of us sitting together back home. There's a blowup of this same picture over our fireplace."

This picture gave Sahra an idea, and she said, "Look at this, Phoebe. Your father has his arm around your sister's shoulder, see? And notice how his hand flops over your chest? And your mother has her hand on your thigh." Phoebe didn't look. She took the snapshot back, stacked them together, and ripped up all three.

This was depression building, and Sahra made a mental note about requesting drugs from Carl again. "You know I'm worried about you, Phoebe. Your mother sounds pretty desperate. Do you ever wonder if she might be covering up for something?"

Phoebe kept her head down. "I asked her about that baby-sitter." The voice was cold, angry. "It was Stephanie, Stephanie Murray. I remember her now. She had brown hair and a gap between her teeth."

"She didn't have blond hair? Brown eyes?"

"No."

"Really? Maybe we ought to go a little deeper, Phoebe. Relax a minute. Sit back. Take yourself to that cottage on the lake again, okay?"

37

Black garbage bags shone in the sun of the Upper West Side and dogs sniffed at the urine-based messages of their fellows as Harvey and Claire entered the central brownstone of the Warburg Clinic in response to Sahra Meehan's phone message: She'd meet with them after all, Phoebe, too. "I knew we'd touched base up there in the park!" Claire had said after Harvey reported the message. Now they followed a secretary into a room marked FAMILY ROOM and found themselves in a beige-carpeted area with a couch and two stuffed chairs, a desk and a metal filing cabinet. They sat in the indicated chairs and the secretary left them. A trim and tanned man their own age with a white shirt open at the neck walked past the door, directing inward an inquisitive look. They shared some breath mints and tried to calm themselves. When a pleasant-looking woman entered, they stood. Then they saw Phoebe. Their daughter did not approach them, did not shake their hands but headed directly for the couch. The brown-haired woman stopped briefly in front of Harvey, extended a cool, long-fingered hand, and again, in front of Claire.

"Sahra Meehan," she announced. Then she crossed the small space between chairs and couch and sat down on the couch next to Phoebe.

Phoebe was looking into her own lap, where Harvey noticed a piece of paper. Sahra Meehan faced them across the small space, her green eyes assessing them. "This is a fifty minute session," she explained. "We will begin with Phoebe. When she has finished what she wants to say, you two will have a turn." She leaned back into the couch and positioned herself slightly sideways to her companion. "Okay, Phoebe, why don't you start?"

Harvey watched his daughter's eyes slide down the paper. He watched them rise and come into the space between them to meet his. He smiled at her a little. How small she was, though older, grown. She was not a big woman. She didn't smile back.

"I want to make clear what has happened," she began in a voice that seemed dry, unstable. "And it begins long ago. It begins when I am three years old. My father, Harvey Fairchild"—here she lowered her gaze to her paper—"began then 'teaching me to be a wife,' as he put it. He began to lift me into his lap and he began to penetrate me, a very small girl—"

"I never did that, Phoebe, I never—"

"Mr. Fairchild!" Sahra Meehan's voice cut into the air. "Mr. Fairchild, you are stepping across your daughter's boundaries now. You must be quiet and you must listen until she is done."

"But I—"

"You are demonstrating a significant lack of control," the brown-haired woman said. "Go on, Phoebe. It's okay."

His daughter looked down at her sheet. "He began to lift me into his lap and he began to penetrate me, a very small girl. 'Momma!' I would cry out, but my mother, Claire Fairchild, didn't come to me. Harvey Fairchild did this to me in the garden behind our house. Each time he did this, I called out 'Momma!' " Here Phoebe stopped and looked across the space at Claire. "But you never came to my aid. You remained obedient to your husband, my father."

Harvey wished to take his wife's hand, to comfort her, but he didn't dare.

"You, Harvey Fairchild, penetrated me repeatedly by putting me into your lap or lifting me up." Phoebe raised her eyes from the paper but she did not manage to direct them to him this time; instead, he realized, she was seeing only to the distance halfway between them. "How could you do that to a three-year-old?" She looked so helpless, she needed so much help.

"I—"

"Mr. Fairchild!"

"She asked me a question."

"You'll have a turn later."

He stayed silent.

"You told me never to mention to my mother the things you did to me. But I did tell her. I told her that you were playing husband and wife with me. She took no action. She did nothing to stop you."

Sahra Meehan put her arm along the back of the couch, as if to shield his daughter, who continued, focusing now into the space between his chair and Claire's: "When I was eight years old, we went camping in New Hampshire, and here my mother was never more than a few feet away from me. But that didn't stop my father." She cleared her throat, twice. "At night you took me to the beach by the lake and you moved me from your lap to the ground. You lay me on the sand and you 'taught me to be a wife' on the sand. 'Momma!' I called out but even though my mother was right there inside the tent, she did not come to help me."

His daughter seemed hollow to him, empty, a form of not-Phoebe. He felt absolutely stunned. How could he have been angry with her? He wanted to reach her, to help her. He wanted her back, the real Phoebe. "Feeb," he said, across the space between them, and he meant to continue no matter what the woman beside her said. "Feeb, this is Dad. I love you, honey—"

"Mr. Fairchild—"

"This is crazy stuff. Come back home—"

"Mr. Fairchild—"

"Come home, we'll take care of you—"

"Mr. Fairchild! Phoebe will leave the room if you don't stop!"

He waited. He looked at his daughter. But she wasn't there. Only the automaton was there. He remembered then, the films they'd showed him before he was sent to Germany—the films of prisoners of war, the lectures about interrogation, about how to resist it.

Sahra Meehan stood, crossed to the desk, picked up two lined pads and two pencils. She approached the chairs and handed a pad and a pencil to Harvey and then to Claire. "If you have something to say, write it here. Do not interrupt again, or I will send Phoebe out of the room and end the session."

The therapist, she had done this. He took the paper and pencil. He looked at his daughter. Kid, he said, silently to her across the space, hang on. Hang on. I'm here. I'm coming to help you. Some way. I'll figure it out. Hang on.

"Very well, Phoebe," Sahra Meehan instructed. "Continue."

His poor little girl looked down at the paper. He understood more of it now. The therapist had done this. He must save her, his daughter. He would save her. First he had to keep still. He had to be more patient and more long-lasting than this determined woman at his daughter's side. He'd need his wits and all his heart to tell his daughter he would wait. That he would never abandon her.

"When we left New Hampshire, the abuse that you perpetrated against me did not end. We took a cottage every summer and you, Harvey Fairchild, taught me how to sail, and while we were in the sailboat you would moor at some spot out of sight of other people and there you would make me disrobe and—"

He blocked out the words. He couldn't waste a minute of this precious time allotted him for understanding what was going on. He kept half his gaze on his daughter and every time she glanced at him, he tried to tell her with his eyes that help was coming. He kept half his gaze on this Meehan person and managed to study her whenever Phoebe wasn't looking at him. This Meehan person sat back against the couch and her body carried a posture of—was it?—possession toward his daughter.

"And something else happened at the lake," Phoebe said, turning her eyes toward Claire. "You, Mother, began to fondle me, too."

"I did no such thing!"

"At the lake you used your fingers to—"

"Never! I never did!"

"I don't lie!" Phoebe shouted, suddenly afire, turning to each of them, finally looking into their faces. "You, Harvey, and you, Claire, appear to be so good, so blessed, but you are wicked!"

"We—"

"Mrs. Fairchild," Sahra Meehan said, leaning forward from the couch, "I must put you under the same stricture as I've put your husband. If you speak again, Phoebe will leave the room."

Oh, Claire, Harvey said silently. Oh, Claire, I'm sorry. He kept his gaze on Meehan, though, and followed her eyes to the clock on the desk: 4:25. Half the session was gone! "Continue," Sahra Meehan said to Phoebe. He picked up his pencil. He wrote *Fuck Her* on his pad and was going to tilt it into Claire's vision. Then he crossed it out instead. He covered it over with heavy pencil markings. It was probably what they'd call evidence.

"Maybe one day I will be able to forgive you," Phoebe was saying, her voice dryer, the voice of not-Phoebe. "You, Claire, were brought up when women were taught to do what men said. But you, Harvey, you strut about the world as if you owned it."

Hang on, kid. Hang on. He began to fill his pad with different words: *intimidation, control, brainwashing.* When he got his chance, he would tell these words to his daughter.

Phoebe read on and on now without interruption. She was looking at them more frequently. Meehan was looking at Phoebe with pride and pleasure. "I am not the only one who knows what my father did, what my mother did." Phoebe said, brighter now, her face flushed. "My sister knows, too."

Bess? Bess sucked into this latest thing too? Harvey took his eyes off the couch and looked at Claire. She was lost, a lost woman, worse than on Twentieth Street. He would have to save them both. He felt suddenly tired, exhausted, out of his depth. But he mustn't stop trying.

Phoebe continued. "Bess knows everything. I'm sure she does. She simply hasn't remembered yet. She's still repressing it."

Harvey checked the clock again: 4:45. He looked at Claire's pad, which was covered with writing in her small script. He couldn't read a word. He didn't want to look at Phoebe anymore. It was heartbreaking. He was beginning to wonder if she was crazy. This was mental illness, wasn't it? He wasn't so sure that he knew what to do. He was going to have to deal first with not cracking under it. A prisoner who loses hope, including the hope of dying with dignity, will crack. He must not crack.

Though he hated the sight of Sahra Meehan, he took up again the task of studying her as Phoebe's list continued. She'd crossed her legs, covered by loose black cloth, and leaned back; she was relaxed now. Late thirties? Early forties? She was wearing a ring on the fourth finger but he couldn't tell if it was a wedding band. A competitor, secure in what she'd won from them, smug, a sergeant of sorts. Some salaciousness? When their turn came, he'd let Claire go first. It was essential that Claire have some time. Then when time ran out, he'd shout his words and grab for Phoebe. No, that would only provide further evidence of his violence.

"Because of this horrendous treatment, I cannot remain a member of your family. The only way that we can ever hope to resume family life is if you will admit to these facts that I have presented before you." Phoebe came to a stop and looked up at Claire and Harvey.

They were to speak? Not to speak? Harvey shook his head in the negative. Claire said, whispering, "No."

Phoebe looked down at her paper again. Harvey thought his daughter's hands were shaking. "If you can't remember but are willing to try to remember through therapy"—Phoebe's voice rose toward a question—"with a sexual-abuse counselor approved by my therapist . . ." She didn't finish the sentence but looked at him and Claire and he thought there were tears in her eyes. They shook their heads no.

Hang on, kid.

Phoebe folded her paper and looked to the woman on the couch beside her. She mouthed some words that Harvey couldn't make out and folded the paper into smaller and smaller squares. Sahra Meehan stood up and said, "That concludes our session."

What? He looked at the clock: 4:50.

Claire's voice was anxious, shocked. "But you said we could—"

"Mrs. Fairchild, the point of this session has been for Phoebe to make clear to you her very real reasons for leaving her family. Since you and your husband remain in total denial and unwilling to even look into your own memories, we have nothing more to say to you. Phoebe? A final word?"

"Do not contact me." Phoebe stood up. "Not by phone. Not by mail. Not at my job. Not at my apartment. If you do so, I will take legal action against you."

"Now, Phoebe," Sahra Meehan said, "you may leave us. You know where to wait for me."

This frozen Phoebe looked briefly at Harvey, briefly at Claire, and walked out of the room. A secretary came and stood what must be guard, he realized, in the doorway. Then without a single good-bye, Sahra Meehan left the room. The secretary explained that she would walk Harvey and Claire to the elevator. The secretary stood with them by the elevator and then stepped into it with them. She walked them to the front door of the building and saw them out. On the hot mica-spattered sidewalk, Harvey put an arm around Claire.

"Our poor girl," Claire said, crying. "She's like the dead. She's lost her mind."

"It's brainwashing."

"Harvey," she whispered. "To be accused—"

He held her closer. "You didn't do it."

"Did you feel dirty all over? Like your mouth is full of—shit?"

"Yes." He saw a cab, hailed it. "Still do."

"I'm sorry." She turned to him. "I shouldn't have left. I shouldn't have left you alone in this."

He opened the cab door. "Will you come home, Claire?"

"I'm here." She stepped inside.

38

"She's four," Fitz said, handing the picture across the booth where they were eating rice and beans.

"Four," Phoebe repeated after him, She didn't want him to have a child. A child meant he'd really given himself to some other woman. Funny, he'd never seemed to be a father, not till now, not till this picture. He'd never seemed to be married. He was the guy you'd meet at the poetry fair on New Haven Green, a knight, knightly. Sir Fitz of the Knightly News. "She's beautiful."

"Some kid," he said, taking the picture back. "I don't show her to everyone."

Meaning what? She looked at him over the chipped vinyl: the blue eyes, the black hair, the five o'clock shadow, the agile body, like hers—but with a purity of eye she no longer dared seek in her own mirror. Her entire moral sense had somehow vanished. She didn't know how to put the world together anymore. There was evil in it, maybe even in herself. "Why me, then?"

"You look sort of motherly." He was smiling.

"Motherly?" She fingered the chipped vinyl. Maybe that's why he'd never taken her to the sunporch in outer Brooklyn where he lived for cheap. Last spring she actually invited him up to her loft for coffee after they'd interviewed a drummer playing down in the Village. The offer is a treasure, he'd replied, wrapping her scarf higher under her chin, but it's 2:00 A.M. and I'm not what you'd call available.

After that they'd begun eating supper together.

"Mother Phoebe," he repeated, handing her a piece of crusty bread. "Eat up, Mother Phoebe. We've got to keep up our strength. This is going to be a long haul."

Meaning what? She ate her bread. They always spoke in this elaborate indirection that suggested so much more. Oh, it was so complicated! His wife, his former wife—well, they were still married—had been born again. That's why she wouldn't divorce him and if he simply abandoned Jenna, he wouldn't be able to see his daughter much. "I'd love to meet her, your daughter."

"It's hard, Phoebe. I mean, it's hard on Deely. She took a shine to Kate, my last, well, girlfriend, and then it ended and Deely was all broken up. I can't do that to her again."

"I can wait," she told him, meaning forever. And tonight she'd made it through a test on some secret course of his: motherly.

"Maybe next spring," he said, as if that much time had already been pledged between them.

"*C'est nada,*" she gave back in two foreign languages at once, the first code to enter her mind.

Would she get herself together by spring? Here's a start, she assured herself. Fitz is real, he doesn't go in and out of focus as if he were an illusion. No, she mustn't think of Central Park. She mustn't think of her parents at the Warburg. The only way to keep a grip on reality was not to think of them at all.

The air conditioner gurgled behind the closed blinds in Sahra's office where Phoebe sat. For the last couple of weeks they'd rehashed the meeting with her parents, Sahra insisting that it had been necessary and fair and Phoebe uneasy and unable to make Sahra understand her reservations. Phoebe actually remembered very little of the meeting—except for how her mother's eyes had filled with tears, how the tears had glittered on her cheeks. That's how she'd known the meeting was wrong. But with Sahra you could only agree or keep silent. There was no point in arguing. Arguing made too much distance between them. So what to talk with Sahra about? Not her parents. Not Fitz! Half the things she told Sahra came back to her twisted. She wanted to keep Fitz the way he was, untwisted. But she had to get ready. If he ever left Jenna, she'd want to be with him without worrying about sex. Survivors had trouble with sex. It brought on pictures, the face of your abuser right in the middle. Sahra was waiting for her.

"How do you know when you're healed enough to . . . have a normal life?"

"When you take charge of yourself," Sahra said, and with that Phoebe felt the irony of something large but couldn't define it. Then Sahra was holding up a piece of paper, saying, "Your father wrote me. He informs me that he won't pay for any more therapy."

"Daddy—" She didn't know why but for a second she was relieved. "I mean, Harvey won't pay?"

"That's right. Harvey Fairchild is taking no responsibility for what he did."

No money, no therapy. Phoebe had a glimpse of the dark and empty world without Sahra: All that was left might be only illusion, shimmering and beckoning into a false brightness. "What will I do?"

"Start here. How would you go about taking charge of your own therapy? Do you have a plan? Some ideas?"

"Well, you could drop me back to one session a week."

"You're not ready for that."

Too sick? God, how long was this going to take? "How about my paying a little less? Do you have a sliding scale? Maybe you'd let me pay closer to the bottom?"

"Sixty dollars is my bottom."

"Insurance?" Phoebe saw by a slight change in the wide-cheeked face that she was getting closer. "Maybe the studio has health insurance?"

Sahra nodded.

"Funny, I don't even know if they do."

Sahra cocked her head, waiting.

"I'll ask."

Sahra smiled. "Good. If you're covered, I'll put you down for a 309.89 this time."

"What's that?"

"Post-traumatic stress disorder."

"Isn't that what soldiers got in Vietnam?"

"What happened to you was traumatic, too, Phoebe. The insurance companies let me claim sexual abuse against PTSD." Sahra tucked the letter away. "Last year I gave you a 311 depression, but this year—thanks to all the hard work you've been doing—you're definitely less depressed."

"Insurance only covers a month though, doesn't it?"

Sahra straightened up. "You can owe me. One day when you've really taken charge of your life, you'll be making plenty of money. You'll pay me then."

"Oh, I don't want to borrow. My father always—"

"Don't worry, this happens now and then. Some therapists don't keep clients who can't pay, but I keep mine. I won't abandon you. Don't worry. You can owe me. I don't have a problem with it."

"What's troubling the Great Mother?" Fitz asked after work as they walked to their separate subways.

"Bucks."

"Ah. I know Him."

"Big bucks."

"Rent?"

"Nope."

"Food?"

"Nope." She was asking him to play twenty questions and she wasn't sure why.

"Don't tell me drugs."

"Not drugs."

"Good. Overdue library books?"

She laughed. "Doctor. It's a doctor. A therapist. I'm in therapy."

"In therapy? I see. Exciting?"

"The usual stuff."

"Oh. You're a changeling, then, like the rest of us?"

She laughed again.

"Hey, you've grown awfully mum. What can it be? You seem okay to me. A little anxious maybe. A workaholic maybe. Perhaps just a tiny bit unsure of yourself on assignment. At times a perfectionist, but other than that? A winner!"

A winner! She liked the picture. "Just stuff."

"You can tell me." He nudged her with his shoulder. "I'm imperishable. I've heard it all. Take a risk. Tell old Fitz."

Now she'd gone too far and, like a tease, brought him in so close she'd have to disappoint him and she hadn't meant to do that. "It's just stuff."

He moved away. "Okay. Stuff. I accept it. It's your stuff."

She said nothing.

"Or is it more serious?" he said, suddenly stopping his steps and, by putting a hand on her shoulder, stopping her. He turned her toward him. "Like maybe, for instance, you're married and have a child but have fallen kind of totally in love with someone else?"

She watched his eyes fill up with light. She gave the smallest shrug. It could mean yes, it could mean no.

"Very well, I can lend you ten bucks." He leaned toward her and kissed her on the temple, right at the hairline, nothing too personal. "You can count on me for a pizza now and then, a couple of beers, or maybe even some Japanese noodles."

The whole thing sounded so much like a lifelong commitment that she made the mistake of mentioning Fitz to Sahra.

Sahra looked the slightest bit hurt. "You have a boyfriend you didn't tell me about?"

"Not a boyfriend, a friend. He's married, remember? He has a child. I told you about him last year. Nothing has happened."

"Married." Sahra looked better. "Another self-destructive choice?"

"Oh, I . . . I'm not choosing him."

"Have you told him about your father?"

"Oh, no. I wouldn't want to."

"Phoebe, any man you choose would have to be told about your father. A survivor always needs special support and special understanding."

"I see." Somehow in this chair, in this office, she'd become a chameleon engaged in intricate mental camouflage to protect herself from Sahra.

"There are materials I can give you for him to read."

"Not Fitz! He'd hate it! His wife has a bumper sticker that says, GOD SAID IT. I BELIEVE IT. AND THAT'S THE END OF IT."

"What does that have to do with you?"

"Oh. Well, you see . . . oh, I'm not sure. Besides, we're just friends."

"Married, with a child. That child needs a father, Phoebe."

"Fitz pays for them. He hardly has a penny to live on." She'd never tell Fitz about her father, she promised herself that, no matter what Sahra said. In fact, maybe it would be better if she kept all the good things, all the things that she was sure of inside herself, secret, safe away from Sahra. Inside, that's where she would rebuild the world. Inside, she'd be real.

Back at the studio, Roseanne Arnold was telling Oprah that her mother had abused her when she was six months old. Phoebe could feel Fitz standing behind her in the editing room, feel it on the nape of her neck. Could he sense her involvement?

Oprah: How can women know if they've been abused?

Roseanne: There are only two answers to that question, One is "yes" and the other is "I don't know."

"Bullshit!" Fitz snorted. "Will you listen to that!"

He must never know!

That night, at the base of her five flights, Phoebe pulled an envelope out of her mailbox. She ripped it open and unfolded a sheet of paper and there he was—the man in the rosebushes. It took her breath away. Who but she could know what he looked like? Bess's handwriting in the margin: *Is this the guy? The Joy of Sex, 1972.*

Bess!

Furious, she crumpled the paper. Could Bess see into her mind? Why didn't Bess mind her own business! Then she smoothed it out and held it this way and that in the inadequate lighting on the stairs. Maybe it wasn't the same man. No, maybe not. It just looked a lot like him, that's all. People were intruding on her! They were getting into her head! They had no right to do that!

She started up the steep stairs. The man from the fourth floor was coming down, a big man, the one who'd shouted at her Christmas morning when her tub leaked. She was afraid to look at him. Maybe his face would change and he'd look just like the man in the Xerox, too.

Upstairs she laid the Xerox in her empty cookie tin and burned it. Whether this was the man in the rosebushes or not, she never wanted to think about him again. She had to get away from him. So she could be ready.

The Xerox burned quickly to ashes. See, Sahra? I took charge of that. But there was an emptiness in the place where Sahra usually was. She could just feel it. She was losing Sahra somehow. She mustn't lose Sahra now! Not now!

In Bess's envelope there was a postcard, too, another one of those cards from her mother. She carried it gingerly, message-side down, and stuck it with the others in the paper bag high up on top of the refrigerator. Even to think about her parents was too dangerous; she must become herself first, or it would destroy her.

39

The catalog they'd ordered from the Warburg School of Social Work featured a number of courses on recognizing and treating sexual abuse and incest. It described semester-long work in hypnosis, in recognizing and understanding such disorders as those of post-traumatic stress and multiple personality. It offered courses on liberating the child within. Harvey and Claire studied it over peanut chicken on their patio—unsure of how to evaluate this curriculum.

Harvey pulled a flyer from the back cover. "Continuing Education Workshops," he said. "The next one is 'Childhood Sexual Abuse: A Review.' "

Claire pulled at the sleeve of her sweater and didn't reply. It was one of those evenings when it's crisp and bright and things start up again—school, life, one's resurrection. Claire was laboring at hers, theirs, but she'd been devastated by the August meeting with Phoebe. Her daughter had accused her. She was finally angry. Except it was herself she was angry at. How could she have let her daughter come between her and her husband?

Harvey had been doing his best to bolster Claire, and the registration form on the flyer gave him an idea. "Why don't you go and sit in? It's chaired by Dr. Carl Mundiger."

Claire let go of her sweater. "He's the one Sahra Meehan wanted us to see."

He'd thought that name was familiar. He handed her the flyer. There were boxes to check: graduate, student, prospective student, other.

"You think we could pass as social workers?" she said.

"You could. They'd spot me in a minute. I'm a guy, therefore an abuser."

"A perpetrator, you're a perpetrator," she said, with a small, sarcastic laugh. "We're perpetrators."

Relieved to hear her laugh, he said, "Let's all join hands and perpetrate."

She did him one better. "I perpetrate, you perpetrate, he, she, or it perpetrates."

"We perpetrate, you perpetrate, they perpetrate," they said together as the lights went on along the street. They stood to clear the dishes and Harvey added, "Somebody in there actually perpetrates. You find out who."

Later they walked up the three flights of stairs together. To resume making love had meant to put an end somehow to the old life with two daughters, the good life, and to move forward into a place where their love was so mixed with pain that practicing it did not quite provide the old distraction. The new life with only one daughter waited to receive them afterward.

The Warburg School of Social Work occupied a substantial building in Lower Manhattan and outside it a woman holding a petition asked Claire to add her name to those of other social workers asking for reform of the Mondale Act.

"It needs reform," the petitioner began. "They really ought not to be able to prosecute us for not reporting suspected abuse."

"I can't, I'm late," Claire said, pleased to have passed as a social worker and hesitant to reveal her ignorance of the law in question. Delayed by traffic, she hurried upstairs and entered a crowded lecture hall where a man's voice over a microphone rose and fell in the tones one uses to a captive audience. Halfway down the aisle, she squeezed past knees into an empty seat. The tanned, trim man at the podium looked slightly familiar and wore a jacket that hung flawlessly from his shoulders and a turtleneck on which swung a gold ankh on a chain.

"To conclude, then," he was saying, "the five cardinal rules." He held up fingers on which to tick off points. "One, always believe your client, even when she herself wavers. In the largest sense, it doesn't matter if her story is true or not. What matters is that the narrative you build together be meaningful to her."

What? Claire looked to the women and the scattering of men around her; they were busily taking notes. The truth didn't matter?

"Two, always be loving and caring—because your client's parents were not."

Not a rustle of objection!

"Three, never show compassion for the perpetrator because your client already feels terribly guilty and will be apt to put her perpetrator's needs before her own." Claire lowered her coat around her shoulders. "Four, always keep the whole family in mind because where there's an offending father, there's usually going to be a passive mother or an aggressive mother or a frigid mother." Claire took out her pen and notepad. "Five, always try to feel the pain with your client. This is a dirty business. Take care of yourselves." Claire looked up at Dr. Mundiger, who had dropped his hand and was using it to cradle the microphone.

"Now, one last comment on this broadening field. You don't have to find the sexual act itself in your client's history. Abuse is more subtle than that. Think of the father who simply shows more interest—perhaps intellectually, perhaps through hobbies—in his daughter than in his wife. We are coming to see that this is emotional incest. It may be more terrible than rape itself because the daughter can never really be sure that anything happened."

It didn't, Claire wrote.

"Be advised, though, that the emotionally incested child will manifest the same signs and symptoms I mentioned before." He produced a list of symptoms so generalized—depression, anxiety, trouble at work, trouble in relationships—that Claire figured she'd experienced almost all of them at one time or another, and so, she guessed, had everybody else in the room.

"Now, with these pointers under our belts, I turn the podium over to our first panelist, the well-known clinical psychologist Dr. Donna Phillips, who will review for us the connection between sexual abuse and multiple personality disorder."

Applause for Dr. Mundiger erupted as an energetic woman came to the podium, blew into the microphone, and smiled at the crowd. "Hi, guys," she said in a deep voice, then repeated herself in a small, shadowy voice: "Hi, guys." Everybody laughed. "Seriously," she said, though she was still at the end of a small laugh herself, "I'm Donna Phillips and I want to talk about how we protect ourselves when we are scared out of our gourds. You all know that repression is what we do when we are shocked and appalled at finding the daddy we trusted over the Product 19 suddenly forcing us into cunnilingus. We can't fight back because Daddy's a heck of a lot bigger than we are. So we deny that it's happening and we tune ourselves out, wa-ay out. Yes," she nodded at the rapt group. "This is the out-of-body experience I'm talking about. . . ."

As Dr. Phillips spoke, Claire looked about the room at the therapists and students. Most of the women were younger than herself. The men, however, seemed her age or older.

The audience laughed at a joke of Dr. Phillips's and she continued: "Now, this kind of depersonalization is a much simpler event than what I specialize in—which is mega-splitting or the forming of new selves called alternates or alters. What happens in MPD, or multiple personality disorder, is that the person in extreme stress creates an alter self into which she may escape. That way she doesn't have to endure the terror or the abuse because it's happening to 'someone else.' If you saw *Sybil,* you know what I mean."

The woman to Claire's left was drawing in her notebook a head with many smaller heads emerging out of it.

"Oh, of note, MPD has been an acceptable category in the *Diagnostic and Statistical Manual of Mental Disorders* since 1980, and it's in today's revision, *DSM-III-R.* This means, new people, that you can make claims on it—you can even bill sexual abuse against it and not even John Hancock himself will turn you down. In conclusion, watch Geraldo next Friday, yours truly will be on."

Amidst energetic applause, Dr. Phillips turned the microphone over to a brown-haired woman who made Claire pull her coat close around her shoulders.

"I'm Sahra Meehan," the familiar voice began, though it was less assured than Claire remembered. ". . . a staff therapist here at the Warburg, and as Dr. Mundiger told you, I'm pinch-hitting today for Dr. Burnett, who was going to run down some techniques effective at getting out repressed memories." She seemed nervous here, as she had not in the August meeting. "Let's start with relaxation and hypnosis." She stopped, took a sip of water, cleared her throat. "You can pick up the *Comprehensive Textbook of Psychiatry* any day and read that hypnosis does not increase accuracy of recall. The establishment tells us that hypnosis creates 'only' "—here she raised her fingers to make quotation marks—" 'a memory filled with vivid details and about which the client feels a great conviction.' " She moved an inch or two back from the microphone and began to hit a better stride. " 'Only'?" She smiled and went on. "We know better, don't we? We've *seen* the reliving of actual events on our clients' faces. No further evidence is called for when a client sobs and calls out, 'Now he's on top of me, now he's putting it in me. . . .'"

"You got it!" a woman chorused from the back of the room.

"Okay." The speaker quieted the audience with a new confidence. "To do hypnosis you don't need to dangle a gold watch. All I use is relaxation or sometimes a countdown. And trust. As Dr. Mundiger said, everything rests on the trust built up between therapist and client. I try hypnosis only after months of gaining that trust. For those who are new to this tool, I suggest choosing the hypnosis breakout after lunch. I will demonstrate there."

Claire missed the voice of science, its observation, identification, and explanation.

"Regression comes next. That's Dr. Burnett's specialty and I must admit I've never used it. She asks her clients to draw something with their left hands. The writing will be childish and producing it seems to trigger the client's memory and put her in touch with her early years. Dr. Burnett says it is truly amazing to watch a grown woman draw a stick figure and say in a child's voice, 'Here is my daddy and now here he is in my bed.' "

How had Phoebe been taken in by this? Her daughter had always been a storyteller. Phoebe tried everything on, experimented with characters and outcome, understood it from within, and cast it off. Only this time she'd gotten caught inside wolf's clothing.

"Dream work," Sahra Meehan was saying. "Survivors report dreams in which they're being held down, unable to move. A larger force constrains them. Who is it? Psychologists today are asking to see the face of the person who is holding the dreamer immobile. At first the client may say she doesn't see any face. That's when the good therapist says, 'Fill it in.' Weeks or months later, the client sees that face and knows exactly who her perpetrator is."

"Hear! Hear!" a man in front of Claire called out.

"Thank you." A blush darkened Sahra Meehan's face. "Which brings us to body work and massage therapy. We don't forget anything that happens to us. Any pain in the body can be a stored memory of violence or rape. A stomachache, a stiff joint, choking, nausea, dizziness . . ."

Tears gathered under Claire's eyelids: This gibberish is what had destroyed her family.

Sahra Meehan grew very serious, grasping the lectern with both hands. "I had a friend in grade school who tried to tell the world what her father had done to her and nobody believed it. Today you and I would have known how to help her. So I close by emphasizing the importance of Dr. Mundiger's first rule: Believe your client." Claire watched as she let go of the lectern and shut her eyes to recite into the microphone. "Only the other day a client of mine asked after more than a year of horrendous memories, 'But what if none of this is true?' " Sahra Meehan altered her intonation in imitation of her client and Claire heard a familiar diction. " 'What if I made this all up, Sahra, the whole thing? Couldn't I have made this all up?' "

It was Phoebe! Was it Phoebe?

" 'You didn't make this up,' I told her. 'You are telling the truth.' Thank you."

Phoebe wavered, Phoebe doubted! Claire heard nothing of the substantial applause or of the next few speakers but when an elegantly suited insurance agent mentioned money, she came to attention to take notes for Harvey.

He told them what categories in that manual they kept talking about could be used for billing but Claire had trouble understanding the terms.

Then he said—not to be whimsical, he pointed out—that there were new things coming down the pike. If any of the abuse took place in an insured home, a therapist might try to bill the home insurance. Or if a client remembered any incidents in the family car, it might be worth a shot to bill car insurance. You never know.

Claire was jotting this down when the meeting was opened to questions. After a few minutes a woman wearing a dowdy collection of mismatched browns took the proffered microphone. She introduced herself as Dr. Elisabeth Walters of Columbia University. "You may know from my work that I don't stand with the feminists on Sigmund Freud. They suggest that he invented the Oedipal and Electra fantasies to cover up real incest on the part of real fathers, including a friend of his. I believe something else. I believe that Dr. Freud may have suggested incest to his first eighteen female patients—some of whom probably belonged to the very constant percentage of the human family we call suggestible. There is, I remind you, an equal complement of skeptics among us at the other end of the spectrum. It includes me. Dr. Freud asked these eighteen young women repeatedly if someone—their fathers perhaps?—had touched them when they were young. Nobody will ever know for sure how many of them who immediately or eventually claimed incest actually experienced it. I thought of this today, listening to some rather surprising things. Ladies and gentlemen, it's time not for anecdote but for science. First, about sleep paralysis. Since Michel Janet cut into the pons of a sleeping cat that promptly got up and began to act out its dreams, we've come to understand that not only cats but humans, as well, are naturally paralyzed during REM sleep. It's for our own safety. Now, if we wake up out of sync with our body-brain systems, we may experience a few seconds where we're still paralyzed, when we can't move. In medieval times, we took this paralyzing force to be satanic creatures sitting on our chests demanding sexual favors. We called them succubus and incubus. Today, you are calling them perpetrators. Let's give these sensations their true name. It's sleep paralysis."

The women to Claire's right began to whisper to each other.

"Now, as for the idea of repression, it was Sigmund Freud who developed it. He needed to explain why his eighteen patients hadn't immediately remembered their incest. He abandoned his theory of repression, though, when he decided that no real incest had taken place. Repression as he and you describe it has never been proved. Prisoners didn't repress the concentration camps. Soldiers who blew up babies in Vietnam are still trying to forget them and cannot. Memory does not lie intact in the brain, waiting to be awakened. For this, see the work of Frederic Bartlett or that of David Holmes, in which he concludes that memory is in part an imaginative reconstruction."

The whispering around Claire increased.

"Abuse exists. Of course it does. How best to treat it? Not by rehearsing or going over and over it. That increases and extends memory of it, which is why I advocate against not reliving abuse. Move on. Build a new life."

Claire made out the whispered words *backlash* and *old* from her neighbors.

"But sometimes there is no abuse," Dr. Walters continued, speeding up as the unrest in the room became more evident. "If so, how do we 'remember' something that never happened? The same way that some of Freud's patients may have, that is, *after* and *because of* interrogation. If we're told by an authority figure that something happened and that we can dig down and remember it, we try. And when we try, things do occur to us because we humans all possess a storytelling brain. When asked for something we don't remember, we tend to fill in the blanks with whatever is waiting around in our storage DNA. We use details from other people's lives, plots from television, scenes from books. A flood of images and information gets soaked up by us all. And there's your narrative."

The unrest could not be ignored.

"Ladies and gentlemen"—Dr. Walters raised her voice—"a faulty narrative is about as useful as faulty directions to a traveler lost along the upper Amazon." She sat down.

At the podium Dr. Mundiger smiled. "Thank you, Dr. Walters, we all appreciate your *long* dedication to our field," he said, gazing in collusion at the audience, "and your *decades* of work within it. Our field, however, is changing. New times have come. The American Psychological Association embraces sexual-abuse theory. It is taught in half the graduate schools today. A *new* group of healers is emerging. By the way, let's have a show of hands. No, no, stand up, will you? If you specialize, or intend to specialize in sexual abuse, please stand."

Half the crowd rose.

"Good, good. You may be seated. Our tool is not the dry debate of laboratory science but the understanding heart. Each and every one of us feels in our hearts the same fine motivation that Sahra Meehan attested to at the close of her inspiring talk. We'll break now for lunch. Students, let me suggest that you not be tempted to sign the petition being paraded out front. The Mondale Act is our friend. It needs no reform."

"We've been had," Claire told Harvey when he picked her up in the car.

They weren't alone. On the Sunday before Thanksgiving they read and reread a piece in *The Philadelphia Inquirer* about a daughter who'd accused her father of abuse but not till after some visits to a therapist. Hers was the same story. There it was, in print. This was happening in several cities, the columnist pointed out, quoting an expert who referred to the phenomenon of false memory recall as part of a growing sexual-abuse industry. Yes, there was real and deplorable abuse rightly publicized in recent years, but there were also false allegations inspired by therapists. The great weight holding down Claire's sky began to lift.

Harvey was exultant. "We've got to get this to Phoebe!"

Claire wasn't so sure. It would have shamed her too much if her own parents had known about or confronted her about her first pregnancy. Phoebe already had Bess at her heels with a clip from *Time*. They mustn't rub Phoebe's nose in it.

"Don't forget that clip about Clarence Thomas and Anita Hill."

"I remember. People's memories are affected if they're questioned a lot."

"The point is, Phoebe hasn't returned Bess's calls since Bess sent her that clip. We mustn't do something that would make it impossible for Phoebe to come home. Phoebe's got to figure this out for herself."

40

Two shapes emerged from the Chambers Street subway station and the young woman spoke: "A person need not make any kind of intimate commitment simply to visit inside another person's apartment. I mean people have been visiting each other for centuries. A person could enter another person's living space without any implications at all except that maybe . . . they'd like a cup of coffee that didn't cost three dollars. A person—"

"A person accepts," Fitz said. "As winter comes on, a person looks for shelter."

"A person likes to feel that a person's private space can be made available to a friend. I mean a friend whom one trusts implicitly and totally and knows has one's best interests at heart."

"A person will not lay a hand on another person."

"Deal," she said, opening the huge door of her loft building. He started up the stairs with energy but slowed by the third level.

"This is a blasted tower! Who are you hiding from?"

"Persons, but present persons excluded." Lately one of those persons seemed to be herself but she couldn't think about that now. It would ruin everything. On the fifth level, she opened her own door. The phragmites in the green vase looked a little tired but it was pleasant to see around them and through the glass door into the softly lighted studio where she led the way.

"Nice place," he said, sitting in one of the chairs. "A mysterious person lives here."

She switched on another light. "Personally, I don't entertain much. It's kind of cool these winter evenings, but it warms up in the morning. Oh, I mean—"

"This is just a test," he replied. "I'm staying here twenty minutes and if I don't touch you and you don't touch me, we're safe."

She sat heavily on the other chair. They put their hands on the table, very close but not touching. They put their cheeks side by side, very close but not touching. He laid his hand about a quarter of an inch from the side of her face, from her hair. She did the same to his dark cheek, dark hair. They looked into each other's eyes, unmoving.

"Time's up," he said, and kissed her, slowly. Then he stood up, and moved backward out of the studio through the kitchen, and she followed. At the door they kissed again, one on each side of the threshold, briefly, and then he was walking down the stairs. Sometimes a person meets a person coming through the rye.

Not knowing,
I retreat to Costa Rica.
Your friend, James
P.S. Only temporary

Bess could laugh at things again, even James. He hadn't found any better answers than she. It was so good to be in Oregon. Half a dozen refugees like herself worked at the store, one of them Nehemiah, whose big secret was that he looked white but had a black father. She'd told him about Phoebe. You can't make friends if you've got a big secret like that and don't tell it. Nobody at the house knew though. They were all staying here for the holidays and were starting the Christmas break with a video marathon. Bess started down the basement stairs with a kettle of popcorn, calling out "Whose is first?"

"Mine," the robust Tanya replied, handing a cassette to a tall man with his blond hair in a ponytail. "It's *Sybil!*"

Mike tucked Tanya's cassette into the slot. "Yuck, maybe I'll sleep this one out."

"No remarks!" Doreen reminded him of the ground rules and settled down with a quilt.

Bess had never seen *Sybil.* She arranged some pillows on the floor.

"Girl stuff," Neil said, stretching out, short and muscular, on adjoining pillows. He always smelled faintly of Xerox machines. "Give me *Blade Runner* any night."

She liked Neil but only as a housemate. "I thought you were bringing *Terminator* 2 again."

"Taking a break."

"Ta dum!" Mike made announcer noises in the dim room. "This is 1976—where were you?"

"Fourth grade!"

"Evanston!"

"This is your Sally Field as the young thing and your Joanne Woodward as the psychiatrist. Let the good times roll."

A tinkly piano tune takes them across the continent to Central Park, where a young teacher wearing glasses concludes an outdoor art class. In a nearby playground a small child is being pushed by a large gray-haired woman on a swing that needs oiling. The creaking of metal strikes the teacher's ear and she remembers something: On the screen of her own memory appears the interior of a barn in which a large gray-haired woman hoists something on a rope.

"Here she comes—Mama!"

"I hardly saw her!"

"Only a glimpse for now!"

In Central Park the teacher shepherds her kids back to school past the creaking swing and again the interior of a barn appears: what is being winched up is a small girl whose legs dangle in their Mary Janes.

"Darling Mom."

"Shhh!"

The teacher is in a hospital where a kindly, intelligent woman in a white coat questions her. The teacher has apparently blacked out and now sees in tunnel vision and talks in a childish voice.

Bess thought of Phoebe, who after no reply about the *Joy of Sex* man had made so much noise after the *Time* clip, shouting: *Never send me anything like that again!*

The teacher becomes herself, resumes her own voice, and doesn't remember the blackout. What's happening? Dr. Wilbur has an idea. It's multiple personalities. She's a psychiatrist; she'll treat the teacher.

Doreen called out, "My mother had those same bell-bottoms!"

"My dad knew about this case," Neil whispered to Bess. "He's an analyst, you know."

In their sessions the psychiatrist manages to evoke different personas from the teacher. The youngest, Peggy, recalls a scene in which an Amazonian-sized mother and an ineffective father tricked her into visiting a house where she was snatched upstairs to a private surgery and given ether for a tonsillectomy. The teenager, Victoria, speaks French and paints. The adolescent, Vanessa, plays the piano. And Marsha yearns for death.

Doreen reached for popcorn. "Good popcorn, Bess. I mean Besses. How many of you are there?"

"I contain multitudes." She gave what she could of Walt Whitman.

"This psychiatrist has all the time in the world," Neil pointed out. "Notice that?"

Woven into the action are references to the color purple and to hands doing cruel things and to the color green, green walls.

Green walls?

Frequently a bare bulb glows too brightly under a reflecting shade.

A hanging lamp?

Nora's stories? Green kitchen, hanging lamp?

On the screen appears Richard, a neighbor of the teacher's on 126th Street. He plays street guitar at night in front of Broadway theaters as the shows let out. Will Sybil go along tonight? She's afraid. Anything promising sexuality is a problem. But as Vanessa—who's not afraid of boys—she accepts and joins him happily until she is distracted by a middle-aged, gray-haired couple coming out of the theater. Then she's tiny again and recoiling as her father tries to fasten her boots with something ominous, a buttonhook.

"Ta dum!" Mike intoned. "The buttonhook!"

Bess whispered, "Neil, what's that hand on my leg?"

"It ees not mine. It ees my alter's, Monsieur Ugo's."

"Shhh!"

In the psychiatrist's unbelievably magnificent apartment, Vanessa sits at a piano and riffles through some Mozart.

"That's me," Doreen said. "I can only play when I'm high."

The doctor hypnotizes her patient: Lie down, shut your eyes, count to five, you're home. On the screen of memory appears the huge and apparently wacky gray-haired mother in full. She is erratic, unpredictable, singing snatches of song willy-nilly. She is malevolent, tripping her daughter on a stairway, slamming a swinging door in her face, hitting her, kicking her, stomping on her crayons. And for a finale, mother takes daughter to a barn and winches her up to God on the second floor. Then mother climbs a ladder, takes the child from the hook, and shuts her into a coffinlike wheat bin to suffocate.

Sybil on 126th Street invites Richard for Christmas dinner. Richard has wisely divined that with Sybil love must be preceded by more than the usual amount of trust. They have gone to bed, tenderly, innocently. Still, they're in bed.

"This was before AIDS."

"It's 1977, you're right."

"Let's hear it for the good old days."

Even without sex, the young woman has a nightmare that turns her into a desperate sleepwalker climbing up a bookcase. Richard tries to help her but she wakes, panics, and runs up to the roof of the building. He finds a pay phone, acquires Dr. Wilbur's number from 411, and urges her to leave her Christmas party. She arrives by cab in her party dress and fur coat.

"Oh sure, you'd better believe she'd get a cabbie to take her to Harlem."

The teacher, as Marsha, stands on the roof about to jump. The young man tackles her, the psychiatrist arrives with hypodermic. All is well, except this kind of girlfriend is more than Richard had bargained for.

"Get out of there, man," Neil advised him. "She's bad news."

Onscreen, our hero splits.

Neil whispered to Bess, "Let me know if I snore."

The psychiatrist leaves to give a lecture in Chicago but detours to Willow Corners, Wisconsin, where she interviews the local doctor. He is the very man who did the little girl's tonsillectomy long ago. Now he's old. The little girl was brought to him often: a torn ligament, a broken clavicle, a burnt palm, a bean stuck up her nose. And once with a bladder infection. Examining her that time, he'd found her vagina scarred, as if by some metal instrument. He doubted she'd ever bear children.

The psychiatrist drives to the child's old house, now conveniently up for sale. She enters the kitchen. It's all green in there. A lamp hangs over the kitchen table: It is Nora's kitchen.

Bess squinted to get the details.

"Okay, okay," Tanya called from the couch. "Get ready. I'll tell you where to shut your eyes."

The psychiatrist is driving again, only this time the young teacher is also in the car. They drive to a pretty field. The psychiatrist has packed a picnic lunch and some new paints for her patient and she's brought along some crocheting for herself. Now she rolls out a blanket, spreads out the food, sits against a tree, and takes up her crocheting. She is the good mother. She has time. When the young teacher delves deeper into herself to remember the last horror, they can eat lunch.

"Watch out! Watch out!" Tanya's voice sounded excited, anxious.

Neil was snoring, or else faking it.

The young teacher is a small child. She is in the green kitchen. She's lying on the cold metal kitchen table, just as Nora was made to lie. She is tied to something, as was Nora. The huge crazy mother is standing nearby at the sink filling an enema bag with very cold water, as did Nora's. She is opening a drawer, eyeing a knife, a buttonhook. Nora's mother used a spoon. Then she is winching something up over the hanging lamp.

"Don't look at the legs! This is the worst part!"

Bess narrowed her eyes, held her breath.

What's being winched up are the little girl's spread legs tied to a broom handle. A broom handle! Nora's mother had used a curtain rod. Bess understood the legs now, though she hadn't quite gotten it when Nora had described it. The spread legs are pointing up under the hanging lamp. The huge mother returns to the sink to the enema bag and the buttonhook.

"Don't look! Don't look!"

Then the kitchen is gone. On the screen there's more happening by a piano but none of it is Nora's tale. Then it's over. The psychiatrist serves up the picnic lunch. After eleven years of therapy, Sybil goes on to graduate school and becomes an art teacher.

Bess thought of Mrs. Mercer at her glass-topped table, waiting to provide chance kindnesses to her daughter's friends. Surely that little woman with the dyed hair had never done any of these things to her daughter.

"Sybil wasn't even a multiple," Neil said, stirring on his pillows. "Her mother was schizy but Sybil herself was probably just a plain hysteric, and very suggestible. My father said Sybil was only producing the other personalities because Dr. Wilbur wanted her to. She wanted a multiple and so did the writer and so did the publisher. They were shooting for a best-seller, an update of *The Three Faces of Eve.*"

Bess nodded, her thoughts on Nora. She had to tell somebody about this. Not her parents—her mother kept telling her not to rub Phoebe's nose in the facts and though she'd love to talk to her father, she felt funny because of what she'd done in Minneapolis. Not Phoebe. Phoebe was freezing her out. Who?

41

Christmas was for being together but Fitz was over in New Jersey hanging Deely's stocking and she was alone with the paper bag full of cards and letters from the top of the refrigerator. Why aren't you going to your parents', he'd asked. They're flying to Florida—Bess had told her that on a Christmas card.

Did she dare open the bag? A terrible unease had been growing and growing inside of her. She felt like the pressure cooker at home that had gone wild and splattered blood-red beets all over the kitchen. The bad things were all she could remember of home now, and she wanted the good things back. Maybe she'd find some in the paper bag. She emptied it suddenly and spread the cards and letters out. Maybe she'd find bad things. Did she dare?

"Dear Phoebe, The snow is inches deep and I remember how you and Bess used to come in from the garden with your striped mittens dangling from those funny strings that go through the sleeves. 'Hello superfriend,' you said. 'Have you got some supersoup?' "

"Dear Phoebe, Today I thought of that hippie cook you introduced us to when you were waiting tables at the Cape, the one with the tattoo. He was so very fond of you. Remember how he gave you his checkered shirt as we drove off? He suddenly stripped it off and stuffed it through the window? We're so very fond of you, too, Phoebe."

"Dear Phoebe, Here I am on North 20th living in the world as it is, full of sirens and hopelessness and fear. I have hope, though, and a great pleasure: I'll be meeting you this Sunday in New York."

"Dear Phoebe, The leaves are all yellow and red and when I was a child we would rake them into huge piles in our yard in Cedar Rapids and burn them. My father would stand with the rake and my mother would make cocoa—the real kind, with shaved chocolate and sugar and milk. We love you and if you feel like coming down at Christmas, I'll make cocoa."

She remembered that hot chocolate—darker shavings on the brown milk in a white cup in the kitchen at home with Haydn in the air. She remembered the kitchen with the rockers and the hanging plants. She remembered the back windows where she'd set the colored glass bottles and where they'd hung the cut-out snowflakes at Christmas. She read more cards. She read letters. And then she put her head down on the round table. Mom! she called out silently. Are you still there? What's real, anyway? She knew she was making it up but nonetheless she felt her mother from those days standing beside her ironing, quiet and comforting, saying, Everything will be all right. You'll work it out.

Sahra ended the session with a surprise. "Do you know what your sister did?"

"No. What?"

"She sent Nora Mercer a videocassette."

"Which one?"

"*Sybil*"

"I never saw it."

"It's about a multiple. Sybil's mother abused her."

"Bess does that. I told you! She sends stuff. I told you how mad it made me!"

"Yes you did. Donna Phillips felt she should share with me how much your sister has upset Nora. She's sent her back into an emergency phase."

"That's awful."

"Dr. Phillips has advised Nora to stop seeing you."

"Me? I don't see Nora anyway."

"Your sister is really a very aggressive person. I don't want you back in the emergency phase. Do you see how hostile she is?"

"I don't know if she's that bad. She gets carried away. She always thinks she's onto the truth about something."

"But she isn't letting Nora have her truth! Bess is trying to take Nora's truth away."

Something about that made Phoebe want to laugh and then the total impossibility of getting what she was laughing at across to Sahra rendered her silent. Bess would have understood.

"Tell you what," Fitz said. "It's getting mighty cold on the porches of Brooklyn. How's this? MWM seeks temporary home with SWF and could pay half her rent, usual conditions apply, separate beds."

"Hey, okay. Great news." She knew he meant I'm ready when you're ready, and she wasn't ready, though getting closer. "I owe my therapist a thousand bucks or something. This'll help."

They lugged his futon up the stairs and put it under the skylight. They were both businesslike about things. He couldn't believe there was no shower. She couldn't believe that all his possessions fit into a Macy's bag. She went to bed first, lying alone in the sleeping alcove, which felt more than ever like a closet, only now she was trapped in it. This was her apartment, after all! The next night they moved her futon out against the other wall of the studio and put all their clothes into the alcove, which once again became a closet. She lay on her futon and discovered how cold it was under the skylight.

"This is a whole lot warmer than Brooklyn," Fitz said, standing by his futon in a funny way.

"Dream on. We're at the North Pole. What are you doing?"

"Yoga. I'm standing like a mountain, Tadasana!" Then he lay flat on his futon. "This is Savasana, the corpse position. I tell Deely that if she can't sleep, she can lie like this in bed and think of me. I'll be standing like a mountain thinking of her."

And that was it. They said good night.

In the morning at her stove she caught a glimpse of him in the bathroom mirror, shaving. "That's the way my dad shaves!" she said suddenly. "That upward stroke."

"What's he like?"

"Oh, he's . . . he's neat." She turned away from him, running water for the teapot.

"You never talk about him."

"I don't?"

"He shaves like me, that's the first thing you've said. It's enough, though. Your father shaves like me. This is not an inquisition."

He came out of the bathroom and they made toast.

"My mom had these lamb slippers," she went on, grateful for the things she'd found in the letters. "She made cinnamon rolls that came apart in segments like an orange. She's a very thoughtful person, and fair. My dad is more like a kid. He made pancakes. He poured the batter like this, from way up high. He liked to pour it into the shapes of animals."

"Mine did that!" Fitz looked pleased. "From high up. He did best with snakes."

"Mine considered snakes a cop-out!"

Fitz laughed, then looked immediately sadder. "My mother tried to make them that way, too, after I told her about Dad's. I got home from visiting my pop in Manhattan and I bragged about his pancakes and she got right to work on her own pancakes. I thought of them as Competitive Pancakes. She didn't want him gaining any points on her. I hate divorce."

Phoebe could see her father, raising the pitcher higher and higher, finishing off the wings of a perfect bird. And her mother, heating milk on the stove to make the coffee French.

"Why are we doing this?" Fitz asked as they lay on their separate futons. "I'm not objecting, simply bringing it up for discussion."

"This is the modern way. Think of AIDS."

"Is that your secret, Phoebe? Have you got AIDS?"

"No! For God's sake! I would have told you."

"Okay. Okay. Relax. Have you got herpes?"

"For God's sake, you're the one who's resisting!"

"It's both of us. But I'm married."

"Yeah. You are."

"You're not a virgin?"

"For God's sake, of course not!"

"Which god is this you keep throwing at me?"

She hurled a sock.

They were walking to the subway Monday morning and Fitz was walking fast, talking fast about his visit the night before to his daughter. "She said, 'I can't kiss you Daddy because nobody can kiss you but your parent. Miss Michaels told us in assembly.' I said, 'But I'm your parent!' 'No,' she said, 'Mom is my parent. You're my father.' Why are they putting ideas like rape into kids' heads?"

Phoebe kept it general. "Some children *are* abused."

"Not mine."

"But Fitz, if somebody else abused her, wouldn't you want her to be able to get help?"

"Of course! But what's all this suggestion going to do to her and her friends? How is a kid to grow up with any innocence?"

"Unmolested."

"But this way it's rape, rape, rape all over the place and it's scary, Phoebe. A parent has no choice over what his kid can bring into the house by twisting a knob on the TV while his wife is in the kitchen making supper."

Phoebe stopped a few feet from the subway entrance and said, icily, "Maybe you ought to be there by the TV, to keep an eye on Deely yourself." Abruptly, she started down the stairs, calling back, "And I hate it when you're macho!"

He followed her, saying, "I hate it that we're still apart."

She stopped on the stair. "Me too."

He stopped beside her. "You mean it would be okay?"

"I'm scared, Fitz. My"—she switched from "father" smoothly—"boy friend, my last one, was a little loony, a little, I guess you could call it, violent in his way, and I need to be sure I feel safe, that's all."

"Ah, Phoebe, I'm sorry. Is that what your therapy is about?"

She took one step down. "Kind of."

He followed and they took the steps one by one together. "Kind of. Well, this is complicated. But I'm real glad you're out there ready to defend Deely, thanks. Tell you what, I'm scared too. My last . . . my wife, sort of broke my heart. She changed so. That won't happen with you, will it? We make love, fall asleep, and you wake up with a firm belief that you can pray cancer away?"

She came to a stop in the dark at the bottom of the stairs. "We're not getting married. We're just going to bed."

"Oh, sweet Feeb." He put his hands over her hair and then his arms around her and said, warm, into her ready ear, "You're so old-fashioned."

Later, on her lunch break she found a phone booth and spoke to a tape recorder: "Sahra, this is Phoebe. I can't make it this afternoon. I've got . . . a fever, a sudden fever. I should be better by . . . by Thursday. See you then."

It was his face, the closeness of it, shifting slightly at the edges and his hair taking on a whiteness under the skylight that frightened her.

"Keep looking at me. I want to see you," she said, her voice unsure, its plea too audible.

"I'm here," he answered softly, to the rhythm of their movements.

She kept her eyes on his, no color now, the shadowed face, the face that mustn't turn into Dad's. And it didn't.

"Phoebe? Hey, Phoebe?"

"I'm here."

"You okay?"

"I'm great."

"So why are you crying?"

"I'm glad, that's all." Something soft and feathery seemed to settle around her shoulders. Everything here was real. She'd keep it to herself until she was sure she wouldn't lose it. That didn't take too long.

Sahra was hurt again. "You made love without talking it over with me?"

Phoebe nodded yes.

"Well, tell me, how it was?"

Phoebe held herself still.

"Were you excited?"

How surprising, Sahra's intrusion on her privacy.

42

1992

The birthday surprise started on the PATH train beneath the Hudson River, where they sat rocking side by side in the tunnel under the water.

"Scared?"

"Nope. Where're we going?"

"You'll see."

She knew, of course, and he knew she knew. There is so much we say without the words. When they reached Hoboken, he led her to the sidewalk in front of a small apartment building and they stood for a minute in the April breeze facing a miragelike view of Manhattan. She waited there while he went into the building; he came out with a four-year-old girl holding his hand. They rode back into the city with Deely sitting on Fitz's lap and telling him about day care while she kept looking up at Phoebe. Phoebe tried smiling. She tried making a face. She tried not reacting. She tried waving. She tried compressing her nostrils. The child did not laugh. Phoebe ran out of things to try. Every time Fitz said anything to Phoebe or Phoebe to Fitz, the child would hit Fitz on the arm.

"This is her time with me," Fitz explained, looking not quite himself.

They sat around a table at the skating rink in Rockefeller Center even though it was too cold for that. Fitz looked from one to the other and said, "It's barely spring and you two are looking as blooming as daffodils." Deely banged her Nikes against the rung of the metal chair. She looked at her father, the dark-haired, blue-eyed man with the beard and at the red-haired woman that Phoebe knew to be herself. She couldn't tell how Deely saw her, how alike or how different from Jenna. What's Jenna like? she'd once asked Fitz, meaning is she more beautiful than me. "Overcommitted," he'd replied, "in a rush for salvation." Fitz was gentle with his daughter, and very patient. He treated her like a teenager until she grew sleepy and then he lifted her onto his lap as if she were a baby. It was sweet to see. It made Phoebe anxious though, and sad.

That night her father appeared in memory. She was in her bed at home, calling out because of a nightmare. He pulled up the covers. Here I am, good old Dad. Now go to sleep, honey, your mother is exhausted. And then he was snoring. He didn't touch her. Had that happened? Or was she making it up? It didn't seem to be specific. It seemed to be generalized, a moment that might have been typical of other moments but not an actual memory in itself. The Towel was specific but so blurred now from examining it with Sahra that Phoebe had to cast it aside. The Rosebushes had been smashed by Bess—one look at that nasty little Xerox and she'd never seen the man in the Rosebushes again. That left scattered images and the two big memories—The Tent and The Sand. They were different, those two, from anything else.

"You know, Sahra, when I go back over my memories—the ones I recovered, I mean, especially The Tent and The Sand—I notice a funny thing. I could, like, get inside those, and walk around in them. What do you make of that?"

"Tell me more."

"Well, in The Rosebushes, there's just a pair of muddy boots and I could never see any further. I couldn't see around them or up above them."

"But that's the man who's exposing himself, isn't it?"

Phoebe pulled at the hem of her dress. "I'm not so sure he was doing that, Sahra. That was one of the things I sort of got pushed into saying in group."

Sahra laughed. "There goes your Rolls-Royce again!"

Phoebe looked straight at Sahra. "What I want to know is why could I get inside some of my memories and not others?"

"I'm hardly a neurobiologist. I'm not even sure they'd know."

"But you must know how these recovered memories work, I mean, don't you?"

"I know they're real."

"But there's real and real. I mean, look, in The Tent I could stand up from my mat and walk around my sister. It was like a film. Only it was still going on. I could get *into* it and change events. I could see things that I hadn't remembered. Like the title of a book, I could read it, *The Lion, the Witch and the Wardrobe.* Isn't that strange? I couldn't do that in The Towel. All I had was a faint sense of my mother helping me out of a bathing suit. I never could get back into that cottage and actually move around."

"But you did last summer!"

"You mean when you were asking me questions? That was different. You said stuff like 'Is the towel striped?' and I'd get a picture. But if I sat here now and tried all by myself to get back into The Towel, I couldn't."

"You could get into The Tent?"

"Yes, probably."

"That gives me an idea. This weekend, get into The Tent and fight back. Scream at your father. No! no! no! Fight him off. Kick him, kick him in the balls if you have to! Could you do that?"

On Sunday when Fitz was gone, Phoebe carried a chair into the bathroom and shut the door. This could be scary. She hadn't had any pictures for a long time but she'd sure never called one up. Usually, she begged the memories to go away. At least there was light under the door. She sat and shut her eyes. Let me see The Tent. Not too close up! Distantly, she heard traffic, a siren.

I want to see The Tent.

A yellow and white tent like the one at Liz Tsui's wedding floated up in her mind's eye. Then a circus tent with elephants marching. The bathroom smelled damp, as if the water were leaking from the pipes straight into the plaster. She heard what sounded like mice but assured herself it couldn't be.

I want to see The Tent.

A lake appeared, two tents. They were made of nylon, blue, and stood a way back from the lake in the mountains. In the morning the lake had ripples on it and birds sang. She and Bess went swimming. The bottom of the lake was ankle-deep in muck, though, and that's why she liked to run back to the tent to read. This was The Tent, but more generalized than specific. She couldn't get into it.

She must be blocking The Tent somehow. Maybe this was a whole new kind of repression, the repression of repression? That made her smile a little. Fitz would love that, if only she could tell him. But she couldn't, ever. Lovers abandon survivors: They think you're creepy.

I want to see The Tent.

There it was again, blue nylon. She couldn't get into it at all. She remembered the nice feeling of lying on her belly inside the great curve of the tent, reading *Are You There, God? It's Me, Margaret.* But that's all. Her father wasn't anywhere about. He didn't come into the tent. He must have been at the lake keeping an eye on Bess as she swam.

I want to see The Sand.

There was the lake, the water rippling on it, a little bit of nice clean sand. There was nobody around. Then she could hear voices and she didn't know if she was remembering them or making them up, but it was time to go home. "Strike the tent, Two Squad!" her father called. He was teaching them to be soldiers. "Private P, uproot the stakes, Private B, gather and fold." She didn't remember the exact words, just the gist. That was her dad, though, the dad she used to know.

They took Deely to the aquarium, to the top of the Empire State Building, and to half a dozen playgrounds in the city. At an Adventure Playground on Central Park West, Fitz went to buy ice cream while Phoebe watched Deely, who brought her a stone, along with a pronouncement: "It's white."

"Yes, a white stone."

Deely looked up at her then, dark hair, blue eyes. "I like my mother better than you."

Stung, Phoebe thought of what Fitz had said about the competitive pancakes. "Of course," she said. "She's your mom."

"But you're okay," Deely added shyly and ran off.

All of a sudden Phoebe thought she understood what it's like to be a mother. Then she was inside her own mother's head, looking at herself as a young child. Hers had been a delicate face like Deely's, red hair instead of Deely's dark, the same blue eyes. The child Phoebe brought her mother a stone, offered it on a flattened palm. It's white. Yes, her mother would have answered, a white stone. What hundreds of words went into those three! All the colors, all the shapes and sizes, all things living and not. All those words had to be taught to the child before she could carry a stone to her mother and say, a white stone. And before words, the hours of singing and nursing, and before that the slow minutes in the womb. Jenna had loved Deely. Claire had loved Phoebe.

And how had she returned that love?

That evening she looked into the mirror and moved her lips without any sound. "Maybe I wasn't sexually abused." She blinked and looked away. She sautéed onions, boiled rice and beans, grated cheese. She returned to the mirror and whispered: "Maybe I wasn't sexually abused." That time she had to shut her eyes. Something large and red inside her seemed to burst: It was all over. She could never face her mother again, or her father.

Or herself.

43

They waited.

Bess could tell them very little about Phoebe anymore, though her own life was picking up since Adrianna's arrival in Portland. Bess listened to whatever they relayed to her from Rachel: that hundreds of families were coming out of the woodwork with the same story; that there seemed to be a set of younger accusers and a set of older, more troubled ones; that certain therapists at the Warburg Clinic could be pinpointed as the radiating centers of circles of accusing clients. Then came the bad news: that very few accusers made their way home—too much rage had been evoked, too much shame swallowed.

"That's why Phoebe's got to come to this herself, Bess. Shame is powerful. It can kill. Sometimes the accusers want to die."

In the middle of July, Phoebe heard from Nora. They met on the Brooklyn Bridge. It was a bright day with the same blue sky, white clouds, and rayed sunshine that Deely so loved to paint. Nora's voice was nearly lost in the thrum of the cars over the metal bridge. Her father had died, a massive heart attack on the Long Island Expressway.

"They had the funeral without me, my mother and my brother."

"How'd you find out?"

"My mother called Donna afterward. Donna told me in my next session."

The gulls swooped over the water and the great city rose behind them.

"That video your sister sent me." Nora started, stopped.

"I don't know anything about it."

"I watched it."

"She shouldn't have sent it, whatever it is."

"It's the same scenes, Phoebe, some of them. It's my scenes. I don't remember ever seeing it. Of course, I must have—some rerun when I was studying or shall we say somewhat engaged on the couch with Derek Block."

"Does Donna agree?"

"She thinks that my recollections of my mother relied on—that was her phrase, 'relied on'—the scenes from the film because 'horrible as the scenes in the film were' "—Nora's voice took on increasing sarcasm—" 'they were far less heinous than what my mother had actually done to me.' You know how it goes. I'm probably still repressing the worst!"

They laughed at that, feeble laughs of recognition that implicated themselves as well as their therapists.

"You don't believe it anymore, then? About your mother?"

"I don't know. I've got doubts."

"It was Donna?"

"I'm not sure. Maybe."

"But you still go to her?"

"It's too late. Not to would make me a murderer. And, besides, you know how it is, how it got started in the first place. It's so delicate. You feel you've got to . . . help them along. Otherwise they'll lose their faith."

Phoebe took hold of a missing piece. "Holy shit."

"It's kind of like school, you know. You've got to keep your mouth shut or everybody hates you. You've got to go along with what everybody else is thinking. But what I came to tell you, buddy, is something else. Your dad could pop off any minute. Don't wait too long."

The safest way was to lie: She had to leave because of the money, the three thousand dollars she owed.

Sahra only replied, "You know you can owe me, Phoebe. Really, I don't have a problem with it."

"It's kind of . . . weighing on me."

"If it's holding you back, we could think about suing your father. They say it's hard to go to court but I understand that there are emotional gains to be had, as well as the financial."

The judge slamming down his gavel, her father in chains: she moved a little closer to the truth. "You don't understand. I want to . . . to take a break from therapy."

Sahra looked puzzled. "A break?"

"That's right. I'll start to pay back what I owe. And maybe someday . . . I'd want to come back."

Lines formed around Sahra's eyes. "You need someone with you while you complete your healing."

"You think I'll go crazy?"

"It's not that. You need more work."

"You think I'll kill myself?"

"Put it this way: You're just not ready to leave."

"You always said I've got myself to count on. Why not now?"

"Because you won't have"—Sahra's lips pressed together and then opened—"a counselor."

"Oh." Phoebe tried again to be gentle. "That's what I want to try. I want to try it without . . . one."

With no warning at all, Sahra stood. There was sweat above her upper lip. "I was afraid of this, Phoebe. It happens every now and then at this plateau. You could stall here and never totally heal. But if this is what you want, I wish you well, I really do. Good luck."

Sahra was trembling and Phoebe said, "It's just a break! I'm just taking a break!"

Sahra's voice took on condescension. "If you leave now, Phoebe, I think it may be too hard for you to return."

"You mean I can't come back?"

Sahra nodded. "That's what I mean."

Phoebe stood, bringing her eyes level with Sahra's, and shook the long, limp fingers extended toward her. She stumbled out onto St. Marks Place, where the light seemed so palpable, so lucid, encasing her.

She'd done it!

There was suddenly so much free time. And money for food! At least for today; tomorrow the debt. Where had she been all this time? She bought an entire take-out dinner for two at the Japanese noodle shop. Climbing the stairs to her loft, she held the carton to her breast.

Now she'd call her father.

No.

She'd call her mother.

Maybe not.

Bess.

Absolutely not.

She'd tell Fitz.

Never.

She was strong enough for Sahra but not for any of them. You need a lot of strength to become a shit forever. The worst thing was that her parents would rejoice. They'd kill the fatted calf for her and if that happened, she'd be the prodigal until the day she died. And Bess would say I told you so.

44

On Harvey's fifty-eighth birthday they cleaned the cellar. It fit his mood. Down in that dim space lit by bare bulbs, they could see the very rocks of their house's foundation. They sorted through the large furniture first, his mother's treasures from the little house in New Jersey. They lifted and tugged at objects having weight; it satisfied, somehow.

"If we'd been born two or three hundred years ago, we'd be out of touch with at least one of the girls by now, anyway," Harvey told Claire. "She'd have joined some migration, sailed to the New World, walked west with the pioneers. A letter would take years."

"I'm more concerned about Bess right now." Claire had heard from Bess that James Buttenwieser had come home with a young woman he'd met on his travels.

Harvey said nothing: he still felt forced about Bess. And if he felt this bad about Bess, he wasn't sure how he'd handle Phoebe if she ever came home.

They reached old trunks moldy at the seams and years of rubber-banded checks. They moved the trash to the base of the stairs and swept up, their faces wrapped in old dish towels against the dust. They aligned the girls' bikes and the crib against a wall. One day they might have a grandchild—whose whereabouts and name they wouldn't know. Not to know Phoebe's child, it was all so unbelievable.

"Sometimes I hate her," Harvey confessed as they hauled the trash up the stairs. "There, I said it."

"You can't hate her!"

"I can hate what she's done."

"She got caught in a fad. We all do from time to time."

"Why didn't she resist?"

"Who knows. She bit at the bait."

"She's going to have to apologize to me!"

"That could keep her away forever." Claire pushed her trash through the cellar door into the kitchen's light. "Okay, I know what you mean." Somehow, it had happened to her, the thing she'd so dreaded. "I'll never feel the same toward Phoebe either." They crossed to the back door and Claire tried to emend herself. "She's not the same person to me anymore and I bet I'm not the same person to her, either. We'll just have to start fresh, when she comes back."

"If."

With his trash, Harvey pushed through to the outside where it was hot and sticky. They reached the overflowing cans and piled the last plastic bags on top of them. Claire looked up at the sky, tranquil, cloudless.

"It's strange what Ezekiel saw in the sky. We never see the things he saw, the wheels of the Assyrian war chariots up there. We don't see what the Puritans saw, either, witches and Indian hatchets. We look up and see UFOs and sexual abuse. It's a mirror, the sky, of what we've already got in our brains, of what our culture worries about."

"She should have resisted it."

"You took LSD in the sixties."

Bess called to say happy birthday and Harvey took the phone. "Guess what your mother gave me."

"New file folders?"

"A plane ticket to Portland. Labor Day. I'm coming out to visit you. See the sights. Just me, a dad visit. You got a symphony out there?"

"Dad, really?" Her voice, too, sounded unnatural.

"Would you rather I didn't?" It ran through his mind that she might be afraid of him, afraid to be alone with him. "I'm hoping you can find me a B & B."

"It's great, Dad. We can go to the zoo."

"The zoo. Good idea."

"Can I bring a friend?"

For defense, he wondered. "Adrianna?"

"No, someone else. From work."

"Sure thing. Looking forward. See you."

One by one, Claire told herself, they were coming together.

"We've got to start talking to people," Claire told him over the birthday cake. "We're as moldy as those trunks. We're green from darkness. It can't be good for anyone, the girls or us."

They'd have a party, after all. It would be a buffet: chairs situated gracefully in the garden and strawberries floating in white wine. The guests arrived on a July night as thick with heat as those when the Constitutional Convention met to slap at flies and shape a democratic government, or at least a start at one. And here they were, the heirs of that, most of them in their fifties, wearing linen and cotton that gripped too tight at the waist.

"Perot is too brittle. He'd crack under the strain."

"Bush will pull it out. We're already beginning to see some result from his economic policies."

"Are you kidding? We're falling further into debt!"

"I'm for Clinton. Except that if he's elected, he'll be the first president younger than I."

That was true for most of them. It would be the end of an era, theirs.

Claire found it hard to get back into the middle ground of life. She passed to the serving table and began to make up plates. Maxine Bender, Adrianna's mother, was looking at her strangely across the table. Bess had told her Mrs. Bender was struggling for thought control, so she wouldn't get cancer again, even though Adrianna kept trying to explain to her that it was partly an environmental disease and she ought to be suing Philip Morris instead. Claire carried plates around, touched guests on the arm to indicate the waiting table. When the last of the berry pies was gone and the decaf hot in the pot, everyone seemed to be on to travel. New Zealand has a lot of sheep, China has bugs in the bathtub, in Japan don't be surprised to find a stranger sharing your hotel room, in Fiji there's no TV. Maxine was studying her again, so Claire leaned across the whipped cream to whisper, "Eternal vigilance is the price of freedom."

Maxine didn't laugh and whispered back: "I'm so sorry, so sorry. Is there anything I can do?"

"About what?"

"Harvey and Phoebe."

Luckily, there was plenty of noise around. "What do you mean?"

Maxine's small face took on confusion. "Well, Bess told Adrianna. I'm sorry. . . ."

Bess again, Harvey mustn't know. Suddenly she didn't care, she wanted everyone to know. She wanted to stand on the table and announce it, get it over with, have it behind them.

". . . and I want you to know," Maxine continued, "that I don't for one minute believe that Harvey did it. I mean, it must have been something else. Some small event that got blown up—"

"I don't think so, Maxine," Claire interrupted her guest. "I used to think so. But Harvey and I don't blame ourselves so much anymore. We were good enough parents. Not perfect, good enough. And Phoebe's a good enough daughter. Not perfect, good enough. She got caught up in a storm, like those girls in Salem who saw witches among their neighbors, or like those families of schizophrenics who used to send their sick ones to have chunks of their forebrains scooped out because the experts said it would help them. Remember lobotomies? We're part of an epidemic, that's all."

Maxine gave her a pitying look and Claire moved away. If this was real life, she might never get back to it. She'd moved outside of this somehow, outside of peace, outside of reason—well, there'd be plenty of company, much of North Twentieth Street, for instance. And, appropriately, here came Lacey Quinn, who'd been back from Rome almost a year now.

"I miss you, Claire. It's been ages. Junior and I are thinking of starting up a gallery together, his bucks and my talents. And maybe your contacts. Want to advise us?"

"Lunch, Wednesday!"

45

The leaves were off the trees when Phoebe and Fitz drove to Philadelphia in the big studio van with two cameramen aboard to shoot their One-Minute Birthday special on Benjamin Franklin. If things moved smoothly, they'd be able to get their footage in four hours and clear out of the city as daylight faded. Fitz wanted to meet her parents but she wasn't ready. Maybe someday. Oddly, it was Dad who'd forgive her sooner. He'd be the easier one. Mom measured with a finer spoon. Mom expected more of a person, full responsibility. She'd hurt them enough, destroyed enough. But she wasn't able yet to try to fix it. Bumbling would only hurt them more. All she could do, anyway, was try to explain how it had happened, step by step. But not until she could keep from being sucked back in, defined by them, by what she'd done, an idiot for life.

They double-parked in front of Franklin Court where Ben had built a house, now gone, for his wife, Deborah. Phoebe led the men under an eighteenth-century brick archway and into a paved courtyard fit out with a "ghost house" made of steel girders. When she'd come here as a little girl, she hadn't understood why the girders were called that. Does a ghost live here? She'd asked her father. He'd explained it all to her, walking her around the strangely outlined space where a house had once stood. Her father seemed to be here, in Franklin Court, himself a ghost, waiting for her to restore him to life. Someday, Dad.

"Shoot the girders to show how they represent the main outlines of the house that isn't here anymore," she instructed the cameramen, both younger than she. This was their first big job, too.

"Get a couple of those," she said, pointing at the courtyard stones engraved with excerpts from Ben and Deborah's letters. Excitement mounted in her. Dad would be so proud of her, Mom too.

"Now down here," she called out, beckoning them after her. She liked to lead. She liked to call out. She liked to toss her newly cut and crinkled hair. She liked to stand close to Fitz, their jackets only a quarter of an inch apart. The cameramen had figured out there was something going on between them. Phoebe led the men down a long ramp to the underground museum. This would be hard, keeping the tourists out as they filmed. They had to block off the central area where railings ran to keep visitors from dropping into a recessed "room" below. Down there, pint-sized papier-mâché men in white wigs stood on the floor of a miniaturized British House of Commons. Of course, she'd called the museum director long ago and now she marked the area with yellow tape. Incoming tourists were impressed. Look, it's TV!

The cameramen leaned over the railings to capture a two-foot-tall and balding Franklin as he pled the cause of the colonies across the sea, that is, here. They needed audio. She pressed the audio button on the railing and one of the men taped its spiel. That wouldn't copy well enough. She'd have to arrange a reel-to-reel transfer later when they knew exactly how many seconds of it they wanted.

Around the walls of the actual underground room were life-sized cutouts of famous and lesser-known people of Franklin's day. And in the center of the room stood scores of little podiums, each supporting a telephone. You could dial up any of the personages silhouetted on the wall and hear what they had to say about their contemporary statesman and friend.

"Wait!" Phoebe held up her hand and called out to a family of tourists about to enter the room. "Could you wait, please?" Obedient to media, the family waited and when Phoebe finally gave them the high sign, they rushed in. The father explained to a little boy that he could dial a number on the phone—and hear what George Washington had to say about Ben Franklin. "No! No!" the boy shrieked, "I want to call my friend Zephyr!"

Fitz laughed and Phoebe with him. The cameramen weren't into children yet. They all moved out of the museum and through the damp air to drive to a restored eighteenth-century tavern near the river. They shot the tavern doorway and the bar inside and came back out. The wind was quick off the water and Phoebe leaned briefly against Fitz for warmth. They all ran part of the way up Second Street to Market and then hushed themselves to enter the light-filled Anglican church. Phoebe had always loved it in here. It sure beat the Quaker Meeting House, Bess's favorite, where all the light was Inner.

Everything was going amazingly smoothly, not a single glitch. Except they were about to finish too soon. She couldn't tell Fitz why they were avoiding her parents, because she couldn't bear to lose him the way she'd lost everybody else. Fitz walked back for the van while she guided the cameramen as slowly as she could up to Betsy Ross's house and on to the intact eighteenth-century alley, then back to Independence Hall, then even more slowly to the Franklin tombstone. But it was still light and they were already folding their scripts, with the cameramen opting to return to the tavern for a beer. Phoebe and Fitz promised to join them when they'd found a parking lot. In the van, Fitz put the key into the ignition and said, "Hey, chief, we've got time for your folks, after all."

"But we've got lots of work to do later, in the studio."

"You're putting me on, aren't you?" He caught her eye in the rearview mirror as he pulled out of the parking place. "You don't want them to meet me, is that it?"

"No, I do. I do."

"I'm not good enough for the Main Line, is that it?"

"They aren't the Main Line!"

"We Irish are the Celts, you know. We're more ancient than you ordinary English."

"Don't be dumb!"

Was Fitz really hurt? Maybe she could handle it. The day had gone so well. Here she'd led this whole shoot, her first shoot, and not a single thing gone wrong. Fitz did look mad, very mad. "Okay, then," she said, unable to stop herself. "We'll try my father. Take a left."

When he pulled into the traffic on Walnut, her temperature seemed to drop eighty degrees. She tried to appear nonchalant, calling up all her acting tricks from long ago, draping her hand over the back of the seat and deliberately relaxing her body. It was Dad. It was only Dad. Bess and Mom wouldn't be there. It would be all right.

"Turn right. That's my park, where we used to play."

"Nice territory."

"There's my goat. See it?"

He didn't have time to spot the bronze goat on its pedestal, and soon they were turning right again, onto Market, near the blue granite towers. "Looks like you can't double-park here," she said. "Maybe we should skip the whole thing."

"We're double-parking," he replied, snapping on the disabled light. "If the studio won't pay the ticket, I will." He got out of the van, took her hand, and she followed him.

This was wrong. She knew it then. But it was too late to stop it. Maybe her father would be out on a site visit. She couldn't stop it without telling Fitz everything. They were in the marble lobby, they were skirting the reception desk, now they were in the elevator to the seventeenth floor. Oh, please, Dad, I didn't mean to hurt you. I don't know why I did what I did. I was crazy. It was totally dumb, rotten. This was the end of her life. They hurried out of the elevator and followed the rug to the end of the hall, turned left, then right, and then they were standing in the doorway of the office with the big window.

He was sitting at his desk, working on some papers. He was older, his hair a little thinner.

He looked up. He didn't move. Then he stood. He said her name. He came toward them.

"Oh, hi, Daddy!" she said, letting go of Fitz's hand.

"Phoebe, Phoebe." He approached her, his voice strangled.

He put his arms around her and she put her arms around him and they were standing together. She shut her eyes tight and hugged him. He smelled familiar and good and the tears were welling up behind her lids.

His arms around her tightened. He was steady. He was there. She let go first, even though she didn't want to let go at all. This was getting too odd. It would seem creepy to Fitz, born again. She had to act more natural.

"I wanted you to meet my friend Fitz," she said, and her voice worked better than she'd expected. She stepped aside to let Fitz move in between her and her father.

Her father cleared his throat. "Hello there," he said, extending a hand toward Fitz, who took it smoothly. They were just about the same height. Fitz was maybe a quarter of an inch taller. He was smiling at her father.

"Glad to meet you, sir," Fitz said. She hadn't known he'd use a sir. It was kind of charming, if you weren't going out of your mind.

"We've got our van running," she said. "Maybe I didn't tell you we're doing a documentary on Ben Franklin. It's just for kids, really, nothing important. But I'm an assistant director now. Here"—she felt her way into her pocket—"here's my card. We've got to run. It's great to see you, Dad. Say hi to Mom."

"Wait, I'll go down with you! You can tell her yourself. We can take a cab up to the museum."

"Sorry, can't. Not now."

"Call her, at least. You could do that."

"Later, later." Her voice began to shake.

"Okay, sweetheart," he said, stopping. "Do what you can do. I'll tell her everything."

She pulled at Fitz's hand and they were out the door.

"You've got to tell me what this is all about," Fitz said in the elevator. "I have to know."

On the way to the bar, she told him. He looked at her as if she were Jenna. He told her that she had to call her mother, right now, this minute. They stopped outside the bar.

"No," she said. "I was right the first time. We shouldn't have gone to my father's. I'm not ready."

"What about them, Phoebe?"

"It has to be right. I have to be able to stay intact."

"But how can you keep them waiting?"

"Look, Fitz," she said, knowing she was memorizing him, his face, his hands, in case he left her now. "I went to my father's because I couldn't withstand your wanting me to. That was wrong. I'm not going to be able to follow through with him, or to call my mother. I'm not strong enough to withstand their hurt or their forgiveness yet. And now they'll be expecting me to call. I've hurt them even more."

"You're only thinking of yourself."

"Maybe so, but I can't do it simply because you want me to. Don't you get it?"

"No."

"That's exactly what I did wrong in the first place! I did what Sahra wanted me to do. I didn't wait for myself. I've got to stop doing that. Even if it means I lose you. I'm not ready. I can't call her."

He understood. But somehow the light had gone out of his face and she knew that this was the end of romance. From now on, things would be the way they are in real life.

Harvey and Claire flew to Portland for Christmas. Bess reported a couple of phone calls from Phoebe.

"Your mother still has hope," Harvey told Bess, as they waited for Nehemiah to join them for dinner.

"Don't you, Dad?"

"Less and less."

Claire didn't know if hope would be enough. In the long wait, she'd felt her anger shifting away from Harvey, away from herself, away from the therapists, and onto Phoebe.

46

1993

Phoebe stared at the small type in the *Times*. There was no picture. *Sahra Meehan, M.S.W., to Wed Carl Mundiger, Ph.D. Ms. Meehan has recently been appointed Associate Director of Young Adult Services at the Warburg Clinic for Women, a branch of the Warburg School of Social Work, where Dr. Mundiger is Director of Family Services.*

It's wild what you don't know about your therapist. She hadn't thought about Sahra in a while now. People were saying that lots of young women had done what she'd done. Thank God her parents didn't know that. She'd better get to them before they found out. The initiative must be hers or otherwise it would end up the way it had with Bess, a half truce. She'd apologize, but not until she'd told them how she'd gotten into it. That way she'd have a chance of not falling apart. Of not groveling.

When?

The Sunday before Phoebe's twenty-seventh birthday, they took Deely on the Staten Island Ferry. The sun felt warm and a great lucid sky arched above them, as if the whole world were at once both entirely simple and entirely mysterious. Nothing could be hidden in that sky, yet nothing was revealed. Fitz went off to buy a couple of coffees and she stood leaning on the railing with Deely. Across the deck, she saw a woman her age with a baby who'd smeared the front of her jacket with an ice cream sandwich. The mother was wiping it up with a napkin, rubbing and rubbing. The child was screaming. The woman smiled at Phoebe, mother to mother, as if to say, ain't it the way. Phoebe smiled back.

Now.

The Sunday after her twenty-seventh birthday, she walked from the train station over the Schuylkill and south to Rittenhouse Square, which was beginning to leaf out. The fountain had no water in it yet. The bronze goat had been rubbed shiny by a million kids. Little guys in knitted caps were fighting over it this very minute. "No! No!" one screamed while the other pushed him from the pedestal. "It's mine!"

Walking slower and slower, she reached her own short, narrow street and almost kept right on past. Something like antigravity was repelling her from it. She resisted, struggled into it and through to turn onto her block. Careful on the cobblestones, she walked toward the house with the ginger-colored shutters. Another force was pulling her toward the house. If this were years hence and her parents dead, this gravity would lead her irresistibly to the door. One more step and she stood motionless, caught between the two forces. Then her arm moved. Her finger pressed the bell.

Nobody came to the door.

In the fringed shoulder bag she found her ancient keys. She put a gold key into the lock and opened the door. The house smelled a little musty, as it always did. The afternoon light was shining into the pleasantness of the kitchen. She smelled lemons. Nobody was home. She stepped inside. Hello? Nobody answered.

"I'm home," she wrote on the message pad by the front door. "Don't be scared. Everything's okay."

She climbed up the stairs past the parlor and the family room, up to the third floor. She called up the stairway toward the fourth, just in case they were in their room. But there was no answer. Usually the house was full of music but now there was only the faucet dripping in the third-floor bathroom. She reached her landing and turned into her old room.

Someone had cleaned up a little, but essentially it was the same—bed, pillows, bookcase, window seat, leaded windows onto the back garden, posters from when she was a teenager. She sat down on her bed. She was so much older now. And, if not wiser, at least a little steadier. All there was was the truth. She stretched her legs out on the spread and lay down. Okay, Fitz, here I am in corpse position. Stand by me, but not too close. I'm ready.

Claire saw it first. She looked at Harvey. He read it. Phoebe hadn't signed her name but of course they knew the handwriting. Then they were running up the stairs, calling out her name; she was sitting on her bed, standing, coming to the landing. They all stopped there, pausing, poised, held back. The love was there, but the trust would take so much longer, if it ever returned. Nobody reached out because every move, every fraction of an inch mattered and all three of them needed to hold together, first themselves, before each other.

"I . . . I . . . Hi. Hi, Mom. Hi, Dad."

"Hi, Phoebe."

"Hi, honey."

"Look," she began, touching a hand to the crinkly hair, moving her fingers along her neck to comfort herself. "All I can do is try to tell you what happened. So, you guys remember when Bess and I went to New York . . ."

Author's Note

Among works consulted in trying to understand and imagine a tale of memory recall, I am indebted to: Ellen Bass and Laura Davis, *The Courage to Heal: A Guide for Women Survivors of Child Sexual Abuse*; Beverly Engel, *The Right to Innocence: Healing the Trauma of Childhood Sexual Abuse*; Renee Fredrickson, *Repressed Memories: A Journey to Recovery from Sexual Abuse*; Eleanor Goldstein and Kevin Farmer, *Confabulations: Creating Memories, Destroying Families*; Alice Miller, *Banished Knowledge: Facing Childhood Injuries*; Richard Ofshe and Ethan Watters, *Making Monsters: False Memories, Psychotherapy, and Sexual Hysteria*; Mark Pendergrast, *Victims of Memory: Incest Accusations and Shattered Lives*; and Carol Tavris, *The Mismeasure of Woman.* Shorter works: the 1994 and 1995 issues of the *False Memory Syndrome Foundation Newsletter*; Richard Gardner in the *Academy Forum*; Robyn Dawes in *Issues in Child Abuse Accusations*; Paul McHugh in *The American Scholar*; Judith Herman and Mary Harvey in the *Harvard Mental Health Letter*; Elizabeth Loftus in the *American Psychologist*; Darrell Sifford in the *Philadelphia Inquire*; Bill Tayler in the *Toronto Star*; and Lawrence Wright in *The New Yorker.*